TIES THAT BIND

DESPERATION DRIVES THE HARDEST BARGAINS

MARIA FRANKLAND

AUTONOMY
PRESS

First published by Autonomy Press 2025

First edition

Cover Design by David Grogan www.headdesign.co.uk

A mother's love crushes down remorselessly all that stands in its path.
Agatha Christie

JOIN MY 'KEEP IN TOUCH' LIST

To be kept in the loop about new books and special offers, join my 'keep in touch list' here or by visiting www.mariafrankland. co.uk

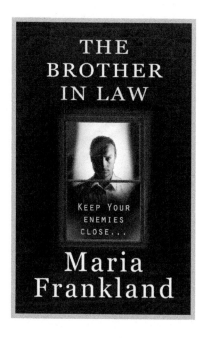

PROLOGUE

SERGEANT JON SHEPPERD - APRIL 19

'IT'S BEEN A QUIET SHIFT, hasn't it, Sarge? Considering it's the weekend.'

Bella glances at me, her voice light but laced with a cautious optimism that makes me uneasy. I'm a big believer in the power of tempting fate, and referring to our shift as being *quiet* is doing just that.

'Don't speak too soon.' I take a right off the main road. The scenic shortcut over Otley is a route I drive by habit, especially at times like now when the sky has brightened and a picturesque sunrise is imminent. The station isn't far away, but I've learned better than to assume a shift is over until I've completed all the paperwork at the end of it and walked through the door. Due to holidays and sickness, we already started well before our usual clocking-in time of eleven pm so I want to get out without delay. I'm yearning just to sink into my bed beside my wife before the rest of my house starts stirring for their morning routine.

'I hate finishing at this time – having to go to bed when the rest of the world is waking.' Bella slumps back into her seat. 'I prefer the evening finishes when we can all meet in the pub.'

'Oh, I don't know. After the state of the place we threw that crowd out of last night, I'll quite happily settle for a nice cup of tea rather than a beer. That pub was enough to put *anyone* off alcohol.'

'Yeah, it was a right dive, wasn't it?' She pulls a face.

'It was a case of wiping your feet on the way *out*.' I laugh. 'Anyway, those two lads going at each other will be regretting it this morning as they wake in the comfort of our cells.' The image of their bloodied faces fills my mind. 'With sore heads for all the wrong reasons.'

Bella's laughter suddenly stops short as a huge bang echoes through the emerging dawn. I don't just hear it – I *feel* it resonate through my body. Then all is quiet again, save for the hum of our engine.

'What the *hell* was that?' I ease off the accelerator and scan the horizon. 'It sounded like a bomb.'

'Over there, Sarge!' Bella's blonde ponytail swings out as she twists in her seat, her eyes locked on a spot to our left beyond the tree line. 'Pull over – quick!'

I swerve our patrol car into Surprise View car park, slowing as we crunch our way over the loose gravel. 'Shiiit.' Against the backdrop of the morning sky, plumes of smoke curl into the air. The source, a medium-sized vehicle, looks to be crumpled against the dry stone wall in the far corner.

'Jeez.' Bella's hand flies to her mouth. 'How have they managed that? In a car park, of all places?'

As we reach the scene, I slam us to a halt and throw open the door, my hand already poised over my radio.

'Stay well back,' I order Bella, waving at her as I scan the wreckage. 'We don't know if this is going up in flames. Let's assess first – then I'll call it in.' This is why I'm often paired with newly-qualified officers. I'm calm under pressure and always remember to explain the procedure to those who are shadowing.

'Oh my God.' Bella's voice is barely a whisper. 'People are trapped inside.'

I resist the urge to ask her what she expected since the crash has only just occurred. I could also remind her that this is what all her training has been preparing her for. But that would be insensitive. After all, the first time is always the most difficult. I'll never forget my first road traffic accident when I had to stand by, redirecting traffic as all four deceased passengers, a family, were cut free by the fire service. After that, I didn't sleep for several nights. But that was on the M1 at rush hour, not in a sunrise car park at a tranquil beauty spot.

I reach for my radio and tilt it to my face as I edge closer to the vehicle. 'This is Unit Twelve, Sergeant Shepperd.' I wait for a moment. Why does Control always take longer when we're calling in something urgent?

'Come in Unit Twelve.'

'We've got a serious one-vehicle RTA at Surprise View Car Park, Otley.' I glance at the mangled bonnet. 'Substantial front-end impact with smoke and leaking fuel present.' I wrinkle my nose against the stench of petrol. 'Two casualties are trapped inside, and a third has either been hit by the vehicle or has been ejected with the force of impact. Requesting immediate backup, ambulance, and fire service. Over.'

'Received. Stand by.'

Bella is still frozen in place, her eyes fixed on the motionless figure sprawled in front of the crash site amid the shattered stone wall and the bent metal fence in front of it.

'Ambulance ETA four minutes. Fire service, six.' The radio crackles.

I nod toward the casualty on the ground, my voice steady. 'Four minutes, they're saying, Bella. It's four minutes too long. We need to intervene.'

She doesn't move. She's probably terrified that it's going to burst into flames. I'd be lying if I said I wasn't, but still – we're trained to preserve the lives of others. If there's a chance of getting them out, we have to take it. I can't see any sparks from the electrics so we should be OK.

'Come on, I've got you. We've got this.'

Still, she doesn't move.

'There's no time like the present to put that First Aid training into practice. Come on Bella – *now!*'

PART I

1

TEN MONTHS EARLIER – OLIVER HOLMES - JUNE 13

'IT FEELS like there's a storm brewing.' My wife lowers her lipstick-rimmed glass to the table as her dark hair flutters in the evening breeze. Every time I look at her, I thank my lucky stars. I must have done something incredibly right in a previous life to have attracted such a stunning, not to mention, *younger* woman. When I first took her to a work event just after we got engaged, the eyes of many of my colleagues were out on stalks.

'You could be right.' I tug at my shirt sleeves which are sticking to my body in the heat. 'Much as I'm not keen on them, we could certainly do with one to clear the air.'

'You're not keen on storms? You never said.'

'I was terrified of thunder when I was a boy. Mum'll tell you.' I glance over to Mum's *Granny Pad,* as dubbed by my girls, over in the far right corner of our grounds. Really, it's a modern cottage with two bedrooms and its own garden space and I love that she's so close by.

I'd like to hear more tales about Ellen's childhood but she won't tell me any, reasoning that most of her memories are difficult ones. She tells me that she wants to leave the past where it belongs, enjoy the present and look to the future.

'How come your mum never wants to join us out here?' Ellen reaches for her nail file.

'She isn't feeling a hundred per cent tonight.' I nod towards where my phone's resting on the bistro table between us. 'She sent me a text earlier.'

'You never said.'

'It's probably just the heat – it's never agreed with her and with a storm on its way, it might have brought on one of her migraines.'

Ellen nods but she doesn't look very sympathetic. Hopefully, in time, her relationship with my mother will become less strained.

If an imminent storm has a scent, it's hanging in the air, along with the June flowers in the pots which dot the patio. I glance across at the pond which I could cheerfully jump in to cool off.

'What about Jasmine? Isn't it your weekend to have her to stay? Maybe she's turned up while we've been sitting out here.' She pauses the sawing at her crimson nail and glances back at the house.

'She's gone with her sister to some spa.'

'Really?' Ellen's voice rises but her face falls.

'I thought I mentioned it.'

'No, you didn't – anyway, it's got nothing to do with *me*, has it?'

I can tell what she's thinking, *why don't my stepdaughters ever want to include me in their plans?*

'If you must know, they're with Carmen.' My ex-wife's smile fills my mind and I blink it away. It took meeting Ellen for me to fully get over her, since our separation was entirely my fault. If it had been hers, splitting up might have been easier to bear. 'I can't imagine the two of you wanting to share a hot tub.' I pull a face.

'Oh, right.' Ellen reaches for her wine. 'Well, hopefully,

she's got something more worthwhile to talk to them about than *me* for a change.'

'What makes you think they're talking about *you*?' I rest my hand over the back of hers. No new wife could feel more insecure about an ex, especially since Carmen and I have always been on such good terms. 'I reckon that both of them, because they worship their mother, possibly just feel like they're somehow betraying her if they get too close to you.'

'It's more than that.' Her face falls. I hate having this discussion. We have it so many times.

'Honestly, it'll get easier.'

'Will it *really*?' Ellen rests her nail file on the table. 'I'd love to have a better relationship with your daughters, but I'm convinced that Carmen purposefully turns them against me.'

Oh God, here we go again. One tiny mention of Carmen's name and the pleasant evening we've been enjoying is suddenly tainted. 'Let's just try and forget about them all, shall we?' I clasp my arms behind my head and lean back in my seat, surveying the striped lawn beyond the patio. The gardener's done a brilliant job.

'OK. Look, I'm sorry. I know you keep trying to smooth things over.' Ellen sighs as she stands from her chair, peeling the fabric of her dress from the back of her thighs. 'With *all* of them.' She looks over to Mum's cottage.

'Shall we go inside and start dinner soon? I don't know about you but I'm getting hungry.'

'I might take a quick shower first. I'm just so hot.'

'You don't need to tell me that.' I grin. 'I'd be joining you in that shower for a repeat performance of last night, but I'd best check on Mum – make sure she's alright.'

'Shall I come over with you?' The look on Ellen's face suggests she's secretly hoping I'll say no.

'No, it's fine, love. You get your shower and I'll be back in ten minutes.'

'Will Phyllis not want to see me, is that what you mean?' She folds her arms across herself in an almost protective gesture.

Gosh, she's hard work tonight, this wife of mine. 'If she's not feeling too good, Mum won't even want *me* bugging her. You know what she's like.'

'*Fiercely independent.*' Ellen mimics the phrase I've repeated so often. Mum *does* love living in the grounds of my house, where she can *choose* when and whether she'll spend time with us, but more often than not, especially lately, she prefers to do her own thing, saying she doesn't know how she ever found time to work before she retired.

Since Ellen moved in three months ago, just after we got engaged, I'm seeing Mum less and less. As well as my daughters. And there doesn't seem to be a whole lot I can do about it.

2

THE BREEZE IS WHIPPING around my bare legs as I wind my way past the summer house. The surface of our pond is radiant in the light of the fading day as I edge around it and along the stepping stones by the vegetable patch. I'm so proud of this garden – after all, along with the house, I designed every inch of it with my own fair hands. I had my daughters in mind as I worked out what was needed – the hammocks hanging in between the trees and the walk-in wardrobes in their rooms. Of course, I couldn't leave out my man-shed complete with a pool table and dart board. I'd like to say it cheered me up after the divorce was finalised, but really, it didn't.

I never envisaged another woman coming along to enjoy this house with me, but now Ellen has, I can't imagine my life as it was before she arrived. I'd hate to return to those days. Lonely evenings of sitting around in baggy boxer shorts, eating pizza when there was only myself to cook for during the week, and binge-watching box-sets on the TV.

'Mum.' I tap on her door. Since Dad died, she's been far happier living here than she ever would have been rattling around the sprawling Ilkley home I grew up in with my sister.

Dad never wanted to move further out to The Dales, but Mum loves the space and the peace here. She still repeatedly tries to pay me something for living here, but I wouldn't dream of taking her money. Ever.

When Dad was in the hospice, I said I'd look after her and I'll always honour that promise. It's the least I can do after the towers of strength both of them have always been throughout my life. I can tell that Ellen's not been anywhere near as fortunate as I have which makes me count my blessings even more.

She throws the door open. 'What on earth are you knocking for, son? Come on in.' As always, she's dressed as if she could be expecting visitors at any moment in her knee-length denim dress and without a hair out of place. She's one of the few women I know whose bobbed hair looks better grey since she gave in and allowed nature to take its course, rather than carrying on, as she put it, with lengthy and expensive trips to the salon to have it highlighted.

'I thought you weren't feeling well.' I follow her through to the kitchen, innately knowing that she's been spinning me a yarn. With her rosy cheeks and sprightly gait, she's a picture of health this evening.

'Drink?'

'I'll have one of them if there's one on offer.' I point at her wine glass. 'So I take it you've made a miraculous recovery since we were messaging?'

'I wasn't feeling all that sociable earlier.' She gestures to a seat at the table then heads to the fridge. 'I'm sorry.'

'Why?'

She looks thoughtful for a moment as she glances across at my house. The sky appears to be several shades darker and all is still. There's a real calm before the storm sense about things. 'Oh, it's nothing.' She reaches up and slides a glass from the cupboard.

'No, go on, tell me.' I watch as the wine glugs from the

bottle into my glass. I always feel at home in Mum's kitchen. It's half the size of her old one but she kept lots of her old stuff from our childhood home, including the table which we've all had many happy times around. Meals, games, conversations...

'If it had been Carmen you were sitting outside there with,' – Mum rests the bottle down, – 'I'd have been out to join you like a shot.'

'Don't you think Ellen can sense this?' I sigh and run my hand over my beard. No wonder she keeps going on about what she senses in Mum.

'Don't get me wrong,' Mum replies. 'I get along fine with her on a superficial level – for your sake as much as—'

'I don't want you just to get along for *my* sake.' I sigh. 'Come on, Mum.'

'It's just that every conversation has to be so *intense*.' She rolls her eyes to the ceiling. 'You know what I mean, don't you?'

'You mean she likes to keep talking all the time?'

'That's part of it but sometimes I just like to sit and be quiet – even when I'm in company. But it's like she's scared of silence.'

I raise an eyebrow. She's nothing if not forthright, my mother. Too forthright. 'I hear you, Mum, but you could make more of an effort with Ellen. Especially with her not having a mum of her own. It would make such a difference to her.'

I joked about us sharing mine after our wedding last month, but as Mum said at the time, *I'll never be Ellen's mother, just her mother-in-law.*

She screws the lid back on the wine bottle and looks in the other direction. She's always been uncomfortable with Ellen being her *new* daughter-in-law. It's obvious that my daughters aren't the only ones who feel like they're betraying Carmen by having anything much to do with my second wife.

'I'm coming for dinner on Sunday, aren't I?' She slides into the chair facing me, sending a waft of her perfume my way. 'So I'll try to be more sociable then.'

'Are you?' I reach for my glass and sip at the full-bodied red. 'It's the first I've heard of it. Ellen invited you, did she?'

She nods. 'Will the girls be gracing us with their presence for a change?'

'I doubt it. I barely see them these days – Jasmine's going through a spell of preferring to be with her mother.' I rest my glass back down on the table with a click.

'So it'll just be me, you and Ellen?' She points from herself to me, and then in the direction of our house. The tone of her voice says everything, even if she's doing her best to disguise it.

'I've no idea but I should imagine so.'

'Oh.'

'Is mine and Ellen's company really not good enough?' I study my mother's expression. It's veering between discomfort and indecision like she's searching within herself for an excuse to get out of it now I've confirmed her granddaughters won't be there. She's becoming increasingly *honest*, the older she gets. Brutally so, at times.

'It's just that Ellen *always* wants to discuss topics that we go around and around in circles with.' She rests her fingers on the stem of her wine glass. 'It wears me out.'

'I think I know what you mean.' For once, I can't disagree. I love the ground my wife walks on but I know *exactly* what Mum's getting at. She was starting one such episode in the garden and I just hope it's not going to continue over dinner.

'If she's not quizzing me about Carmen,' Mum goes on, seemingly relieved to be getting this off her chest, 'then she's going on about how she wishes things were different with the girls, and if it's not them, then dare I say the word, we end up talking about the *reversal* of your vasectomy or lack thereof.'

'Alright, Mum.' We're now on delicate ground here and I don't like the way she's just emphasised the word, *reversal*. I've had enough salt rubbed in this particular wound over the last few weeks. It's not that Ellen makes me feel inadequate – I do a good enough job of that all by myself.

'Do you know how badly she's got her hopes pinned on things being *second time lucky*?' Mum fiddles with the necklace Dad gave her for their golden anniversary. 'You'd think her life depended on it to listen to her.'

I take a big gulp of wine, feeling like I need it more than ever. 'Ellen *knows* we've only got around a five to ten per cent chance of her becoming pregnant. God, I wish the odds were higher but it is what it is.'

'I told you at the time the vasectomy was a mistake, Oliver – you were far too young.'

'It was what Carmen wanted.'

'You should have listened to *me*, Oliver.'

'Anyway, I'm paying this new specialist a lot of money,' I say. 'He claims to be able to work wonders even though fourteen years have passed.' The expression that crossed the consultant's face when I first specified the number of elapsed years swims into my mind. I knew immediately that things weren't as hopeful as Doctor Google had suggested.

'Shall I tell you what I think, Oliver?' Mum's voice is the firmest its been since I arrived.

'I expect you're going to tell me whether I say yes or no.' Sweat pools in my armpits and runs down my sides. Perhaps I *will* go and jump in that pond after I've finished up here.

3

I WAIT for Mum to give me her sage words of wisdom. She'll feel better once she's said her piece, so as always, I'll indulge her. It's not as if I don't spend all day, every day trying to keep the women in my life happy. If it's not Ellen, Mum or my daughters – it's my ex-wife, my PA or my sister. Dad was also a master at this, his motto being, *anything for a quiet life.*

'I'm sorry to be so blunt.' Mum stares into her glass. 'But I'm going to just come out and say it.'

'Go on then.'

'I think you could impregnate Ellen with *quadruplets* and she still wouldn't be happy.'

I usually trust her judgement but not this time. 'Ah, come on, Mum,' I begin. 'That's—'

'There's a deep dissatisfaction in her that I've never been able to put my finger on.' Mum lifts her eyes to meet mine.

'What do you mean?'

'You've given her the commitment, the beautiful home, and the extravagant lifestyle,' – she checks the items off on her manicured fingertips, – 'but there's *always* a yearning. You'll *never* be able to give Ellen enough – it's written all over her face.'

'I think you're wrong, Mum, I really do. She just wants to be a mother.' I stare down at my wedding ring, my shoulders sagging. I was in a reasonably good mood when I was sitting outside with my wife, looking forward to a relaxing weekend of pottering around the house together, a few drinks and some good food. Mum couldn't possibly understand how Ellen's biological clock must be ticking. After all, she's been a mother twice over and a grandmother four times. I'm not even a woman and I seem to understand this more than my mother even does.

'Why did you have to rush into things like you have?'

I shrug. Here we go again. We did race from meeting to engagement to marriage, all the while, Ellen making no secret of her desire for motherhood. But this is *my* business and somehow I need to impress this on my mother.

'Look, I do understand you didn't want to remain single for the rest of your life, but why couldn't you have gone after someone nearer to your own age and...' Mum's voice becomes more gentle – bordering on sympathetic. 'Someone who's already had their children, someone who's a little less, how shall I put it – *needy*?'

'We can't control who we fall in love with.' I frown. Poor Ellen. She tries so hard to win favour with my mother but really, no second wife, in Mum's eyes would have ever been a patch on Carmen. Not Ellen, not *anyone*.

'Will Ellen still love you when all hope of the two of you having a child has failed?' It's Mum's turn to arch an eyebrow. 'Will she even *stay* with you?'

I drain my glass as I shuffle in the seat to which the backs of my legs are sticking. I'll be pouring another large one when I get back to the house, which I think will be my fourth drink of the evening. I'm already feeling the effects of the alcohol on an empty stomach so it could even be my fifth.

Honestly – my bloody mother. I only popped in to make sure she wasn't in agony with a migraine or some other ailment. 'I'll cross that bridge if and when I come to it,' I reply. 'In the meantime, like I said before, the specialist I'm seeing can work wonders.'

'The only *wonder* that specialist will be achieving is parting you from several thousands of your hard-earned pounds.' She clasps her hands together on the table. 'It'll be a wonder for *him* when it's sitting in his bank account.'

'Ellen's more than worth every penny.' I stare at her, hoping the look on my face tells her that she's going too far. 'Making her happy means the world.'

Mum's expression becomes even more discernible or maybe that's down to the wine I've drunk. 'Money can't fix everything, Oliver – nor can it buy happiness. Ellen's or anyone else's.'

I stand from my chair. 'Look it's been nice having a drink with you but I'd better be getting back to Ellen.'

'There's no need for sarcasm, Oliver.' She presses her lips together. 'Just keep in mind that some things aren't meant to be, no matter how much you want them.'

'On that happy note, I'll bid you goodnight.' I head towards her. She might have annoyed me since I arrived but I'll never leave without my usual peck on the cheek as a parting gesture.

'It looks like the rain's started anyway.' Mum tilts her head. 'Look how dark that sky's turned.'

A little like my mood. I kiss her still-soft cheek then head towards the door. 'I'll get back over there before it *really* comes down.'

'And don't be having loads more to drink,' she calls after me. 'Get some food down yourself – you're already staggering.'

By the time I've dashed back to my house, I'm soaked to the skin.

'You don't *need* a shower,' Ellen chuckles as I arrive at the patio doors into the kitchen, my clothes clinging to my body. 'Wow look at that. I've never seen lightning like it.'

I turn just in time to see a magnificent fork light up the sky and then slide the glass door behind me, grateful to be out of the bouncing rain and away from my mother's well-meaning words. 'I might be a middle-aged man now, but I'm still not a fan of thunderstorms.' I laugh.

Ellen strides to our American-style fridge and pulls out a wine bottle. Her damp hair hangs in waves down her back and it's impossible not to notice that she isn't wearing a bra beneath her linen shirt-style dress. I could never have imagined a new wife living here with me when I designed the place but as she pads around the kitchen tiles in her bare feet, she's become just as much a part of this house as I am.

I rest my elbows on the counter of the breakfast bar to watch Ellen as she pours from the bottle of Sauvignon Blanc.

'How was she?'

'Mum?' I accept a glass from my wife, taking care not to let it slip through my wet fingers. 'Ah you know, the usual. She's alright – just a bit tired.' I won't mention a word about her feeling *anti-social*. 'She's looking forward to Sunday dinner.' I give Ellen what I hope is my best jokey hard stare then raise the glass to my lips. I'd better get some food down me soon. The fresh air as I ran over from the granny flat has made the wine go to my head even more. I should have stuck to beer – I don't drink that as quickly.

She smiles. 'I thought having her over might defrost her a little.' She rakes a finger through the front of her hair. 'Hopefully, your girls will join us as well – safety in numbers. I've sent them both a text but they haven't replied.'

I stay quiet and take a sip from my glass, not wishing to get

Ellen started by telling her there's not a cat in hell's chance that my daughters will join us on Sunday. The poor love has done everything in her power to win them over but it's just not happening. 'Nice drop of white, this.' I hold my glass aloft.

'Cloudy Bay,' she replies. 'New Zealand. It'll go well with the chicken.'

'I'll just grab a fresh change of clothes.' I head towards the door. 'Then I'll be right with you.'

My feet sink into the deep pile of carpet as I make my way up the stairs and to our bedroom for some fresh shorts and a T-shirt. My house still has the bachelor pad feel I was craving when I built the place with its slate greys and sparse walls, but I can't deny that I'm enjoying things having the woman's touch nowadays. A bunch of fresh flowers here, a fluffy cushion there.

I pull the door to my wardrobe open, leafing through my endless designer shirts in the hope of finding a comfy t-shirt. I'm enjoying being at home more and more these days, so a shop might be necessary for some more leisurely clothes. Gone are the days of being wedded to my career as an architect. Now that I'm four years beyond my fiftieth birthday, I know what's important in life and it isn't just work. Whoever lies on their deathbed and says, *I should have spent more of my life in the office?*

The ensuite smells of Ellen's floral-scented shower gel and the sink is littered with her many lotions and potions. Her clutter took some getting used to when she first moved in, but now I wouldn't have it any other way. I hunt around in the mirrored cabinet, my hand falling on a pile of unused ovulation and pregnancy tests instead of the comb I'm seeking for what's left of my hair.

I sigh deeply. My new consultant has told us that my fertility could suddenly improve at any time, but this doesn't mean I want my wife stockpiling these bloody tests. But as she keeps reminding me, just because my previous check after the operation hasn't been what we'd hoped for doesn't mean I'm *completely* infertile. He really gave Ellen something to hang onto when he said that things can and often do change. And even if they don't, we'll have other options.

The rain is now hammering so hard outside that it's splashing through the open ensuite window onto my arm. I tug the window towards me, squinting against a sharp bolt of lightning, followed immediately by the rumble of thunder.

'That smells divine.' My stomach rumbles.

'Did you hear that just now?' Ellen looks up from stabbing a skewer into the chicken I began roasting earlier. 'The storm must be directly overhead – the thunder wasn't even a second after the lightning.' With the oven gloves slung over her shoulder, and her face bathed in the under-cabinet lighting, she's the vision of a domestic goddess.

She's almost childlike in her excitement about the storm, reminding me of how much I love her and how lucky I am to be spending this Friday evening, with just me and my wife in our beautiful home – babies or no babies. I only hope Mum was wrong and that I *can* be enough for her.

Then, as I settle down on a stool at the breakfast bar to watch as she continues to move around the kitchen, the doorbell echoes through the hallway.

4

'ARE YOU EXPECTING SOMEONE?' Ellen wipes her hands with a towel.

'Of course not.' I frown. 'I hope there's nothing wrong.' Nine o'clock on a Friday evening in torrential rain is not the time for social calls. Mum's at home and the girls, as far as I know, are at the spa with Carmen. I can't imagine who else it could be at this time of the night.

'Are you going to answer the door?' She shakes her mane of hair behind one shoulder. 'Or do I have to break off from sorting the dinner?'

'I've got it.' I wink at her, and then stride along the wooden tiles of our hallway towards the main entrance, unable to make out the shape beyond the frosted glass. At least only one person is standing on the porch. I expect there'd be two people if it were the police with something dreadful to relay.

It's a visitor who doesn't know us, as most people know to use our side door. This front door's only ever used by people delivering something – like bad news.

'Where's the key?' My voice is strangely loud in the usually serene hallway. *Am I the only person who ever puts keys where they're supposed to go?*

The doorbell rings again, far louder in my ears now I'm so close to it. The rain's still bouncing down out there. It's little wonder that whoever is waiting beyond the door is dying to get in here where it's dry.

'Hang on. I won't be a sec. I'm just finding the key.'

As I'm about to instruct our late-night caller to go around to one of our other doors, my hand falls on what I'm looking for in the top drawer of the Welsh dresser.

'Coming,' I call, lurching to the door. I slide the key into the lock and pull the door towards me, blinking at the person who stands dripping on the porch. 'Can I help you?'

Like me, the stranger outside is dressed casually in shorts, a T-shirt and trainers. Unlike me, he's got a full head of sandy-blonde hair, has far fewer wrinkles around his friendly blue eyes, and must be around twenty years younger. He steps forward. 'I'm so sorry to bother you mate, but I've gone and broken down.' He pulls an apologetic face. 'Yours was the first house I came to.'

'Oh, I'm sorry to hear that – where has it happened?' Hopefully, I don't sound too irritated at this man who might end up delaying my dinner. The poor bloke – the last thing he'll need is someone being irked at him asking for help.

'Do you mind if I come in for a minute?' He rubs at his bare arms. 'Just to get out of this rain.'

With the storm still gathering pace, the rain's hitting him almost at a diagonal as he stands on the porch. I don't really want to ask him in – after all, we're just about to eat, but my manners get the better of me.

'Of course. Wow, it's gotten even heavier since I last looked out.' I hold the door wider and he rushes towards me. 'Come in.'

'Thanks, mate. I hugely appreciate this.' He steps off the

doormat into the hallway. I push the door closed after him. 'I didn't want to have to disturb your evening, but I didn't have much choice.'

'You've broken down, you say?' I've no time for small talk – the quicker I can get him sorted, the faster I can get back to enjoying my evening with my wife.

'Yeah, I've been walking for around forty minutes. I can't tell you how relieved I was when I saw the lights from the end of your lane.' He rakes his fingers through his sodden hair. He doesn't have a bag, a coat, or *anything*. Despite my initial irritation, these observations evoke a twinge of sympathy. I'd hope that if one of *my* girls broke down somewhere, someone would take them in and offer to help. And what goes around, comes around, after all.

'Who is it, love?' Ellen calls from the kitchen as she bangs the oven door. 'The chicken needs a few more minutes.'

'Fetch a towel through, will you?'

'Sorry,' the man grins, pushing his fringe back from his forehead. 'I'm dripping all over your floor.'

'Oh, don't worry about that – so, are you with a breakdown service?'

He hangs his head. 'If only things were that simple. I know I'm ridiculous but I've only recently set up as a kitchen fitter and am trying to keep my costs down.' I feel even worse now for being irritated. Breaking down tonight is probably the last straw.

'Oh.' There's an element of surprise in Ellen's tone as she emerges from the kitchen, probably at this hunk of a man who's descended on our home. 'Erm, here you go.'

'Thanks, love.' I turn to take the towel from her, wishing she was wearing something more substantial than the skimpy shirt dress. 'This gentleman's broken down about a forty-minute walk away. I think we'd better put the kettle on.'

'Oh gosh, I can think of better nights to be breaking down.'

She laughs as she jerks her thumb in the direction of the window and pulls a face. Thankfully, she doesn't seem as bothered as I initially was. She's more easy-going in this respect – and one of the things that initially drew me to her was her inclination to support the underdog. I first saw it at the bar she was working at before we got together. Someone evidently on his uppers had called in. While everyone else gave him a wide berth and looked at him as if he were the dregs of society, Ellen made him welcome and offered him something to eat and drink. Meanwhile, I found myself compelled to hang around until the end of her shift, hoping for a moment with her.

'Let me cover the cost of that man's drink and sandwich,' I said as she loaded glasses into the dishwasher. 'I noticed you took it from your own purse.'

She spun around, looking surprised. 'You're very observant, aren't you?'

'The way you treated him and paused to chat with him will have made a huge difference to his day.'

'I didn't do it to win any praise.' There was an almost defensive tone in her voice. 'Anyone can end up like he has – what are the stats – something like we're all three paychecks away from homelessness?' She looked me up and down, probably taking in my tailored suit and expensive shoes. 'I can't imagine that's anything you need to worry about though.'

There was something in her eyes that seemed to view my affluence and good fortune with derision, and for reasons that baffled me, I longed to close the gap between us. 'We're all *people*,' I said, wishing I had something more profound to come back with. 'Money's just a tool.'

'Yeah.' She went back to the dishwasher but jerked her head up when someone whistled her over and she disappeared into the shadows at the opposite end of the bar. I hoped it wasn't a boyfriend who I'd offended by paying her some attention. Anyway, I hadn't said anything untoward. Rather than trying to see who she was talking to, I busied myself with how I was going to get home and opened the Uber app on my phone. Then after a few minutes, she reappeared.

'Sorry if I was a bit off before – it's been a manic shift, that's all. We're short-staffed.'

'I could see that. Have you worked here for long?'

'Long enough.' She rested her elbows on the polished bar. 'I haven't seen *you* in here before.' It was framed as a question rather than a statement.

'My girls are away with their Mum. I usually have them at the weekends and didn't feel like going straight back to an empty house. I took a chance on this place.' I was about to add that it wasn't my usual sort of establishment to drink at but she might have been insulted by that, so I stayed quiet.

'You're separated then?' Something in her voice told me she was interested.

'Divorced.' I hated the word and hated being a divorcee even more. 'How about you?' Blimey – had I just said this? It was the first time I'd shown a flicker of interest in a woman since Carmen. But something about this woman intrigued me beyond measure.

Disappointment bubbled in the pit of my stomach when she hesitated before replying. 'Never married,' she eventually said. But she still hadn't confirmed whether or not she was in a relationship.

'So you're single too?' I hoped I wasn't looking at her *too* intently. We were poles apart, granted, but I wanted to keep talking.

She glanced over at the group of men at the other side of the bar, the last people other than me who were making a move to leave. 'Sure am. I tell you what, how about I get rid of these last few customers and then we could perhaps find somewhere else for a drink?'

I was happier at her suggestion than I'd felt in a long time.

'Thanks so much.' Our impromptu visitor accepts the towel from Ellen which he begins to rub over his head and face. 'I'm so sorry for interrupting your evening.'

'Not at all.' She turns back towards the kitchen. 'But I'll have to leave you in my husband's capable hands as I have to attend to a chicken.'

'Do you have anyone who could pick you up from here?' I hook my thumbs into the belt loops of my shorts. 'Anyone you could call?'

5

'MY PHONE'S as dead as a doornail.' The man laughs as he pats his shirt pocket. 'But no, there's no one I can call – I live alone. So, I think I need to bite the bullet and join a breakdown service sharpish.'

I laugh back at him – not that what he's just said is funny. Nor is having this adonis standing in my hallway.

'Hopefully, they'll be able to tow me to a garage tonight.' A sudden seriousness exudes from him and he looks almost vulnerable. 'Everything I own, my entire livelihood, is in the back of that van. If anything were to happen to it...' His voice trails off.

The poor bloke. From his physique and rough hands, it's obvious he's a grafter. As Ellen's reminded me so often in the short time we've been together, not everyone has enjoyed the trappings of their parent's wealth like me and my sister. Private school, university, a gap year, and a trust fund from my grandparents to get us started in life to name but a few of our privileges. 'Right, let's get your phone on charge, shall we?' I hold my hand out for it. 'Come on through.'

'Ah, that would be awesome.' He slides his feet from his

soggy trainers and then follows me into the kitchen. 'Cheers, mate.'

I bite down on my lip, possibly to prevent myself from asking him *not* to call me 'mate.' Holding the door open for him, I glance back to see the trail of wet footprints he's left along the hallway. 'What phone have you got?'

'A Samsung. I hugely appreciate this, you know.'

His gratitude is tinged with an air of something else – inferiority perhaps? It's *me* who should feel inferior beside *him*, the way he looks. 'To be fair,' I say, 'maybe you could use something stronger than a cup of tea. I've got some beers in the fridge if you'd like one?'

'Oh, now you're talking.' His face relaxes with gratitude. 'It doesn't exactly look like I'll be driving any time soon, does it? This is so good of you.'

'Have a seat.' I point at the breakfast bar. 'Ellen, do we have a charger for a Samsung?'

She spins on her heel. 'Top drawer – there are a few chargers in there but I don't know what's what. It's just a mass of wires.'

'I'll start by getting you that beer.' I head toward the fridge and slide two bottles from the shelf. 'I might as well have one with you. Do you want a glass?'

'I'll just drink it from the bottle.' He looks even broader, hulked over our breakfast bar, and from the size of his shoulders, it's clear he works out. 'Save you on the washing up.'

It's on the tip of my tongue to tell him we've got a dishwasher but that would sound crass. I can't deny that it's a little inconvenient for him to turn up like this right before dinner but it is what it is. I also wish that Ellen was dressed a little more conservatively now that another man's eyes could be on her.

But if he's noticed anything about how attractive she is, his face is revealing nothing. If he's watching anyone, it's me, not

Ellen. I open both beer bottles before passing one to him along the counter. 'Cheers.' I hold mine aloft. 'Let's drink to getting you back on the road.' I take a swig.

'You never drink from the bottle.' Ellen's voice is tinged with shock. 'What's got into you?'

'There's a first time for everything. Now, let's have a look for that charger.'

I riffle around in the drawer. 'Ta-da.' I plug it into the wall and connect his phone.

'Thanks, mate.'

'Call me Oliver.' Hopefully, I'm managing to keep how peeved I'm feeling out of my voice. Continuing to fight it, I hold out my hand. 'What's your name? We can't have a beer together without being on first-name terms.' I sound like my dad used to. The thought warms me.

'Anthony.' He holds his hand out too and I return his hand-shake. 'I can't tell you how grateful I am for your help.'

'And I'm Ellen.' She turns from slicing a loaf, knife still in hand. 'We were just about to eat actually.'

'No, I'm really so—'

'Don't be apologising – I was just about to say that you're more than welcome to join us while you're waiting for the breakdown service.' She points the knife towards the oven. 'There's plenty to go around. We always cook too much.'

'Oh, I couldn't.' Anthony shakes his head. 'You've both been kind enough already.'

He really shouldn't be staying for *dinner* but I can't retract my wife's invitation without sounding rotten. And it's going to take at least a couple of hours before a breakdown service will come to his rescue. A man on his own, who isn't at risk will receive little to no priority. My dad's face fills my mind. He was renowned for his service to waifs and strays and wouldn't have hesitated to invite a man in this predicament to stay for dinner. I should be more like my dad. I *want* to be more like my dad.

'Seriously.' I peel at the label on my bottle, wondering if I'm slurring my words with all I've drunk so far this evening. 'We've got a whole chicken. So have you eaten?'

'I can't deny that I've got a bit of an appetite after all that stressing and walking. Are you absolutely sure I wouldn't be imposing?'

'Not at all.' She drops the knife into the sink. 'Besides, I'm sure Oliver will welcome some sensible male conversation for a change.'

'She's not wrong there.' I force a laugh. 'I've got two daughters, a sister – obviously a wife.' I point at Ellen. 'Oh, and a mother out there in the granny flat.' I gesture in the direction of Mum's cottage. 'You'll have to close your ears, love.' I smile at Ellen. 'It might be all football scores, fast cars and what's the best beer over dinner.' I can do this – of course I can. It's only for an hour or two and I'll start to sober up a little once I get some food in me. Ellen and I have got the entire weekend in each other's company. We've got the rest of our lives.

'Is that charger working?' He nods at it.

I glance down and squint at the screen. 'Not yet, but if your phone's completely dead, it'll take a while for the charge to kick in.'

'I'll start ringing around breakdown companies once there's some life back in it.' He swigs from his beer bottle. 'Can you recommend anyone?'

'There's the service *we're* with.' I pull my phone from the back pocket of my shorts, hoping I'll be able to read without seeing three of everything. 'I'll have a look – I think we could both get a referral discount if I give you a code.'

'A discount sounds good,' he replies. 'Like I said, It's still early days for my business.'

My goodwill can't stretch beyond him staying for dinner. Perhaps if I'd known him better, I'd have stood the cost of the breakdown cover. However, because I've only known him for ten minutes, that feels like a step too far.

But as Anthony rests his beer bottle down on the marble worktop and grins at me, I have a sense that tonight, with my inhibitions so lowered, we're about to get to know one another a whole lot beyond anything to do with football, beer or cars.

6

'YOU'RE RIGHT, love. The wine really does go well with this chicken.' Really, I'm pretending to be able to taste my food and wine. I'm onto my umpteenth drink and I'm probably blathering rather than speaking coherently. While Ellen put the finishing touches to our meal, I've had two beers with Anthony. *Never mix grapes with grain.* I can almost hear Mum's voice. She was right when I left her house two hours ago – I was already staggering.

'I take it you're local, Anthony?'

'Fairly,' he replies. 'I've got a flat a few miles away. I wouldn't mind a place like this one day though.' He casts his gaze around the room. 'You've really fallen on your feet here, Oliver.'

For reasons I can't pinpoint, his use of my name in relation to his observation of my status feels almost as irksome as him calling me *mate*.

'I've worked hard for it, as it happens – anyway, it sounds like you're cut out of the same piece of cloth – you just need to keep on building your business.'

'I know you mean well but I don't think so.'

'All businesses start from zero.'

'Your idea of zero will differ from mine.'

Ellen's watching us intently. This is a dodgy subject, always quite emotive to her when comparisons start to be made about wealth and backgrounds.

'My childhood,' Anthony continues, 'consisted of me, my mum and my sister hiding behind the sofa from loan sharks when they kept hounding us and threatening to kick the door in.'

'What about your dad?'

'I never knew him.' I can tell from his closed expression that he doesn't wish to be pushed any further on the subject of his father.

'So you've done good – you should be even more proud of yourself for getting your own business off the ground.'

'Barely.' He grins. 'But I'll get there.' For what he lacks in financial security, he certainly makes up for in his looks and the strength of his presence at our table.

'Is your sister older or younger than you?' Ellen seems to be trying to steer the subject away from money and I'm grateful. She hasn't made a great deal of conversation with Anthony but to be fair, we haven't let her get much of a word in edgeways.

Much as I'm getting along with our dinner guest since his arrival, I can't deny how inadequate I feel sitting across the table from him which would probably come as a surprise to him. For all the personal training sessions I attend, I still feel puny beside his muscles and ancient beside his youth. But most of all, my lack of virility is almost palpable. I bet if Anthony had a wife who yearned for a baby like Ellen does, it wouldn't take him five minutes to make her pregnant.

'So you're single, you say?' I rest my wine glass on the polished surface beside my plate and look at Anthony across the table. All two of him. Then I turn to Ellen. 'Can I have some water please, love? I think I've had quite enough wine for one evening.' I'd usually get the water myself but I don't think I can be trusted to walk in a straight enough line from the dining room without looking foolish.

'I was thinking the same thing.' She laughs as she stands, tugging her shirt-dress down from where it's risen as she's been sitting. 'You have put away rather a lot. Would you like some water as well?' She points at Anthony's glass.

'I'd better had,' he replies. 'I don't know when I'll be driving again. Soon, I hope.'

'I'll be back in a moment.' We both watch as Ellen walks to the door and then look at each other.

'It's a great meal – this.' Anthony stabs at a piece of chicken. 'I didn't realise how hungry I was. You're a good bloke, Oliver. I couldn't have turned up on a better doorstep.'

'Oh, well, erm, thanks – we're happy to be able to help.'

'Did you answer Oliver's question while I was in the kitchen?' Ellen rests a glass in front of Anthony's plate.

'What question?'

'Whether anyone's waiting for you back at home?'

I don't like my wife's interest in whether this man is single even if she *is* just being polite. I don't like it one bit.

'I was with someone a few years ago but things didn't work out. To be honest, I'm far happier on my own. I can do what I want, when I want, how I want.'

'I knew someone like that, and then *bam*, I upended it all and turned his life upside down.' Ellen's hand on my shoulder sends bolts of electricity through me as she arrives at my side with a glass of water.

'You certainly did.' I reach for her hand and cup my own over it.

Anthony coughs, looking somewhat uncomfortable with our sudden display of affection. 'Well, you certainly seem to have a good life together here.' As Ellen retakes her seat, he sweeps his gaze upwards, at the beams and the skylights above where we're seated. The rain's still drumming against them, though not as heavily as before.

'I designed the place myself.' I gesture to the doors into the conservatory – my favourite spot for reading. 'When I was still single.'

'It's a huge place for just one bloke.' He returns his attention to his meal.

'I've got two daughters as well.' I gesture to a photo of them on the sideboard.

'Really?'

I don't like the rise of interest in his voice. I'm uncertain whether it's because he could be interested in *them,* or because he believes I might be ancient enough to have daughters who could be of an *interesting* age to him.

'They live with their mother. Well, the fifteen-year-old does. My twenty-three-year-old has a shared house with some girls she works with.' I feel the need to make their ages known to him - so he knows they're off-limits.

'Do the two of you have any kids *together?*' He casts his eyes around the room again, possibly looking for a photo of a younger child or a stray toy discarded on the wooden floor. If only.

'No.' Hopefully the strength I place behind this single word will shut down the conversation.

'Not yet,' Ellen adds.

I glance at my wife, surprised she's weighed into this subject that's so emotive for the two of us, but seeing, as always, the hunger in her eyes. 'But it's not for the want of trying. Oliver's had—'

'Ellen,' I exclaim. 'Far too much information.' I'd say that she's had a little too much vino down her neck as well to be elaborating on such matters. 'I'm sure Anthony doesn't want to hear about our...' My words fade out. I'm not going to use the words *fertility problems* at the dinner table. Especially not to someone I've only known for an hour.

'It's OK – my sister had some issues so I'm no stranger to this sort of talk.' Anthony offers me a knowing look as he reaches for his water. 'Don't worry.'

'Your sister had issues with *what*?' Bloody great – Ellen's clearly going to pursue this topic.

'You know, having a baby.' A cloud seems to enter Anthony's eyes. 'It nearly broke their marriage up at the time. So yeah, I've heard it all from them – chapter and verse.'

'And are they alright – now?' I can hear the hope in Ellen's voice. What she means to ask is, *have they now got a baby?* She usually tries to hide it but I can tell from the watch list on our TV what things she's viewing. Then there's the curated list on our shared Apple News feed which tells me what articles she's reading. She's pretty obsessed with this baby thing, so no amount of money is too high to pay that specialist to increase our odds of success. Whatever my mother might say.

'Yeah – but they ended up having to use a donor.' Anthony scoops some peas onto his fork. 'It was a last resort but at least it saved their marriage.'

We continue eating in silence for a few moments. Silence apart from the incessant drum of the rain against the skylights. The way this conversation has gone is all too close to the bone, being that using a *donor* is one of the *options* that my consultant has put forward. But Ellen and I haven't discussed it yet, not properly. Besides, I'm certain it's *my* baby she wants – not just *any* baby.

'You wouldn't know my niece isn't my brother-in-law's,' Anthony continues. 'She's got his dark hair, his blue eyes, even his temperament, so my sister says.'

'Do they know who her father is?'

'Ellen – what a question for the dinner table.' I reach for my water. Thank goodness Mum stayed at her granny pad tonight and didn't join us. She'd be mortified, however I'd like to think that Ellen would have restrained herself from this line of questioning had Mum been here.

'Oh yes – the donor was cherry-picked. They wanted someone who looked like my sister's husband and someone with a proven amount of intelligence. They certainly ran their checks on him beforehand.'

'So they used a clinic?' Ellen asks. 'They run plenty of checks from what I've found out.'

'Shall we return to talking about how Leeds are doing in the play-offs?' I force a laugh. 'I'm sorry the conversation has got so personal about your family.'

'It's fine,' he replies. 'I don't mind at all.'

'And I want to know.' Ellen sips her wine. 'So then what happened?' She looks at Anthony.

'Well, he just, you know, turned up and did his bit until it was successful.' He pulls a face. 'It took several attempts but when it was, successful I mean, he took his money and then left them alone. He hasn't bothered them since.'

'I thought paying a sperm donor was illegal in this country,' Ellen says.

'*Officially* it's illegal.' Anthony pauses as he raises the fork to his lips. 'But what nobody knows, nobody can prosecute. I can't understand why a donor would be expected to donate for *free*. After all, it's quite a gift they're bestowing – the gift of a family.'

What a topic of conversation. The silence hangs heavily between us all again, the clattering of forks and the click of glasses against the polished table sounding louder than usual at this late hour.

'There's more to our lives anyway than children,' I say quickly, keen to break the mood. 'We have lots of things to enjoy, like our home – and we have some fantastic trips planned, don't we, Ellen?' I'm so keen to fill the void hanging between us that my words are coming faster and probably sounding jumbled. 'Where have we got planned? We've already been to Iceland, we're hoping to go to Florida – we're–'

'I could help you if you wanted.' Anthony stares down at his plate, evidently nervous about meeting our eyes.

As well he should be if he's suggesting what I think he is.

7

'WHAT DO YOU MEAN, ANTHONY?' My heart's thudding so hard I feel it in my throat. And I wish to God I was more sober. At this rate, I'll be following in my father's footsteps and ending up in an early grave.

Ellen's sitting at a right angle to me, her eyes wide, not even attempting to conceal her shock. She looks like she wants to melt into her chair and vanish into thin air. And honestly, I don't know where to put myself either.

This man — this stranger — has waltzed into our home on a Friday night, is sitting at our table like he belongs there, and has somehow dismantled every defence we didn't realise we'd let slip. I can't believe what we've already divulged and I can't understand how we've let the conversation wander so far into this territory.

Anthony leans back in his chair, seemingly unfazed. 'It just seems such a shame,' he says, slow and smooth, 'for you to live in such a huge house,' — he gestures from left to right, like he's trying to sell it to us — 'and not be able to enjoy the sound of a little one running around.'

I stiffen. Ellen doesn't move. The silence that follows isn't empty — it's loaded.

'So what are you saying?'

He turns to me. Calm. Almost amused.

'It's simple, really. If you can give me what I want,' — he taps his chest with three fingers — 'then I can return the favour.'

My voice hardens with the tightening of my jaw. 'And what *do* you want?' Like I don't already know.

I reach for my wine glass again, even though I swore I'd had enough alcohol for one night. But water isn't going to cut it now.

Just an hour ago we were talking about jobs, TV, and the best places in Leeds to get a curry. Somehow, in the course of a single meal, the conversation has swerved into something that feels like a violation.

'I can give you both the baby it's obvious you're yearning for.' His voice is soft. 'I—'

'Look, I don't know what impression we've given you here, but—'

'We haven't even exhausted all options,' Ellen cuts in, folding her napkin with shaking fingers. 'There's still a good chance we could—'

'I don't even want kids of my own,' Anthony says, as though she hasn't spoken. 'But what I *do* need — as you've probably gathered — is some decent money behind me. The launchpad I've never had.'

He says it with such brazen ease I almost forget to breathe.

Ellen's hand tightens around her glass. 'Don't you think there must be better ways than preying on people's desperation?' Her tone is sharp, and brittle with discomfort. 'Look, you probably mean well, but this is all just... too much.'

Anthony's expression is neutral. Even apologetic.

'I *am* sorry. And I *do* mean well. But,' — he clears his throat

— 'I guess there's not a lot I wouldn't do to turn things around for myself.'

'Evidently.' I place my cutlery down in the centre of my plate. The clink is louder than it should be.

The room is heavy with a silence that feels like it might tip over into something else — a fight, a scream – or a deal. I don't know which it will be yet.

Ellen won't meet my eyes.

And Anthony? He just watches us both. Calmly. Like he expects to make the sale. Like it's only a matter of time.

I'm thankful this conversation didn't materialise until the end of our meal, and that I managed to get some food down myself while I still had an appetite. I'd have felt pretty rough in the morning without a meal in me.

'If you could excuse me for a moment.' Ellen pushes her chair back with a scrape and heads for the door without looking at either of us. 'I need to be on my own.' I can't be certain but she sounds like she's fighting back tears. Why did the subject of our fertility problems even have to raise its ugly head? And why the hell has he pushed it to this extent? I stare across the table, wondering what to say or do. Should I go after my wife or should I be forcing Anthony to leave? I never really wanted him here in the first place but I can hardly throw him back out into the storm until we've got him sorted out with his breakdown recovery.

'It was a serious proposition, you know.' Anthony leans forward in his seat as Ellen disappears along the hallway, followed by the familiar squeak of the kitchen door. 'I honestly wasn't trying to cause any trouble – or upset your wife.'

'I think we should just focus on getting you back on the road.'

'I saw first-hand how the donor fixed my sister's marriage.' Bloody hell – the man's like a dog with a bone. 'I've witnessed the happiness he brought into *their* lives, that's all.'

'Please, Anthony.' I slap the palm of my hand against my leg. 'Enough.'

'And I can do the same for the two of you. If it comes down to a choice between saving your marriage, or—' His hands spread across the air in front of him, as if he's already planning to bless the very walls of our home.

'There's nothing wrong with our marriage,' I snap. 'And I need to go after my wife.' I can tell by the level of clattering coming from the kitchen and the slam of the fridge door that Ellen's far from happy. If I know her correctly, she'll now be expecting me to get rid of him.

'I can't believe this, can you?' I close the kitchen door behind me with a click.

'*You* invited the man into our home.' She swings around to face me, her usual pale face flushed with anger. 'And what are you doing – leaving him on his own in our dining room, you heard what he said, he's broke. He could be filling his pockets with *anything*.'

'I don't think he's that way inclined.' I stride over to the breakfast bar and lean against it. If I don't I might keel over. 'He might be a wide boy, but he's not a thief.'

'I can't believe what he's just suggested.' She wrenches the lid from yet another bottle of Sauvignon Blanc. 'As if we could consider paying *him* to donate his sperm.'

A vision of her lined-up ovulation kits and pregnancy tests swims into my mind. Why, oh why, did I ever have that vasectomy? At the time, I was certain my family was complete and I would never have envisaged Carmen and me separating. I gave her everything she wanted, materially speaking, but as she said herself, it was *me* she'd married, not a big house or a designer handbag. I had so many warnings that my constant desertion of her and her needs would one day lead to our divorce, but I never took them seriously. Not until it was too late.

'Well, we must have given him *some* sort of the wrong impression.' It's on the tip of my tongue to say, *I'll have one of those*, as she slides a wine glass from the cupboard, but I'd better not. Anthony's suggestion has gone some way to sober me up, but not far enough.

'It's *your* baby I want, Oliver, no one else's.' She slops wine into a glass. However, I can tell by the way she pushed the conversation in the dining room that her words aren't necessarily filled with the truth.

'But what if,' – I lean my elbows onto the counter, – 'what if a donor arrangement or adopting a baby ends up being our only chance to be parents? What if it's either one of those options or no baby at all?'

'But the consultant said—'

'Five or ten to a hundred isn't a horse I'd get behind.'

She slams the bottle on the counter. 'I just can't believe how we've allowed him into our lives like this.'

'I know.'

'We were having a perfectly nice evening until he came along and *you* invited him in.' She points at me. Her voice rises and I can only hope the incessant drumming of the rain in the dining room is somewhat drowning Ellen out. Anthony probably feels crappy enough as it is for upsetting her.

'Shush. He'll hear you.'

'I really don't care.'

'If we're playing the blame game, love, it was *you* who invited him to stay for dinner.' I rise, somewhat unsteadily, from the counter and reach for her hand.

She looks sheepish for a moment. 'Look, whoever invited him for *whatever*, *you're* going to have to get rid of him. I feel uncomfortable with him in the house.'

'I can't just throw him out into the rain. It's still coming down a bucketload out there.' I jerk my head towards the patio doors. The thunder and lightning have stopped but it sounds like it will never stop raining.

'Help him get his breakdown service sorted,' – She points at his phone, – 'and then get rid of him.'

'OK. I'll be as quick as I can.'

She picks her glass up. 'And just for the record, *if* we're forced to go down the donor baby route, then it'll be through a *proper* clinic, not with some chancer that's quite literally wandered in off the street.'

I pause as I unplug Anthony's phone from the charger, trying to order my drunken thinking. *Does what she's just said mean that Ellen's beginning to consider the donor-baby route?* If she is, then surely it doesn't matter whether we use a proper clinic or like she put it, some *chancer*. The result will be the same, however one is likelier to provide a far speedier outcome.

'Let's just think about this properly before I send him on his way.' I close my fingers around Anthony's phone and look at my wife.

8

ELLEN PAUSES from raising the wine glass to her lips. 'What do you mean? Stop and think about *what?*'

'All I want is for you to be happy, and this arrangement potentially stands to assure that, much more than my five to ten bloody per cent odds.' What I don't add is that I can hardly bear to imagine the continued misery etched on her face when her time of the month continues to arrive.

'You can't be serious.' Her eyes glitter with emotion. 'Besides, what would people think? Your mother, for example – she'd know as soon as she saw–'

'Anthony has the same colour eyes as me,' I cut in. 'And hair, when I had some to speak of, that is.' I smooth my hand over the greying remains of what used to be my crowning glory. 'And he's as sharp as a knife, you can tell that a mile off.'

Ellen glugs more wine into her glass. 'You're not telling me you're *seriously* considering this,' she snaps. 'Are you insane? How much have you had to drink?'

'I know, you're right – it *is* insane. But I want to give you what you want, that's all.'

'Then we'll do this properly.' She turns away as if to let me know the subject is well and truly closed.

'It's not as if time's on our side though, is it?' I reach for her arm. 'As the consultant pointed out, you're at the wrong end of your thirties now – even *your* fertility's declining.'

'There's absolutely *nothing* wrong with me.' She swings around and squares herself up in front of me. 'Not according to the ovulation test I did when I went up for my shower. There was a faint line last night, but tonight it's as clear as a bell.'

I hold my breath. 'So why didn't you say something?'

'I was going to but we got sidetracked by our *visitor*.' She pulls a face. 'Listen, I know the chances are slim but it's *your* baby I want. So, let's not give up, Oliver – not yet. You've already had an attempt at reversal so there *might* be a bit of something going on in there.'

'OK, I hear you.' I let go of her arm, steeling myself to return to the dining room. 'I'll get him sorted then. I just wish you'd said something earlier.'

'About what?' She looks puzzled.

'You know – about tonight being your *window of opportunity*.'

'Why, what difference would it have made?'

'It's just that.' My stomach plummets with what I'm about to admit. *What a failure.* 'After the amount I've had to drink tonight, I don't think...' My words taper into nothing. Ellen doesn't need me to spell out what happens, or more to the point, *doesn't happen* when I've had too much to drink.

'I'll finish up in here.' She turns back to the sink. 'Just let me know when he's gone.'

Her *not* reacting to what I've just said is probably as bad as if she had.

'I'm so sorry if I overstepped the mark.' Anthony twists in his seat as I enter the room. 'I could hear how much I've upset Ellen – but my intentions really *were* honourable.' It sounds weird hearing such a middle-class statement emitted from a working-class mouth. At this thought, I hate myself. *Since when did I become so judgemental?* He's probably a decent enough human being – he's just made a rather off-the-wall offer.

'It's come as a shock to us both, that's all it is.' I head to the other side of the table and sit facing him.

'I can tell a mile off that you're a great couple.' He gestures to our wedding photo sitting beside the photo of the girls on the sideboard. We might not have had the same number of guests as I had the first time around but I was the happiest man alive when I married Ellen.

'Thank you.' *Where is this leading?*

'I mean, look at how you've treated me since I turned up at your door.' He jerks his head in its direction. 'If I was going to help *anyone* like that guy helped my sister, I'd want it to be the two of you.' He gives me an uneasy smile.

'Cheers.' I don't know what else I can say. All I know is that I've promised Ellen I'll get rid of him sharpish, so that's what I need to do. 'Anyway, shall we get you registered for the recovery service – now that your phone's regained some life?' I slide it across the table. 'I'm only sorry I can't give you a lift back to your van.' I gesture to the bottles between us. 'I've put a fair bit away tonight.'

He picks up his phone. 'While you were in the kitchen, I was thinking...'

'What?' I do hope he's not returning to our previous topic of conversation.

'That me, you know, ending up here like this tonight – well, it could be fate. I mean, how else would our paths have ever crossed?' He shrugs. 'I fit kitchens for the local council while you're clearly a good deal more successful and move in very different circles.'

Ignoring his philosophy, I plug my passcode into my phone. I'd better find him a recovery number to ring.

'Are you a believer in things happening for a reason, Oliver?'

His question pulls me up short. This was one of Dad's favourite sayings – one that he'd trot out at every twist and turn of mine and my sister's lives, whether it was something positive or negative. *Everything happens for a reason, son,* he'd say. *People enter one another's lives for a season or a reason.* And it's true. I really believe it. Slowly, I raise my eyes to meet Anthony's.

'You're beginning to consider this, aren't you?' He rests his phone on the table. 'I can tell.'

9

'HASN'T HE GONE?' Ellen's staring into her wine glass as she hunches over the breakfast bar. Anthony's really opened a can of worms with his proposition and somehow, I've got to smooth this over. After all, I was the one who let him into our home in the first place. But no matter how Ellen's reacting, after my conversation with him, I mostly feel like I can trust what he's saying. When he told me his intentions were honourable, I had no reason not to believe him.

'I think we should at least *talk* about his offer.' I pull up a stool beside my wife. 'We haven't discussed it properly yet – not without Anthony in the room.'

She looks at me as if I've got two heads.

'While I was speaking to him just now, he told me this is our *only* chance to take him up on this.' The direction I'm taking here could be the drink talking, or maybe it's my fear at Mum's suggestion that Ellen will leave me if I don't give her what she wants. Either way, I can hardly believe what I'm coming out with, and only hope I don't live to regret it. 'He'll be leaving soon and says we'll never see him again. Before he goes, I need to make sure you *definitely* don't want to consider what he's suggested.'

Still, Ellen doesn't reply but I can almost hear the cogs in her brain whirring at a hundred miles an hour. *What is she thinking?*

'What if we let him leave and then regret it?' More words are out before I can hold them back. 'Like he said, it's now or never.'

'So he's piling on the pressure?' She lets out a long breath. 'Don't you think that smacks of nothing but desperation? I don't know what else to make of it.'

'He's made no secret that he's desperate for money. And *you're* desperate to be a mother, aren't you?' I tear off a length of kitchen roll and mop at my brow. The storm's done little to lower the temperature or permeate the clamminess of the night. When I built the house, I only installed air conditioning in the bedroom and now wish I'd installed it *everywhere*. However, there's not usually much call for air conditioning in England. Especially not in the middle of the Yorkshire Dales.

'And you're *not* desperate for us to have a baby? Is that what you're saying?' Her eyes fill with fresh tears.

'I'm a father already, Ellen. This isn't about me, it's about what *you* want.'

Her shoulders appear to slump further, probably at the mention of my daughters.

'Hey, just because I'm not as *desperate* as you,' – I pull my stool closer to hers, – 'doesn't mean I don't want the same thing. Hell, haven't I proved that already?' I glance out of the window. It's pitch black outside. I should have removed the umbrella from where we were sitting on the patio earlier, as well as all the seat cushions. Everything will be drenched.

'I hate that you've shared an experience with Carmen that *we'll* probably never have together.'

I reach for her hand. 'But we *can* have it. That's what I'm saying. Listen, while I was in the dining room, we talked this through some more.'

'You were supposed to be getting him to leave.' She points in his direction. 'I wondered what was taking you so long.'

'He wants a hundred grand.'

'You're joking, aren't you?' She spins back around to face me, knocking her wine glass to the floor. 'Oh bloody hell.'

'He said he won't stop producing *the goods*,' – Ignoring the smashed glass, I draw air quotes around these words, wincing as I say them, – 'until there's a baby on the way. *Our* baby. Then that's it – he'll be off and we never have to set eyes on him again.'

'*A hundred grand?*' Her voice is a squeak. That she's now focusing on the amount of money that's being discussed might indicate a sudden shift in her thinking.

I jump from my stool to fetch a dustpan and brush. 'It would be worth every penny to—'

'Is everything OK in here?' I look up from where I'm bent into the cupboard beneath the sink as Anthony peers around the kitchen door.

'Why wouldn't it be?' I can't put my finger on the note in Ellen's voice.

His expression's sheepish. 'I heard glass smashing, that's all.'

'Don't worry, we're not killing each other — yet.'

I look at Ellen as I begin to sweep the glass up. Something in my face must soften her.

'Look, I'm sorry I'm upset, Anthony – it's just – well, you've given us a lot to think about.'

I continue sweeping the glass, hardly daring to breathe. The trouble with a smashed wine glass is that it's so thin the broken glass seems to reach every nook and cranny. We'll have to wear something on our feet until one of us has the chance to get the hoover on it. The smell of spilt wine tomorrow will probably turn my stomach when I get up to make our morning cuppa.

'So you *are* thinking about it, is that what you're telling me?' Anthony comes further into the room and the door falls closed behind him.

The tension between us all tightens, Ellen's silence seeming to say it all.

I rise from my crouch. Still, nobody says a word. Clearly, it's up to *me* to break the deadlock.

10

'WOULD we need to draw up an agreement?' I look from Ellen to Anthony. 'Of course, I'm speaking hypothetically.'

Anthony's eyes glitter with what is probably hope. 'As Ellen mentioned while we were eating, it's *illegal* to pay a donor in the UK.'

'But there'd need to be some parameters to shore things up, surely?'

'I guess a gentleman's agreement would have to suffice.' Anthony comes further into the kitchen.

'Supposing, we *did* go forward with this—'

'Oliver!' Ellen cries.

'Just supposing.' I raise the flat of my palm in my wife's direction. '*When* would we actually try?'

'Do you mind if I have another beer?' He arrives at the breakfast bar. 'I think I could use one.'

I hesitate. He's had three already so a fourth would surely put him over the drink drive limit. We're going to be stuck with him overnight at this rate.

'It sounds like we have things to discuss,' he adds.

I tip the broken glass into the bin. The fact that Ellen's not throwing Anthony out on his ear speaks volumes. The moment I mentioned my daughters seems to have been a turning point in her deliberations. She's thinking fast, I can read it in her face.

And so am I. Mum gave me a right earworm when she suggested that Ellen might not even stay with me once all hope has vanished of the two of us conceiving. I can't get it out of my head.

I was alright before I met Ellen in that bar just after the New Year. The girls, especially Jasmine, were far happier then to spend their free time with me. But now, I know how empty my life would be without Ellen if I were forced back to single-man status. No, more than empty, it would be utterly unbearable. It's not as if I'm getting any younger. I slide two more beers from the fridge. 'Do you want another drink, love?'

'I'll have another glass of wine.' Her acquiescence to another drink and her not dismissing Anthony's suggestion of a discussion are a strong signal of the U-turn that's evolving within her. It's both exhilarating and terrifying in equal measure.

'Thanks, mate.' Anthony accepts the beer.

'So when?' I face him across the breakfast bar.

'There's no time like the present.'

I nearly choke on the swig of beer I've taken as Ellen sits on the stool beside me, facing straight opposite Anthony.

'When you say, *the present...*' Her voice is filled with uncertainty. 'What exactly do you mean? *Tonight? Tomorrow? Next week?*'

He looks straight back at her, his gaze unwavering. With those intense blue eyes, and that physique, he could have any woman he wanted. The thought of it being my wife is unbearable. 'Whenever you'd like it to mean.'

Oh bloody hell. She's done an ovulation test – she mentioned it earlier. However, if we do go ahead with this, we can't start the ball rolling *tonight*. We all need time to get our heads around the situation.

'We'll be waiting another month.' Ellen stares down at her hands. 'Unless we act straightaway.'

Panic rises in me like the bubbles in my beer. 'I don't think—'

'But I'm ovulating right *now*.' Her voice is matter-of-fact.

I swallow a large glug of my drink.

'If we're really going to do this.' She reaches for my hand and entwines her fingers with mine. 'We should get on with it before I change my mind.'

Anthony clears his throat. 'There's just the small matter of my payment.'

We both look at him.

'Fifty grand up front and fifty grand once Ellen's passed through her twelve-week scan.' He must have been rehearsing his terms while he's been waiting in the dining room. 'That's how it worked with my sister's arrangement.'

My wife's fingers tighten around mine as she hears the words, *twelve-week scan* and something inside me gives way. More than anything, I want her to have the magic of hearing the wonderful sound of the heartbeat at that scan. I want her to hear the words, *meet your baby, Ellen* as the screen is tilted towards where she's lying. And it'll be *my* baby too. Perhaps not biologically but if it's a part of my wife, I'll love it just as much as if it were my own. I can do this, I know I can.

'The money's not a problem,' I reply. 'But how would we know you won't just take it from us and do a runner?' We might be nearing a decision here but I'm still speaking in woulds and coulds.

'Gentleman's agreement, remember.' Anthony stands from his seat and stretches his arm across the counter. 'You have my word.'

This is the point, it seems, when the *woulds* and *coulds*

become *wills* and *cans*. Once I've returned his handshake, there's no going back.

'So are we going ahead?' His arm is unwavering as it remains outstretched across the counter.

I glance at my wife, her slight nod barely perceptible. My breath catches in my throat. She wants me to go ahead and what Ellen wants, I can't deny. I look Anthony straight in the eye, then stand from my seat to return his handshake. 'I'll sort the transfer shortly.' As I drop back onto my stool. I turn, trying to meet Ellen's eye again but she's staring into her glass. She hasn't tried to stop me from sealing the deal.

We sit for several moments as if all digesting the enormity of what we've just agreed. My mind's going round and round like a spinning top, but, mixed in with the alcohol I've poured down my neck this evening, my thoughts are making little sense. Eventually, I break the silence. 'So the next million-dollar question is *how* are we going to do it?'

'What do you mean, *how*?' I'm not sure if it's my imagination but Anthony's eyes seem to be dancing with amusement.

'I've seen these things on the TV, these sorts of *agreements*.' Suddenly, I'm only too aware that I won't be involved in the *how*. From this point forward, I'm taking a back seat. Nobody says anything so I continue. 'What is it I've heard them use? Oh yes, a turkey baster.' I lurch over to the drawers, trying to picture whether I've ever bought such a thing, perhaps at Christmas, as I wrench the utensil drawer open. 'And we'll need to find an airtight jar. And—'

'We don't have a turkey baster.' Ellen twists around in her seat to watch as I continue to open and close all the drawers. Whether I find one or not, it feels good just to be doing something, instead of us all sitting there and just staring at one another.

'A medicine syringe then. I'm sure I used to have them for the girls – or maybe that was when I was still—' I stop my words in their tracks. I need to stop referring to my former life with Carmen – it's already colouring Ellen's judgement.

'Wouldn't it be easier to do things as nature intended?' Anthony asks. 'Especially if Ellen's ovulating *now.*'

I stop rifling through the drawer and slam it shut, spinning on my heel to look at him. 'Surely, you don't mean–'

He shrugs. 'It'll mean nothing to me. It'll just be a part of the overall transaction.'

Ellen drops her head into her hands. 'This is mortifying.'

'It doesn't have to be,' he replies.

She glares at him. 'Can I just have a few moments alone with my husband?' Her snappy tone towards Anthony makes me wonder whether she's already having second thoughts. I suppose we've only *shaken hands* on the deal – gentleman's agreement or not. We could still send him packing. Do I *want* to send him packing? Really, I want him to have never turned up at all this evening. If I could turn the clock back by two hours, I probably wouldn't answer the door. But I *did* answer and this *is* happening.

I jerk my head in the direction of the dining room. 'Would you mind just waiting back through there for a few minutes?'

'Sure.' He rakes his fingers through his fringe and sets off across the tiles to the door. 'Take all the time you need.' This might be strictly business for him but right now I hate the man. Whichever way we slice this, part of our *deal* is a suggestion of him taking my wife to bed.

As the door closes after him, followed by a click of the dining room door, Ellen spins on her stool so she's completely facing me.

'What are you thinking Oliver?' She crosses her legs but all I see are her shapely breasts, the outline so visible beneath her shirt dress. There's no way Anthony won't have noticed them as well. 'What do you want me to do?'

11

ELLEN'S QUESTION hangs in the air along with the cloying smell of wine and traces of the chicken we started to roast before our existence was blown so spectacularly off course. 'I don't know what you want me to say.'

'What do you want me to do?' She repeats her question, enunciating each word this time.

'I just can't bear the thought of you having sex with another man.' I gulp from my beer bottle, surprised I've nearly finished it already. 'That's the bottom line.'

'It would be just sex – totally perfunctory sex.' Ellen's face is as straight as if she was telling me about a trip she wants to take which doesn't involve me going with her.

'Sex is sex,' I reply. 'No, I couldn't stand it.'

'You've already looked to see if we've got something we can use.' She points at the utensils drawer. 'And we haven't got anything.'

'So, this *arrangement* will have to wait until next month.' I slap my palm against the counter as if to affirm the finality of my decision. 'And we'll get hold of whatever it is to do things *artificially*.'

'What if he changes his mind?' Ellen's voice bears a similarity to Jasmine's when she's after something I've said no to.

'Fifty grand says there's no chance of that.'

'But what if we change *our* minds? No, Oliver – if we're going to do this, let's do it tonight.' She tugs at my arm. 'We've made the decision so we need to act on it *now*.'

'But we've both been drinking.' I move my arm from her grasp and peel at the corner of the label on my bottle, needing to do something, anything, with my hands. 'In fact, I'm starting to think this is something we need to reconsider in the cold light of day.' Dad's voice enters my head again. *If in doubt, do nowt*, was another one of his regularly imparted nuggets of wisdom.

'It'll be too late by tomorrow.' Ellen stands from her seat and reaches for me. I flinch at first, wondering what she's going to do but then she cups my face in her hands. She knows what she's doing – this action always turns me into putty. 'Do you trust me?'

'Of course I do.'

She brings her face closer to mine. 'Do you love me?'

'Do you really need to ask?'

'Just answer me.' She tilts her head to one side and stares at me with her soft grey eyes as she waits for my response.

'Yes, more than anything.'

'Then listen to me, Oliver. It *needs* to be tonight before any of us have second thoughts.'

'But—'

'I promise you, I'll just lie there with my eyes squeezed together and I'll think about you the entire time. It'll be over within a few minutes.'

'No, Ellen. How can I be in the house while you're in bed with *another man*?' I shake myself from her grasp. 'I can't do it – I just can't.'

'It's not *you* having to *do* anything?' She sits back down.

'Look, do you really think I want to lie beneath someone who isn't you?'

I squeeze my own eyes together. I can't bear to imagine it.

'But if it gives us our baby at last, we'll quickly get beyond it and be able to move on.'

'Will we? I'm suddenly not so sure, you know.' I slump onto the stool beside her. If I don't sit down, I might just fall down.

Her face falls. 'Are you saying our marriage isn't strong enough?'

'No, that isn't what I meant.'

'We're still together, even after all the hostility I've been putting up with from your daughters, from your mother—'

'Alright, alright.' I clasp my hands over my ears. 'I hear you. But this, what we're considering here is in another league entirely, don't you think? We're not just talking about a few hurt feelings.'

'You were all for it a few minutes ago. I watched you shake the man's hand.'

'That's when I believed a *turkey baster* would be involved, not...' My voice trails off. How the hell did a normal Friday evening sipping wine in the garden with my wife turn into *this*? I rise from the stool, throw my bottle into the recycling bin and wrench the fridge door open again. I don't know what else to do with myself.

'Don't you think you've had enough to drink?' Ellen's voice is gentle. 'You're always saying you're too old for hangovers.'

'Maybe I need to knock myself out. Perhaps I don't want to hear you both—.' Oh God. What I've just said means it's going to happen. I feel like I have no choice. I'm damned if I do and damned if I don't. Shit. Shit. Shit.

'You won't hear a thing from me.' Ellen comes up behind me and threads her hands around my waist. 'I love you and only you,' she says. 'What's about to happen is merely a means to an end.'

'Have you done anything about your van?' I curl my head around the dining room door.

Anthony glances up from his phone. 'I've got a number ready to call but I thought I'd wait to see what's happening with the two of you first.'

'We're struggling.' I step further into the room. 'I can't lie.'

'No shit.' His face breaks into a grin as he rests his phone on the table. 'It's a biggie – I'll grant you that. To be honest, if it wasn't for the fact that I've seen such a happy outcome for my sister, the whole thing would never have entered my head when we were talking over dinner.'

'Ah, come on – you're not doing this for the warm and fuzzies.' I resume my position facing him. 'You've got pound signs in your eyes.'

'I can't deny it'll be easy money.' He wipes the condensation from his bottle with a downward thrust of his fingers and I have to look away. They are fingers that may soon caress my wife. Whether or not she claims that she'll just *lie there*, he's going to have to touch her to some extent. 'Not to mention tax-free income if you pay it into my crypto account. But look, Oliver – I can see how you live.' He sweeps his gaze around the room. 'A hundred grand is pocket change to you.'

'Hardly.'

'But for me, it's *life-changing*.' He points at himself. 'And what I'm giving to both of you is also life-changing.'

'What if it doesn't work?' My voice is flat. This is like a bad dream. When Ellen and I first met, we watched a load of films together – films we said we'd have watched if we'd been together for years instead of only just meeting. One of them was *Indecent Proposal* where we'd hypothetically discussed what we'd do in the shoes of the characters. We'd thrown the figure of a hundred million into the ring instead of the *million* that was offered back in the early nineties. However, both of us agreed there was no chance we'd risk our relationship like that. So what's changed?

'We can try tonight, and then again in the morning.' He makes it sound like they're needing to get through on a phone call. 'And then I'll just come back again next month if it doesn't work out *this* time? If she's ovulating *now* though, it seems pretty promising.'

'How do we know you'll come back next month?' As if this man knows that my wife is *ovulating*. The whole thing's becoming more and more surreal.

'You'll still be holding my other fifty grand. Anyway,' – he nods down at his phone, – 'I've been Googling all this and there's apparently a two or three-day window in the run-up to a woman's ovulation. So next month,' he stabs his finger into the table as if to further drive his point, 'there'll be plenty more chances to hit the spot as it were.'

I swallow, not liking his turn of phrase one iota. I can only hope and pray that it happens *this* month. The thought of this man returning to my home month after month and writhing around on top of my wife makes me feel ill.

'It'll have to happen in one of the spare rooms on the top floor. And Ellen's not staying with you *all* night. She'll have to come back to you in the morning.' The question is, do I want her to get into bed with me after the act? She won't be able to shower straight away so I'll be able to smell him on her. My stomach twists and for a moment I wonder if the chicken I ate might be about to make a reappearance. I swallow, hard.

'Of course not. I wouldn't expect her to *sleep all night* with me in the same bed.'

'And then when you've done what you need to in the morning, I'd like you to leave straightaway.'

'What about my money – the first fifty grand?' He tips his head to one side as he waits for my answer.

Without replying, I rise from my chair and head to the sideboard for a notepad and pen. Ellen's silent in the kitchen. After a few minutes on her own, she's possibly having second, third and fourth thoughts about the whole thing. We seem to be chasing one another in and out of indecision. As I return to my seat, my soul seems to sag along with my movement. If we're going ahead with this, it probably makes sense just to get on with the transfer.

'Here – write down your crypto wallet address. I'll check with Ellen one last time that she wants to go ahead, and then I'll make the first payment.'

'It'll be alright, mate.' Anthony takes the pen. 'You have my absolute word. I'll take really good care of her.'

That's what I'm worried about. I grit my teeth and lurch from the room towards the cloakroom under the stairs. I'm just in time to spill the contents of my stomach down the toilet.

I'm about to let this man take my wife to have sex in one of our spare rooms.

12

'YOU OK, LOVE?' Ellen's filling a pint glass with water as I stagger into the kitchen. 'Here.' She passes it to me as I reach her. 'You look dreadful.'

'Well, that meal was a waste of time.' I lean against the counter.

'I could hear you,' she replies. 'The chicken wasn't that bad, was it?'

'It's all *this*.' I nod in the direction of the dining room, my head swooning with the movement. Ellen doesn't *look* to be having second thoughts. In fact, she looks happier and more together than she did before. Nervous too, I think.

'And the rather large wine and beer cocktail you've put away this evening.' She points at the overflowing recycling bin. 'Grapes and grain, remember?'

'You sound like my mother.' I try to smile but there isn't a lot to smile about at this moment. 'God, I feel lousy – to be honest, I just need to go to bed and sleep this off.'

'Do you want some aspirin?'

'Have we got some?'

She opens a drawer beneath the breakfast bar and pulls out a packet.

'What would I do without you?' I take it from her, my words a painful reminder of what I hope I don't ever have to find out. 'So are we really going through with this? Have you totally made up your mind?'

'As much as anyone *can* with a situation of this magnitude,' she replies. 'Have you made up *yours*, more to the point?'

I rest on a stool and drop my head into my hands. This is going ahead. It's just about gone too far for me to call a halt.

'If you're really struggling, we can forget it all.' Ellen sidles up beside me and presses three aspirin from the pack. '*Nothing's* more important to me than *you* being happy.'

'Ditto.' I raise my head and grimace as I try to swallow the tablets. One sticks in my throat. It tastes disgusting as it foams back into my mouth and for a moment, I think I might hurl again. I take a big swallow of water and shake myself. 'Ugh – I need my bed, love – our bed.' I stagger back to my feet.

'So what happens now?' She suddenly looks terrified. I don't want to leave her alone but obviously, I have to.

'If you're certain you want to do this, I've got his payment details ready to make the first transfer.'

'As soon as it's over and done with, I'll join you in our bed.' She also stands from her stool and kisses my neck.

'No – I feel too rubbish.' Stepping away from her, I clutch my stomach. 'Sleep in one of the other spare rooms or send *him*,' – I can no longer say the man's name, – 'to the lounge to sleep on the sofa.'

'It's not that you can't face *me* afterwards, is it, Oliver?' Ellen sounds wounded. 'If you're going to feel like that, it's stupid to go through with this. We have to be able to carry on afterwards.'

'No, I'll be fine.'

'Will you really?' She peers at me curiously from beneath her long eyelashes.

'It's like you said – a means to an end.' I reach for my glass. 'I'm just praying it happens the first time and that he doesn't have to come back next month.'

I never want to see him again after he leaves in the morning. We'll be in contact after the twelve-week scan, as he stipulated, and then that will be that. Everyone will believe it's *my* baby and no one ever needs to know the truth.

'Me and you both.' Ellen lets a long breath out. 'I can hardly believe what I'm about to do.'

'Right, I'm off up.' Such normal words. Words we've said countless times since we moved in together in March. Being a little older and having manically full days means I often go to bed before my wife. Gone are the days when I can reliably keep my eyes open beyond ten o'clock. I refill my glass with water and head to the door without looking back. 'Night then.' I just hope she isn't right with what she just said about me being unable to face her afterwards. I can't even face her *now*.

I shuffle across the carpet, feeling dizzier with each step. I need sleep and I need it soon. I've had enough for one day. Enough sun, enough alcohol and enough of being made to feel like a fraction of a man. I hate myself right now and I'll probably hate myself even more in the morning.

I sit heavily at Ellen's dressing table beside our open bedroom window, dripping with sweat and misery as I try to gulp in some of the fresh air from outside. The scent of her perfume and face cream is making me feel worse and I'm fighting the urge just to march back down those stairs and call the whole thing off. I mean, what *normal* sort of husband allows the woman he loves to go to bed with another man – whatever the reason? Things haven't gone too far tonight, not yet. If I act now, I'm not too late to stop it all.

But if I change my mind, what will become of our marriage if I can't give Ellen what she craves? Mum was right – she'll probably leave me. It's not as if I can change the odds – the *five to ten per cent* odds we've been given. But this donor arrangement is something I *can* affect. As Ellen said, it's one mere night of our lives and then we can all move on. At least I'm numb enough with all the alcohol I've poured down my neck to be able to cope with it. Then tomorrow, the whole thing will all be a blurry haze. Perhaps, within a few weeks, it will become like it never happened.

The numbers on my screen are a blurry haze too. But I have to try. Anthony said he won't be taking Ellen upstairs until the money's safely in his account. Apparently, it takes a while to clear so I've agreed to text him the transaction confirmation screen in the meantime.

I painstakingly type in each number of Anthony's crypto wallet. If I make a single mistake with this transfer then the money will be gone forever and some other random recipient will gain themselves a sweet fifty-grand bonus.

All is silent downstairs. Is one of them still in the kitchen and the other in the dining room? Or are they now together but talking in low voices so I can't hear them? What could they be talking about? The best position to make a baby in? Oh God, the thought of what's about to happen between them is eating me alive.

I check and re-check the numbers several times. I should go downstairs and get one of them to go over what I've typed in as a precaution, but I can't face it. I take a deep breath and hit send. As Anthony so rightly pointed out, this sort of money *is* pocket change to me – if I've made a mistake, I'll cut my losses and just send it again. I screenshot the confirmation screen and send it to the second number he's written down on the pad of paper. Then I rise back to my feet, wondering what the hell I'm going to do next.

I should shower but fatigue's winning the battle. So instead, fully clothed, I crawl into bed and reach for the lamp to plunge myself into darkness. Then I bury my head into my wife's pillow, needing her scent to send me swiftly to sleep.

I *can't* bear to listen out for the creak of their footsteps on the stairs, indicating they're on their way up to do the business. Nor do I want to hear any rhythmic bedsprings or perhaps even Anthony moaning.

Oh my God, what am I doing? This is madness. Absolute *madness*.

13

JUNE 14

A COMBINATION OF BIRDSONG, sunshine and heat wakes me from what must be the deepest sleep I've ever sunk into. Not that I feel rested – instead I feel like I've done ten rounds in a boxing ring. I reach across the bed towards Ellen but my fingers connect with the space where she should be. *So where is she? And why am I fully dressed?* I usually sleep in my boxers, or when it's as hot as it has been, nothing at all. My head swoons as I lift it from the pillow and then feel around the duvet for my phone. Tapping the screen, I see that it's just after half past seven. I normally rise at six, especially in the summer, and usually bring Ellen a cup of tea at around this time. That's where she must be – putting the kettle on. She'll come back up to bed with a brew for us both and we can spend some time together before getting on with the rest of our day.

Then it hits me like a brick. *Anthony.* More to the point, Ellen *with* Anthony. We agreed they'd have sex last night and then again this morning in an attempt for her to conceive.

I've even paid him for the privilege.

Oh God. I throw my head back against the pillows, twice,

and then three times. What have I done? *What the hell have I done?* I lie back, desperate not to hear any evidence of their second time of trying. Thankfully, the house is in silence.

The half-open blind taps against the edge of the window in the breeze. There's little evidence of the storm that raged out there last night. It's been and it's gone. Much like I hope Anthony has.

My mouth feels like something's died in it. I need water and I need it fast. Swinging my legs out of bed, I haul myself unsteadily to my feet before heading to the ensuite. The first thing I do is shut the cabinet door so Ellen's wretched ovulation kits are out of sight. It's because of *them* we're in this hellish situation.

I refill my pint glass and then take it back into the bedroom. Perching on the edge of the bed, I unlock my phone. I would *never* have made the agreement with Anthony last night, had I been sober. Ellen's mournful eyes and the desperate edge to her voice also fed into things. My message screen is still open from last night with a screenshot proving I'm fifty grand lighter.

It's been transferred.

Received safely. Thanks mate.

He's no mate of mine. I might have thought he could have been for the first hour after he washed up here – when we were discussing, amongst other things, Tesla's latest model and England's chances in the cricket. But that was before we moved on to my bloody fertility problems.

I slap my hand against my forehead. If I'm honest with myself, I can't really blame Anthony. He saw an opportunity for easy money and grabbed it with both hands. It was *me*, a supposed level-headed and mature, fifty-four-year-old man who loves his new wife and is content with his lot, who agreed to this madness. I could have put an end to it at any time before I staggered up here. And to think I was deliberating over whether to help him by shelling out for his breakdown cover. I'd be a lot less lighter than fifty grand if I had. Another text slides over my screen from Jasmine. It was sent just after three in the morning.

> Can't get hold of you, Dad so I'm grabbing an Uber. I've got my key.

Wait - *what*? I hope to hell Jasmine didn't mean she was getting an Uber *here*. Why would she? Last night, she was supposed to be with her sister and mother. Unless she was fibbing for some reason. Or I've made a mistake. I'm often accused of not listening properly when one of my daughters is trying to tell me something.

I need to find out for myself whether Jasmine's here and what Carmen's playing at if she's allowed our fifteen-year-old to travel around in an Uber on her own at three in the morning. I also need to know what's going on with Ellen and Anthony – I can't bear not knowing. My gut twists as I put their names side by side in my mind.

Right, come on, Oliver. Sort it. First, I need to freshen myself up to face the day. Ellen probably won't look at me with the same eyes she used to after what transgressed last night, so I need to look and feel better than I do at the moment.

As the water runs over me and I soap my body and what's left of my hair, I begin to feel slightly more human. If only the guilt and regret could be washed down the plughole as easily as the lingering traces of sun cream and sweat from yesterday. I *never* usually go to bed without showering – it shows how far that man, not to mention the drink, separated me from my norm last night.

I brush my teeth, trim my beard, and then squirt on deodorant and aftershave. It's shaping up to be another scorcher out there so it's looking like another shorts and T-shirt day. If only I was looking forward to a normal Saturday. However, it feels like things will never be *normal* again. I rifle around in my cupboard until I find something to wear.

As I head along the landing, I tap on the door of Jasmine's room. There's no answer, not that I'd expect there to be at this time of the morning. I gently push the door ajar, taken aback to see her blonde hair spilling over the edge of her bed and her clothes in a heap on the floor. I'll have to wait until she wakes to grill her about last night. Not only about what she's doing here instead of being with her mother and sister, but I also need to work out whether she's seen or heard anything she shouldn't have.

On the face of it, everything could be perfectly normal as I head down the stairs towards our sun-dappled hallway. My framed seascape still hangs where it did, in pride of place halfway up the staircase. The photo of my girls when they were six and fourteen smiles out at me from the hallway windowsill and the fluffy rug we got as a wedding present from my sister still sits squarely in front of the main entrance, showing no signs of the imposter who stood on it last night as he dripped with rainwater. The trainers he slid off are not there so hopefully he's gone too.

I poke my head into the kitchen, where a pot of coffee sits on the hot plate. As I head over to it, I look for residual evidence of *him*. The only thing is the Samsung lead still plugged into the USB port, and a discarded coffee cup in the sink which may or may not have come from him. I'll have to give the cleaner a call. I want this place scrubbed from top to bottom to eradicate all traces that he was ever in my house.

I pour coffee into a fresh cup and head back out of the kitchen in search of my wife.

'There you are.' She's curled up at the edge of our L-shaped sofa with her feet tucked under her. She looks small and forlorn and I wonder whether she's regretting last night as bitterly as I am.

She looks at me with wide eyes and I quickly look away. 'I thought I should leave you sleeping,' she says. 'After the state you were in, I mean.'

I should thank her, but how can I? 'So you admit I was in a state?' I sit at the opposite end of the sofa, unable to bear to be in her proximity.

She forces a smile – a very weak one.

'Yet you still went ahead with...' My words fade out. I can't possibly verbalise a description of what may or may not have taken place between the two of them after I crashed out. 'So tell me – *did* you actually go through with it?'

14

'YOU WERE the one who agreed to this arrangement, Oliver.' Ellen's avoiding my eye now as she replies. 'In fact, if I remember correctly, you were much more fired up than me – at least to begin with.'

This means it *has* happened. No matter how drunk, fired up or whatever I may have been last night, my wife has had sex with another man. There's no way of sugar-coating it.

'So how was it then?' My words drip with sarcasm and my wife looks as bereft as if I'd just shot a small rabbit. 'With *him*.'

'I told you it wouldn't mean a thing – and it didn't. It was a means to an end, just as we agreed.'

'You must have enjoyed it to some extent.' I have no idea why I'm tormenting myself in this way. Or Ellen, for that matter. Yet, I can't seem to help myself.

'I can't believe you're saying these things.' She drags a cushion over her stomach as if protecting herself from me.

'Did it happen *twice*?'

'That's what you paid him for, wasn't it? Look Oliver, it was a two-way transaction – that's all it was. Our chance to be a proper family. He's gone now, so for God's sake, let's keep our fingers crossed that it was successful and try to put it in the rearview mirror.'

'What if I can't do that?' How stupid I've been. Assuming it *was* successful, I'll have to live with a permanent reminder of my mistake. And knowing my luck, the baby will be a dead ringer for Anthony. Born with a six-pack and muscles like Arnie.

'Then I could end up pregnant and facing single motherhood on my own, couldn't I?' Ellen's face falls further. I try to feel at least a twinge of guilt but I can't. All that's snaking through my veins is jealousy.

'I told you to wait a while, didn't I?'

'Did you?' Her head jerks up. 'Don't start blaming—'

'I said we should look at what he'd offered us in the cold light of day – but you just wouldn't listen.'

Ellen hangs her head. 'I suspected you'd change your mind.'

I stay quiet. She's right – I would have *definitely* changed my mind.

'Look, what's done is done.' She twists herself around in her seat so she's completely facing me. 'We *have* to go forward now – together.'

'So you still want me then? After *him?*' I wish I could blast this jealousy from myself. I was so drunk last night that I'm struggling to bring Anthony's face to mind. All I can remember is his intense stare and assured grin. Not to mention his bulging biceps.

'What I'm trying to hang onto,' – Ellen ignores my question, – 'is that his sister and brother-in-law have been where we are – where they felt there was no other option than to use a donor to help them. We've gone for the same solution to our problem, that's all.'

'Yeah, but did their donor actually go to *bed* with his sister?' I tilt my aching head so it rests on the back of the sofa. 'We should have spoken to them first. We should have—'

'You've got to let this go, Oliver. If you can't, then I'll have to go and stay with Kirsteen for a few days.' A tear escapes down her cheek and she brushes it away. 'I can't cope with you being like this.'

The thought of her clearing off doesn't bear thinking about. 'OK - you're right. I'm sorry.' The only way forward is to work through this together.

'I've got enough turmoil swirling around inside me without you making me feel even worse.'

'We both have.' I shuffle along the sofa so I'm sitting beside her.

'I feel disgusting after what I've done.' She stares down at her hands. Hands that must have touched *him* no matter how much I don't want to admit it.

'Have you showered?' Part of me wants to hug her to feel better. But the knowledge that she's been with another man is stopping me.

'Not yet. I wanted to do the same as I've done with you – after, you know.'

A vision of my wife with her legs up against the wall fills my mind. I just wish it could have been because of *me – not because of* him.

'Say something then.' Her voice has a pleading edge.

I clear my throat, unsure of what she wants me to say. 'So how did you both leave things?'

'I asked him to go - straight away.' She lets a long breath out. 'As you might imagine, I didn't want him sticking around.'

'Me neither.'

'But all this aside, Oliver, Anthony *does* seem to be a reasonable bloke.' She tucks a stray hair behind her ear.

'Do you reckon?'

'He's on his uppers financially but he's filled with a desire to do something good – like someone did for his sister. He says it's transformed their lives.'

As long as that's the only thing Anthony's got a desire for. I look properly at my wife now with her hair loosely piled at the top of her head, still wrapped in her dressing gown. She's always beautiful to me but she looks knackered. I can only hope it's because she's been lying awake half the night, agonising over the decision we've made, as opposed to a different reason.

'So what happens now?' I want to ask her if I'm just supposed to act normally and go about my business. It's a stupid question really. After all, what else am I going to do?

'I'll know in around a fortnight if I'm pregnant, or not,' she replies. 'Either way, he said you've got his number to keep him posted. If I'm not, he'll come back. And if I am, we just have to let him know everything's OK after the twelve-week scan and then pay him the other fifty grand.'

'I don't know if I can go through it again next month, Ellen.' I stare at my wife's pink-polished toenails, unable to erase an image which seeps into my mind's eye of her feet straddling Anthony while I was lying in a drunken stupor all night.

'Like I said last night, you didn't have to go through *anything*, did you? It's *me* that feels like shit this morning. Not to mention cheap and nasty.'

'Let's just hope it's worked the first time.' I stare at the fluffy white cushion covering her midriff, praying I'll be able to celebrate a positive pregnancy test result and that we can get back to normal. What if every time I look at my wife, I only see *him* from now on? *What have I done? What the hell have I bloody done?* I don't know when I'll stop asking this question of myself. What an idiot I've been.

'No one can ever find out about this, Ellen. What would people say if they knew I'd encouraged my wife to sleep with another man – no matter what the circumstances?'

My eyes fall on our wedding canvas above the fireplace. It was a simple day with only a handful of people in attendance. Mum and Ellen's friend, Kirsteen, were our witnesses. My girls didn't want to come – they both said they couldn't face it. The way they've carried on at times, anyone would think I'd had an affair which split up my marriage to their mother, instead of just being a husband and father who worked too hard. They took it incredibly badly when I first left our home but I really thought they'd come to terms with our new way of being. That is, until I met Ellen.

'Is that all you care about?' Her voice is haughty. 'What other people might think?'

'No, but it's got to be a consideration. Which reminds me.' I glance at the door. 'Did you hear Jasmine come in last night?'

'No – *when*?' She looks puzzled.

'I had a text from her – at about three in the morning but I was out of it. I've just checked and she's fast asleep upstairs.'

'You're joking!' Ellen wraps her arms more tightly around herself. 'No, I didn't hear a thing. I went to sleep in the top guest room,' she jerks her head upwards. 'The one right above ours.'

'Why didn't you come to our bed?'

'You told me not to – remember?'

I shake my head. 'Last night's a complete blur but bits and pieces are swimming back. Really, I'd like to forget it completely.' I force a smile for the first time since I woke.

'Besides, it was best that I didn't disturb you. Especially since you'd been sick before you went to bed.'

'Was I? Bloody hell, so I was – I can barely remember it.' No wonder I have a burning sensation at the back of my throat. 'So you promise you didn't spend all *night* with him?'

'Of course I didn't. It was all as we agreed. He wanted a coffee this morning after...' She cuts herself off mid-sentence. 'But I told him it was better if he just left. After all, it's not like he can't afford breakdown cover now, is it? Or a new van.'

'He can have a fleet of the bloody things.' I close my eyes. 'It sounds like he should have been asleep when Jasmine came in with a bit of luck.'

'Well, she wouldn't suspect the truth in a million years, would she?' Amusement dances in my wife's eyes which I'm not sure I'm happy about. After what's gone on, I think I preferred her to be looking miserable about it.

'We need to get our stories straight, just in case,' I reply.

'Say he was a friend of yours if she mentions anything.'

'But why would he be sleeping here?'

'Tell her he'd had one too many to drink. After all, if we're going to do this *properly*, no one can ever suspect the lengths we've gone to.' She moves the cushion and pats her belly. '*You're* the baby's father,' – she points at me, – 'and that's all there is to it.'

My wife has an air to her that I haven't been around before. It's an air of tranquillity, one of being at peace with herself. Yes, all this might not be the conventional way of having a child together but she's getting what she's been longing for.

'What are you staring at?'

'You just seem, different, that's all.'

'Pregnant – hopefully.' For the first time since I've arrived downstairs, her face breaks into a smile.

She wasn't like this when we started trying after my reversal in March. Instead, she seemed blasé and often used the phrase, *if by some miracle* when we'd been talking about it. This morning there's a sizeable shift between us and all I've done to cause it is to put up fifty grand.

However, I have to put Anthony's involvement out of my jealous mind. If I don't, I risk cracking our relationship wide open.

Which is what my mum and my daughters seem to have been waiting for since Ellen and I got together.

15

'Whose were those shoes on the mat, Dad?' I jump at the sound of Jasmine's voice behind me, her flip-flops slapping against her feet as she crosses the patio.

'What shoes?' I raise my head, slightly peeved at being disturbed from my hangover recovery in the midday sun with just the company of birds and a few butterflies. The nearest house, other than Mum's, is a couple of miles away, so the peace and solitude I can bask in out here is most welcome. With nothing but the familiar sight of emerald fields, the rolling hills of Yorkshire and clear blue skies above me, I was beginning to feel more human. But I'm also relieved to finally have a chance to talk to my daughter about last night – to ascertain what she may or may not have seen or heard.

'The trainers – the scruffy ones. I tripped over them on the way in.'

'Didn't you use the side entrance as normal?' I adjust my lounger so I'm sitting up to face her.

Jasmine throws herself onto the other sunlounger, the one Ellen usually lies on, and stretches out her long limbs, tanned from the recent South of France holiday she spent with her mother. 'I didn't have my keys. I had to go into the lockbox for the key to the main door.'

'What were you doing, catching an Uber and turning up here at *three in the morning*?' I shield my eyes from the sun with my hand. 'Weren't you all supposed to be pampering yourselves at some spa?'

'That was during the day.' She rubs her eyes behind her sunglasses. 'I was out with my mates last night.'

'Until three in the morning?' My voice rises. As I stare at the willowy girl before me with her fair hair on end, I still see my gap-toothed seven-year-old with her hair in pigtails and plasters on her knees.

'Alice's parents were away for the night.' Jasmine keeps her gaze fixed on the water fountain, seemingly avoiding my eye. 'So she had a house party.'

'Did she indeed? And do Alice's parents know about this?'

She shrugs. 'I guess they will have done.'

I make a mental note to find out – I'd want them to tell me if the shoe was on the other foot. 'You'd better not be getting any ideas.' I wag my finger in her direction.

'*You* had a party.' She glances back at the house. 'It was boring though – you could even talk above the music.'

'It's *my* house to have a party at.'

'It was only so you could show off what you've built.' She pulls a face.

'Did your mother know where you were last night?' The million-dollar question. I can't imagine Carmen allowing Jasmine to go to an unsupervised house party. I might have given in but I'd have insisted on picking her up before midnight. Not that I was in any fit state. If only I'd known, it might have stopped me from agreeing to what I've managed to get us into.

'She thought I was with you.' She also brings her

sunlounger into a sitting position, as though she's trying to level herself with me.

'Great,' I reply. 'You've lied to your mother and now you're expecting me to corroborate your story. Did *anyone* know where you were?'

She shrugs again. 'I'm fifteen, Dad.'

'Exactly – in the eyes of the law you're still a child. *My* child – *and* your mum's. Therefore at least one of us needs to know where you are at all times.'

'You're not going to blow my cover, are you?' She narrows her eyes in a similar way to how Carmen used to when we had any sort of disagreement. Jasmine is her mother's daughter in so many ways, in her build, her colouring but also her forthright temperament. Occasionally, however, I see flashes of my mother in her as well, mostly in how blunt they can both be.

'I don't know yet. I'll need to have a think.' I reach for my water. My mouth's as dry as shoe leather.

'Please don't tell her, Dad.' Jasmine groans as she throws her head against the sunlounger. 'She'll ground me for the rest of my life.'

'And how do you know *I'm* not going to?' I point at myself.

'Because you love me way more than Mum does.' She smiles her sweetest smile, the one she's always reserved for when she's trying to worm around me. 'Which brings me to what I came out here to ask for.'

'Whatever it is, the answer's no.' I close my eyes.

'You don't even know what I want.'

'The answer's still no.' The faint hum of an aeroplane passes over us. How I wish I was on it right now – heading far away from my normality.

'Dad!'

I open my eyes and grin. 'No doubt it'll cost me in either time or money?'

'I'm wounded.' Jasmine lets her sunbed back down as if

collapsing back onto it while clutching her heart. 'What makes you say that?'

'Because it's always one or the other.' I smile. 'So which one is it then – the bank of Dad or Dadcabs?'

She looks sheepish. 'The bank of Dad actually.'

'How much?' I'll probably end up agreeing to whatever she asks. With her sweet voice and huge blue eyes, Jasmine has always had me wrapped around her little finger. Her older sister often moans that she gets away with more murder than *she* got away with eight years ago at the same age. I guess that's the way it sometimes goes in families. We cut our parenting teeth on our first-borns.

'I just need some extra allowance this week.'

'For?' I lift my sunglasses onto the top of my head as salty sweat runs into my eyes. I'm probably sweating pure alcohol today after what I put away last night.

'Everyone's off into town, and there's this dress I've had my eye on for ages.'

'Jasmine, you've got more dresses than a person could wear in a *lifetime*.' I glance at her pretty denim pinafore. She's always been a dress sort of a girl, refusing to wear trousers or jeans, which she protested were for boys whenever her mother laid them out. She's the complete opposite of her older sister, for whom, it's a good thing that her job calls for trousers and heavy boots. She's also blue-eyed and fair-haired but I never see her wear it loose. It's always tied back in a bun or ponytail.

'*Please*, Dad.'

'I'm still thinking.'

'While you're thinking, you still haven't answered my question.'

'What question?' Really, I know exactly *what question*. I just hoped she'd been distracted from it.

'You never told me who those scruffy trainers belonged to. Did someone stay over here?'

'Erm, yeah, just a friend of mine.'

'A friend?' She arches one of her perfectly shaped eyebrows. 'With trainers like *that*? Was it the man in the shorts who was up so early this morning?'

I lean forward on my deckchair and try to keep my voice nonchalant. 'You *saw* him?'

'He was just leaving.' She gives me a curious look, probably at the shake in my voice. I guess I *have* got worked up since our conversation took a turn in this direction. I need to keep my cool – she can't suspect Anthony's anything other than an insignificant acquaintance.

'How did you know he was leaving?'

'I heard Ellen saying, *we'll be in touch.* They sounded like they were at the bottom of the stairs when I got up for the loo.'

Think fast, Oliver. 'Yes, I was down there too.'

'But I didn't hear *your* voice.' There isn't any suspicion in her tone which is something. 'Anyway, I couldn't be bothered coming downstairs but I wondered who it was so I watched out of the landing window as he walked down the drive.'

'He's someone who did some work for me.' I rub my eyes beneath my sunglasses. Even with them on, the light's still too bright. I'm never drinking again. Ever.

'You just said he was a *friend.*'

'Gosh, do I grill you about everyone *you* know, Jasmine?' Somehow, I need to change the subject. 'Blimey – he's a friend who happened to do some of the work on the house when we were building it.' I can no longer keep the exasperation out of my voice. 'He came around to discuss another project I might have for him, we had one too many beers together so he stayed in one of the spare rooms until he was fit to drive this morning. Is that alright with you?'

Damn – I shouldn't have mentioned driving. After all, there would have been no additional vehicle out there when the

Uber dropped Jasmine off in the courtyard at the front of the house.

'Oooh, what's rattled your cage?' She tilts her head to one side in the same way her mother used to when she was assessing me. At least she isn't mentioning that there were no other vehicles other than my Range Rover, Ellen's Audi and Mum's Mini when she first arrived. Hopefully, she won't have noticed.

'Where's Ellen, anyway?' She glances back at the house, her voice dipping as she mentions her stepmother. Perhaps with the passage of time and a shared sibling, they'll eventually form something of a bond. I'll have to handle how I break the baby news, if it arrives, to her correctly. A few extra pounds on her allowance whilst she gets used to the idea should keep her sweet.

'Ellen's having a lie-down,' I reply. 'She had a rough night's sleep.'

'Looking at the state of you, you did as well, Dad.' Her gaze washes over me, seemingly in silent condemnation. 'You've got more lines on your face than a race track and your beard could do with a better trim.'

'Gee thanks, dear daughter.' I force my face into a smile. 'What time did you say you were going out?'

'When you say yes to giving me some extra allowance.'

'How much?' This is one of my most frequent questions when dealing with either of my daughters. Or it's *what time*? Or *where to*? And now I'm about to go right back to the start – I'll be fifty-five years of age with a newborn. No wonder the consultant looks at me pityingly. He probably thinks I'm crazy. I *am* crazy.

'A hundred quid should cover it.' Jasmine leaps to her feet as I unlock my phone and she comes to peer over my shoulder. 'Oooh, who have you been sending fifty thousand pounds to?'

I shift the phone from her view but I'm a couple of seconds too slow.

'Yesterday? Who's *Anthony Powell*? The man who was here this morning? What work is it he's doing to be getting paid *that* much?'

'Do you want some extra money to spend or not, Jasmine?'

16

JULY 4

IT's like waiting to be hung, drawn and quartered. As I sit beside my wife on the edge of our bed, both of us unable to take our eyes off the plastic stick, I don't know how I want this to turn out. I've already managed to persuade Ellen to wait a few days since her missed period, but I wish I could persuade her to wait a while longer. However, she's woken early, saying she needs to know *now*. Rain drums softly against our window pane and really, I just want to crawl back into bed and pull the covers over my head.

If only we'd never crossed paths with Anthony Powell. And if only I hadn't blasted all sense away with the volume of alcohol I poured down my neck. We haven't heard a thing from him since that night last month and I'd be happy to keep it this way. He's probably super busy spending the fifty grand I've already transferred. His sort can't keep a few quid in their accounts for more than five minutes. No doubt, he'll soon be back to where he started.

But if this blue line doesn't appear, he'll be coming back *here* for round two. The prospect of this kills me. How the hell can I, stone-cold sober, countenance the reality of him and

Ellen going to bed together again? The truth is that I can't, and we need to find another way even if it ends up being a clinic. Or a turkey baster.

If the blue line *does* appear then equally, I don't know how I'm going to handle it. I can hardly jump up and down, roaring with excitement when genetically, the baby's got absolutely nothing to do with me and may only serve to remind me of my own inadequacies as a man as it enters the world and turns our lives upside down.

However, I think I already know what the result is going to be. I watched Ellen as we walked in the park the other day, and I was struck by her sickly pallor, combined with a grace in her I've never noticed before. I could somehow tell she was pregnant – even before she's been able to, it would seem.

'Oh God, this is torture.' Ellen peers more closely at the stick. 'How long now?'

I glance at the timer I've set on my phone. 'Be patient – it's not even been a minute.'

What we've done is illegal. I've been researching it and though it's not clear what the penalty is for paying a donor such a large amount of money, I don't want either of us saddled with a criminal record. Not to mention the damage to our reputations.

'Look, *look*.' Ellen waves the stick in front of my face. 'The leaflet says even the faintest of lines means I'm pregnant.'

'Let me see.' I hold out my hand and scrunch my eyes together, hardly daring to see for myself. But when I open them again, there can be no denying our fresh reality. There, on the pure white background of the results window, is a thin blue line. Slowly, I raise my eyes to look at my wife, forcing myself to smile. 'Congratulations, darling.'

She spins around so she's looking at me. Her eyes shine with happiness. 'I can't believe it.'

Neither can I. And I don't know how I'm going to convince

the rest of the world that *I'm* this baby's father. Especially since I'm already the dad of a twenty-three-year-old and a fifteen-year-old, with a second vasectomy reversal procedure to deal with the scar tissue coming up. Not that too many people know about this. But more than enough probably do. Mum, Ellen's friend, Kirsteen, my sister, Hannah, and a couple of people who work for me know all about it.

'I'm off round to Kirsteen's – I want to see her face for myself.' Ellen leaps from the edge of the bed. 'We should tell Phyllis too. And I'll have to make an appointment at the doctors won't—'

I catch my wife in midflight, holding her against my chest. I'm unsure whether it's her heart thudding so hard, or mine. After what I've endured to get us to this, I want her to share it with me, not go running out of the door to her friend's house. Besides, I need to be certain she won't divulge any of the truth behind the conception.

'We're going to be parents,' she murmurs into my shoulder. 'I can't wait.'

'Me neither.' I keep her pressed against me, not wanting her to see into my soul right now – to know what I'm thinking and feeling. Nor do I want to burst her bubble by reminding her that I'm *already* a *parent* and have been for the last twenty-odd years, thank you very much. Suddenly she pulls back. 'We'll have to let *him* know, won't we?' There's a slight edge of panic in her voice.

'Leave it with me.' I sit back on the bed and pat the mattress beside me. 'You need to be looking after yourself, Ellen. Which means no getting worked up about *anything*, do you hear?'

She nods and sits back at my side. At least this means Anthony has no reason or excuse to come back to the house. If that test had been negative, he'd have returned a week from now. As it is, I never have to set eyes on him again. He's helped us, I know he has, but I can't stop myself from hating the man. Especially since it's happened so easily.

'I'm feeling a bit sick as it happens.' Ellen rubs her belly. 'I don't know whether it's nerves, excitement or pregnancy hormones. I might have a lie down. I'll go and see Kirsteen in an hour or so.'

'It's probably a combination of all three,' I reply. 'I'll fetch you a glass of water.'

Clicking the bedroom door closed, I head down the stairs to the sanctuary of my office, letting a long breath out as I sink into the chair behind my desk. My eyes drift from a photo of the girls taken a couple of years ago to one of me with Ellen, taken by a stranger in Filey, just after Ellen proposed to me.

She'd suddenly stopped and grabbed at my arm as we walked along the beach. 'You know what day it is today, don't you?'

'Erm.' It was a freezing cold day, I knew that much. 'Thursday?'

'It's the twenty-ninth of February.' She smiled. 'So you know what that means.' She didn't take her eyes away from mine as she dropped to one denim-clad knee onto the sand. A passing couple stopped to watch.

'Oooh, she's proposing to him.' A woman clapped her gloved hands together. 'It's a leap year, isn't it?'

'Don't you be getting any ideas,' her companion said.

'Oliver,' Ellen began, her face pink between the white of her hat and scarf. 'I know we've only been together for a few weeks but you make me so happy and I've never wanted anything more than for us to be together forever. So will you marry me?'

By then, more people were gathering around to watch our big moment. Their expectation was palpable beneath the grey and wintery sky. It was too soon though – yes, it had been a magical few weeks since we'd met at the bar at the turn of the year but *marriage*? Already?

'Are you going to leave me down here for much longer?' Her voice trembled as she continued to stare at me from where she was kneeling on the sand.

'Just say yes,' one of the onlookers shouted above the crash of a wave.

I looked from her smiling face back to Ellen's now slightly worried one. How could I reject her proposal with all these people watching? I couldn't do it to her. We could always have a *long* engagement while we got to know one another better.

'Yes,' I finally said. 'Yes, I'll marry you.'

17

FROM BEING happy in my man cave for so many years after Carmen and I separated, I've now found myself married to an energetic woman seventeen years my junior, and with a baby on the way that isn't biologically mine. Did I mean what I said when I promised I would love it as my own? I guess I'll soon find out. But first, I've got to get in contact with Anthony. The last thing I want is for him to turn up here next week, so he needs to be stopped.

> Anthony, it's Oliver Holmes from The Gables in Askrigg. You stayed here three weeks ago.

Stayed here? How crass does that sound? And like he's going to have forgotten who I am. My name is probably imprinted in his head, and fifty grand says he'll have pinned my number to the top of his contacts. So I delete the message and start over.

> Oliver Holmes from Askrigg here. Just wanted to let you know that Ellen's pregnant. So there's no need for you to return to the house and we'll be back in touch after her scan – as previously agreed.

That's all that needs to be said. I toss my phone onto the desk and drop my head into my hands, listening to the continued drumming of the rain against the window. I wish I could feel even a little happy. But what if I can't love this baby? I haven't even been able to look my wife in the eye the same way since I agreed for her to go to bed with Anthony. She's seemed so distracted, probably with her wishing, waiting and hoping for a positive pregnancy test, that she doesn't seem to have noticed any difference in me. Ultimately, we'll probably be OK – if we can only weather the next year or so.

I might as well cancel my second attempt at the vasectomy reversal. Hopefully, my consultant won't ask too many questions. Knowing my luck, the minute he discovers that Ellen's pregnant, he'll want to make an example of me as one of the clinic's success stories and splash photos of us across their website. No way.

> Well, that's just brilliant news. I must be made of stern stuff to have achieved it at our first attempt. Cheers for letting me know. So now there's just the small matter of the other 50K???

Stern stuff? What a pillock.

> Didn't we agree you'd get it after the twelve-week scan? When we know everything's viable?

> To be honest, Oliver, I'm in a bit of a tight spot and could do with it now. Look, I'm sure nothing will go wrong and like I said to you before, I'm a man of my word. If things do go pear-shaped, I'll honour my agreement to keep trying.

Fury chases through my veins, replacing the feelings of

trepidation and inadequacy. We agreed on twelve weeks, so why is Anthony altering the parameters?

> You've still got my crypto wallet details, haven't you?

Bloody hell. I suppose there's nothing else I can do other than to pay. At least then, that's it. He'll leave us alone and there'll be no further dealings.

> If, and I mean 'if' – I agree to pay you early, I'd like you to sign something first.

> Such as?

> An agreement stating in black and white that everything is settled between us and that you won't be back for any more.

> Any more what?

Smarmy sod. If things *do* go wrong from here, I'll pay to get Ellen into a proper clinic for another attempt and we'll do things the way we should have done in the first place. With all the correct checks and balances.

> Money. This next payment is in full and final settlement. So I'd like your email address to send the agreement.

> Wouldn't you prefer me to come around and sign it in person? We can even get some witnesses if it makes you feel better.

I can imagine his cheeks dimpling as he smirks at his response to my request.

> An electronic signature will suffice. After I've received that, I'll release the money.

> You make it sound like we're selling a house or something. OK - it's apowell0101@outmail.co.uk

Perhaps I'm building Anthony into some kind of an ogre unfairly, but he's all I've been able to think about for the past three weeks and he's haunting my dreams as well as every waking moment. The sane part of me tries to convince myself of the tale he told about his sister's happiness.

However the insane part of me keeps taking over, the part which hates his guts, especially since he's been able to bestow such a precious gift to my wife so effortlessly. A gift that should have been *mine* to give. Mum was probably right – I should have gone after someone nearer to my age. But once Ellen had been in my life for just a few weeks, she became like a drug. My girls were probably right that they felt sidelined as I wasn't giving my all to my work, or anything. Ellen was a woman who was making ends meet by working two bar jobs but suddenly, she was all I could think about. And it's safe to say we've come a long way as a couple in the seven months we've been in each other's lives.

I pull up a web page I was looking at last week. In normal circumstances, I'd have had my solicitor draw up a contract. But in this case, I'm having to rely on Rocket Lawyer, an online hub which allows sample agreements to be downloaded.

I load up one for sperm donation and begin scrolling. The word *artificial* needs to be taken out. There was nothing artificial about *this* baby's conception. I take out the *no-fee* clause and replace it with the two payments we've agreed on – in full and final settlement. I delete the clauses about the donor having undergone screening and counselling but keep all the lines pertaining to how Anthony has *no* legal rights whatsoever over this child, that he will not be expected to contribute financially to the child's welfare and that all parties have entered this agreement freely and through exercising his and her own choices.

I underline the clause which states that the donor is not permitted to contact any parties directly or indirectly and will have no interest in the welfare or the happiness of the child.

Then, in a similar way to when I've drawn up contracts to do with architecture, I set it all up on DocuSign, first signing myself as the partner of the recipient, and copying both Ellen and Anthony in for their signatures.

As soon as this is signed and the second fee has been transferred, we'll be able to put Anthony Powell well and truly in the past.

Ellen will have what she wants. *He'll* have what he wants. And then we can all get on with living happily ever after.

There's just the small matter of breaking the news to my family.

18

'She's *what*?'

'Don't sound so shocked, Mum. You knew we were trying to make it happen.'

'You make it sound like– Oh, it doesn't matter.' She rests the tray of tea on the lounge table.

'You're actually the first person we've told.'

I didn't expect my mother to be swinging from her ceiling beams in raptured exhilaration but I'd hoped for a better reaction than her bemused face and shocked tone of voice. And judging by Ellen's crumpled expression, so did she.

'So.' Mum leans forward to pour the tea from the pot she always reserves for visitors, her necklace dangling onto the tray. 'When did you find out this happy news?'

'This morning.' Ellen's voice rises in excitement, seemingly not catching the sarcasm in Mum's words. 'We wanted you to be the first to know that you're going to be a granny.'

Mum sniffs as she looks up from what she's doing. 'I'm already a granny. Speaking of which, your daughters should have been told before me, Oliver.' I don't like the way Mum's looking from Ellen to me. She doesn't look at all pleased for us.

She often claims to know me better than I know myself so can she somehow sense something's *off* about our situation?

'I'll tell them when I see them.' I accept a cup from her, wondering how she can stand to listen to the crap she's playing through Alexa. She's always prided herself on still enjoying chart music and the girls love her for it. 'Actually. Haven't you got anything stronger, Mum?' I'll get a smile back on Ellen's face if it's the last thing I do. 'I think a glass of something bubbly could be more called for than a cup of tea. After all, it's not every day you hear news of a new baby in the family.'

'You two go ahead.' Ellen pats her belly beneath her leggings. I have a feeling she'll be doing a lot more of that in the coming months. 'I'll stick with my brew. Besides, no one makes a cuppa better than you, Phyllis.'

Without saying a word in reply, Mum rises from the sofa and shuffles across the carpet of her sunny lounge in her slippers.

'I'll give her a hand.' I jump up from the sofa.

'With *what*?' Ellen screws her face up as she twists around to look at me from mum's pristine white leather armchair. 'I'm sure she can manage to carry a bottle and two glasses on her own.'

'I just need to talk to her.'

'Right, spill it, Mum.'

'I hope you're not meaning the champagne. It's a drop of the good stuff, this – your Dad chose it.'

Something within me lifts. If she's opening that particular bottle, she must feel at least a *little* happy about our news. My eyes fall on a photo of him in the garden of their old house which was his favourite place to be. He's about five years older in the photo than I am now and I'm acutely aware of the fact that I'm looking more and more like him. I just hope I don't take after him in the health stakes, especially now with another child on the way. Suddenly, it's become even more important to keep myself fit and active in the gym and on the golf course.

'At least he's somehow a part of our celebration then.'

'Celebration?' The tone of her voice says it all.

'What else would you call it? Come on, Mum. We're having a baby for goodness sake – you could at least congratulate us.'

'I'm just not buying into this, Oliver.' Mum turns around to face me, her bobbed hair swinging with the motion. Her eyes are marble-hard and her mouth's set in a thin line, much the same as it was when I announced Ellen and I were getting married. 'It's all too sudden and I smell a rat.'

'What's that supposed to mean?'

'You know exactly what I mean – you haven't even had your second op yet. And it's only been *three weeks* since you told me about your so-called five to ten per cent odds.'

I should have known it would be *Mum* who'd challenge us. 'My consultant mentioned miracles – don't you remember me telling you what he'd said?'

'No, I don't.' She slips her hands inside the pouch of her denim pinafore but she doesn't take her blue-shadowed eyes off me. 'And from everything you've told me so far, it would *need* to be a miracle. Or an immaculate conception.'

'Why are you being like this?' I keep my voice low so Ellen can't hear me above Mum's music. She's always suspected my mother doesn't like her and if she hears all this, she'll have concrete proof. 'Why can't you just be happy for us? Or even *pretend* to be?'

'Because there's something you're not telling me – I can read you like a book.' She turns back to the bottle and begins peeling its foil from the top. 'If this was *your* baby Ellen was carrying, you'd be shouting the news from the rooftops to anyone who'd listen. You did with the other two.'

'That was over two decades ago.' I glance at a photo of them with Mum when we all went skiing, which she's pinned to the fridge. 'Becoming a parent isn't such a big deal to me now.'

'It is to Ellen.' Mum twists at the wire holding the cork in place. 'We both know how desperate she is to conceive.'

'All the more reason for you to be happy for us.'

'Look, you're my son,' – Mum lowers her voice and glances at the door, – 'and I only want the best for you, so I'm just going to come out and say this.'

'Say *what*?' Great, one thing I can count on with my mother is for her not to mince her words.

'That *you* might be blinkered to Ellen's wiles and her ways but I think...' She pauses as though checking in with herself with what she's about to say.

'Go on.' I think I've a pretty good idea of what she's going to come out with here. I lower myself onto a chair at the table.

'I think Ellen's probably been sleeping with someone else to achieve this pregnancy and you'd be lying if you said you didn't suspect the same. There, I've said it.'

I open my mouth to protest but Mum continues before I can gather my thoughts.

'And until I see DNA evidence to the contrary, I'm afraid I can't accept this baby as my grandchild.' She pushes the bottle back across the counter as if she can't bear to open it after all. 'I suggest you take a long, hard look at the facts as well, Oliver.'

'There's nothing to take a look at, Mum.' Her face is set in the expression I used to hate when I was a boy. The one that says, *no way will I change my mind. Not for anything.*

'You've always been far too trusting.'

I freeze at the sound of a footstep in the hallway. It's Ellen – damn. I'm really going to get it in the neck.

'I heard what you said, Phyllis.' Ellen appears in the doorway, a hurt expression across her pasty face.

'I'm sorry.' As Mum turns, there's no reddening to her face

as I'd expect after being overheard. 'But I've only got my son's best interests at heart.'

'I want to go back to ours.'

'I don't want to upset you, Ellen, but I can't go along with this façade.' Mum throws her arms in the air. 'Whatever *this* façade is.'

'Go back to the house, love.' I attempt to load an apology into my expression as I look at my wife. 'I'll be along right after you – I just want a few minutes to talk with Mum.'

'So you're not coming with me *now*?' Ellen's close to tears and I feel dreadful about it, but I can't leave things as they are here. Evidently, Mum needs convincing and somehow, I've got to be the one who convinces her before she causes any more damage, especially once the girls are told.

'Just go back to the house – I promise I won't be long – we'll talk then.'

'I'm going to Kirsteen's.' A tear rolls down her cheek as she looks from me to Mum.

Just as I'm about to try and talk Ellen out of driving to her friend's house, I notice movement from the patio out of the corner of my eye. Oh, bloody hell – it doesn't rain, rather it pours. Jasmine has arrived early. She must have had a free period at school. It's my weekend to have her, but normally, she doesn't turn up before early evening. These days she stays at one of her friends' homes until she reaches a point where she can't put off being here any longer.

Ellen follows my gaze. 'I'll see you later then.' Twisting on her heel, she almost marches out of Mum's back door and towards our house, avoiding bumping into Jasmine by going around to the side of the building, rather than via the garden.

'So how are you going to handle this one?' Mum leans against the counter, looking bemused. 'You're probably as well letting Ellen go now Jasmine's here.'

'Well, firstly, I'm going to give *you* some time,' – I point at her, – 'to get used to the idea that I'm going to be a dad again, whatever your theories are. While I head across to speak to Jasmine.' I push my chair back with a scrape. 'You're right – she needs to know before she works any of this out for herself.'

'What are you going to do about Ellen?' Mum folds her arms.

'I'll give her a chance to calm down, and then, thanks to you, I'll drive over to Kirsteen's place to eat humble pie.'

'I'm taking no pleasure from any of this, you know.' She glances out of the window. Ellen's gone and who knows if she'll even come back tonight after this – especially now Jasmine's arrived.

'You owe Ellen a huge apology.' I shake my head. 'I can't believe how badly you've just treated her. She might not be top of your Christmas card list but she's still my wife.'

'I hope for *your* sake that I *do* need to say sorry, son.' Mum steps towards me but I put my hand up to prevent her from coming any closer. 'I hope that more than anything.'

19

'YOU HAVE GOT TO BE JOKING.' Jasmine stamps from one end of the breakfast bar to the other in bare feet and then back again, not too dissimilarly to how she might have done at three years of age. 'You're old enough to be a grandad.'

'Look, it happens, love.' I'm trying to keep my voice calm and steady in the hope that she'll stop shouting. I've already had just about enough today. When things have calmed down, I'm going for a run. I badly need to clear my head.

'It's disgusting if you ask me.' She pauses and folds her arms, wrinkling her nose like I'm a bad smell that's wafted into the kitchen.

'When people get divorced, sometimes they *do* have second-time-around families later in life.' I reach for her elbow but she twists herself from my grasp. 'But trust me on this, the very last thing I wanted to do was to upset you with our news.'

'I just can't believe it.' She continues marching around the kitchen, only pausing for a few seconds to snatch up a glass from the draining board and fill it with water. 'Didn't you think to mention your *family plans* to me first, especially since they affect me too?'

'*What?*' I stifle a laugh even though the situation is far from funny. I knew Jasmine wouldn't be happy but she's responding *far* worse than I expected. Thank goodness Ellen didn't stick around to witness it, especially after Mum's reaction. 'Should I have asked for your permission beforehand – is that what you're saying?'

'You've changed, Dad.' She wags her finger at me. 'I don't even know you any more.' Finally, she stands still before pulling her denim skirt to cover her modesty as she seats herself on a stool at the breakfast bar. 'Since you met *her*, it's like you don't want to know us.'

'That's not true but maybe you're right in some respects – maybe I *have* changed a little – it happens. People *do* change and so do situations.' I sit beside her and go to rest my hand on her arm again but she tugs it sharply out of the way. 'And that's all that's happening here.'

'Don't touch me. I can't believe what you've done to us.' She slams her elbows onto the counter. 'Everyone's going to be laughing their heads off about this – God, what are my friends going to think?' She pauses as if contemplating this, then asks, 'Does *Mum* know?'

'Your mother and I might be on good terms but what I do with my life and what she does with hers is not each other's business anymore.' I've got to take back some control here. 'Really, Jasmine, what I do with my life is totally up to me. One day, you'll be off, doing your own thing like your sister is, and I'm sure you don't just want me to be all by myself for the rest of my life.'

Judging by the look on her face, perhaps she does. 'It's sick, do you know that?' She jumps off her stool, pushes it back with a screech and storms across the kitchen as if she can't get well enough away from me. 'Absolutely sick.'

'What do you mean by that, Jasmine?' Swallowing my rising anger, I swivel around on my stool to look at her. I've been surprisingly calm up to now but between my mother and my daughter, they're pushing at all the wrong buttons.

'There'll be *twenty-four* years between your oldest kid and your youngest.' She folds her arms across herself. 'Bloody hell - when the kid's my age, you'll be *seventy.*'

'So what. Some men have babies far older than I am. Look at Rod Stewart.'

'Who?'

'OK, so perhaps you've never heard of him.' I laugh. 'Bad example.'

'This isn't funny – you're just selfish – you haven't thought about anybody apart from yourself. And *her.*' She points at Ellen's flip-flops which have been discarded on the doormat by the patio doors. 'She's nothing but a golddigger, we can all see it a mile off, Grandma too – she's probably only married you and got pregnant so she can take half of everything you've got – that's what Mum thinks as well. In fact, she'll probably want it all – there'll be nothing left for anyone else.'

'Have you quite finished, young lady?' My voice hardens – it has to. I expected to have to appease my daughter, but I didn't expect her to kick off to this extent. 'Because shortly, I'm going to collect Ellen from her friend's house and I expect you to find it in yourself to congratulate her when we get back.'

'You have got to be joking.' Jasmine turns her back on me and stares over the garden. 'I hate her – I hate you both – you're ruining my life.'

'One day, when you're a little more mature, you might understand that I'm entitled to a life of my own,' I begin.

'What about *my* life?' She throws her hands into the air. 'You won't want to know me anymore, will you? Not when you've got a screaming brat to take care of.'

'Is that what all this is about?' I decide to ignore the screaming brat reference as I cross the kitchen to where Jasmine is standing with slumped shoulders and her head bowed at the patio doors. I take each of her shoulders in my hands and this time she doesn't try to shake me off. I should have foreseen this. She's insecure, that's all, and it's my job to reassure her.

'No one will ever take *your* place, sweetheart.' I try to pull her closer but she's rigid.

'I won't be the youngest anymore, will I?' Her voice trembles. 'And I like being the youngest.'

'I'll always be your dad and will always be right here for you, no matter what, do you hear me?' I try to turn her around but she's as immoveable as a boulder. 'Nothing could ever make me love you any less – not even when you're acting up.'

She doesn't turn to face me but I can tell from the shake of her skinny shoulders beneath the flowery t-shirt that she's crying. I know from some of the guys at work that this is classic *middle child syndrome*. Jasmine's behaving like the middle child before the baby has even been born.

'I want to go home to Mum.'

'Ah, come on, Jasmine.'

'I don't want to be here when Ellen gets back.' She swipes at her falling tears with the back of her hand. 'I'm going home and there's nothing you can do or say to stop me.'

'We can sort this out, can't we?'

'No, we can't. I'm not coming back here – ever.'

20

SEPTEMBER 6

'IT'LL JUST FEEL a little cold on your tummy.' The lady with the kindly face squirts gel onto Ellen's still-flat stomach as she lies on the bed in the dimmed room. Ellen's been counting the days down to today, more excited than I've ever seen to know that the pregnancy's progressing as in the textbooks she's been glued to. All she wants is to hear the heartbeat.

I grip onto my wife's hand, eager for her sake that all's well but as for myself, really, I want to run off into the hills. I can't believe twelve weeks has already passed. The baby will be here before we know it.

'Perhaps after today, people will start to come around to the idea.' Ellen squeezes my fingers. 'Some of them might even want to see the photo. We *can* have a picture today can't we?'

'Of course.' The sonographer moves the probe up and down and side to side over Ellen's belly. 'Can you just confirm your age and the date of your last period?'

'I'm thirty-seven,' Ellen replies. 'And it was the thirtieth of May. I've already worked out that my due date will be the sixth of March.'

'You're certainly on the ball with your dates.' She continues wiggling the probe, her expression giving little away.

'Aren't most expectant mums?' I ask, stopping myself from mentioning Carmen. Ellen's made it crystal clear that she doesn't want me talking about my first two experiences or drawing comparisons between her and my ex-wife. It probably doesn't help that Carmen and I have always been on such friendly terms, though there can be no denying that relations have soured somewhat since I married Ellen and my daughters have been reporting back to their mother. However, I haven't seen them at all since the news about Ellen's pregnancy. I didn't even get the chance to break the news myself, rather Jasmine stilled the beans to her sister and her mother.

'You'd be surprised how many aren't.' The sonographer keeps her eyes on the screen, the frown that's creasing her forehead not something I want to see.

'Is everything alright?' Ellen squints at the screen before looking at me, as if I might be able to offer some reassurance. Obviously, I can't. I glance at the screen, only seeing a collection of blobs in various shades of grey.

'I'll just be a moment.' The lady rises from her stool, but at least this time, she makes eye contact with me and then Ellen. 'I'm just going to ask the doctor to take a look.'

'Oh no!' Ellen grips my hand as the door closes softly. 'Something's wrong, isn't it? I could tell from her face. I've seen this kind of scenario in the documentaries I watch.'

'She'd have told us if there was anything wrong.' Nevertheless, the hairs are standing up on the back of my neck and I shiver. I'm still not sure about this baby, even if we're nearly a third of the way into the pregnancy, but for Ellen's sake, I hope there isn't a problem. She'll be devastated. And there's no way I want Anthony back in our lives. We haven't heard a thing from him since the day of the positive test and that's the way I want things to stay.

'There can't be a problem, surely. I've had so much sickness and Kirsteen says that's a positive sign – it means my hormones are acting as they should be.' She scrunches her eyes together. 'Oh, Oliver, I hope everything's OK.'

'Let's just wait and see, shall we?' I don't want to give her false hope. I just hope this doctor doesn't take long as I fear Ellen will explode with anxiety if she's forced to wait much longer.

I jump as the door bursts open. It's a white-coated doctor with a stethoscope dangling from his neck, and he's closely followed by the sonographer.

'I'm Doctor Elliott,' he announces, smiling at us in a businesslike way. I'm mildly reassured by his confident air and trustworthy face. However, if there's anything wrong, it's not as if he'll be able to fix it – nobody will. 'You must be Mr and Mrs Holmes,' he continues. 'Right, shall we take a look at what's going on in there?'

He takes hold of the probe with steady hands, professional and clinical — but I'm watching him so closely that I can't fail to notice the flicker of tension in his jaw.

He tucks the tissue paper deeper into Ellen's waistband, then turns the screen away from us and into his own line of sight.

I stiffen. Why the hell would he do that? Is there something he doesn't want us to see?

Ellen's body tenses beneath his touch as the probe glides across her abdomen. Her eyes are fixed on the ceiling now, at its square polystyrene tiles, her lips pressed tightly together. Before we came into the room she was chatty, joking about craving chocolate ice cream. Now she's silent and still.

The room is heavy with the quiet hum of a fan and the other machinery. But there's something else — something less tangible. A kind of dread.

The doctor's expression is blank as he presses a button.

Then another. And another. Each one is a quiet click that lands like a blow. His focus is unbroken as he moves the probe slowly, deliberately — up, down, side to side — scanning every corner of Ellen's womb like he's hunting for something. Then he turns to the sonographer standing behind him.

'You were right,' he tells her quietly.

My stomach drops. 'Right about what?' My voice comes out sharper than intended, cutting through the silence as I grip the edges of my seat.

'Please.' Ellen's eyes dart between the two of them. 'Just tell us.'

The doctor hesitates for a second, then finally tilts the screen towards us. It takes my brain a few seconds to catch up with what my eyes are seeing. Shapes. Shadows. Movement.

And then it lands. Oh God. I drop my head into my hands. A cold sweat breaks across the back of my neck.

'What is it?' Ellen gasps. 'What's wrong?'

21

I CAN'T LOOK at my wife. 'There's bloody *two* of them.'

My voice is muffled by my hands. I can't lift my head. I can barely *think*.

'Congratulations to you both,' the doctor says, when I eventually raise it – like he's just handed us a bottle of champagne. He wipes his hands on the paper roll with the same detachment someone might use to clear crumbs off a table. 'Multiple pregnancies aren't uncommon in older women. Unless either of you have a history of twins?'

Slowly, I meet Ellen's eyes and we shake our heads in unison. She looks stunned. Pale. Almost childlike with the enormity of it. And of course we can't say what's really going on.

That these babies have nothing to do with me — not biologically. That we made a deal. That there's a third party in this equation, a man who should be nowhere near this room and yet is everywhere in it.

'Do you want to hear their heartbeats?'

Ellen clasps her hands together. There are tears in her eyes. 'Yes please.' Her voice is almost a whisper.

The doctor keeps watching us as the sonographer pushes at

some buttons on the computer. His gaze lingers just a moment too long, like he's trying to figure us out. Or maybe he's already worked it out and is letting us stew.

'Have you undergone any fertility treatment?' he asks. 'That can increase the likelihood of twins.'

Again, the glance. Again, the silence. We both shake our heads. What else can we do? How the hell would we even begin to explain?

'Here we go then — twin one,' announces the sonographer. 'I'll just turn the sound up.'

A whooshing sound fills the air. A fast, powerful rhythm. A heartbeat. A new life. I've heard this sound before — with Carmen. It was magical back then. Now it makes me want to crawl out of my own skin.

'And twin two.'

The sonographer moves the probe to the other side. Another heartbeat. Just as strong. Just as real.

Ellen is close to tears. A part of her is already in love – I can see it. And me? I don't have a name for what I'm feeling. Not joy. Not fear. Something messier. Heavier. I want to laugh, cry, yell, and knock back a bottle of whisky — all at once.

'I realise this must be a shock for the two of you,' the doctor says gently, 'but as it sinks in, I'm sure you'll start to see this as a blessing.'

Ellen gives a watery laugh. 'I'm going to be the size of a house.'

Normally I'd make some joke. Rub her shoulder. Lighten the mood. But I can't. Because all I can think about is the fall-out. The sheer, unavoidable chaos this will bring. I've already had grief from my daughters, my ex-wife, and my mother over the prospect of *one* baby. Their reaction to *two*? I don't even want to imagine it.

'Two for the price of one,' the sonographer says brightly as she wipes the gel from Ellen's stomach. She smiles like it's a punchline.

She doesn't realise how close to the bone her comment is.

'Cheers.' Ellen and I clink our mugs together in the outdoor seating area of the hospital cafe. It's a beautiful late summer's day out here, perfect for welcoming good news, so I'm going to have to force some joy, even if I'm struggling to feel any.

'Oh my God, oh my God, oh my God – twins!' Ellen rests her mug down as the people at the next table, one attached to a drip and the other on crutches peer at us curiously.

'We're having twins,' I explain.

'Congratulations.' The man nods in our direction before turning back to his muffin.

Ellen lowers her mug and grips my arm. 'Are you starting to get used to the idea – even just a little?'

'I'm shellshocked.'

Not to mention fifty-four years old. How the hell am I going to cope with *two* newborn babies? As a young man, I could run on empty but I'm not as good at it these days. I enjoy my sleep, my peace and quiet, and the freedom to do what I want, when I want. I was crazy agreeing to this in the first place but in my defence, not only did I just want to make my wife happy, I was also looking at the whole thing through rose-tinted glasses. But now reality is beginning to set in.

'We'll be fine.' She must be able to read my mind. 'Two of us – two of them.' She points from me to her and then to her belly. I can't believe she isn't showing yet, not now that we know she's carrying twins.

'Hopefully Mum will pitch in too,' I say. Judging by the way she's been acting since we broke the news of the pregnancy, I doubt this very much. She's always been independent and enjoyed doing her own thing but over the last few months, it's as if she's been going out of her way to avoid me. I miss her and can only hope that once she sets eyes on the babies, they'll win her over.

'Are we going to tell her when we get home?' Lines of concern etch themselves into creases across Ellen's forehead. 'And the girls?'

'It's best if I tell them all on my own, love.'

'But it's *our* news.' She pouts. 'I'm sick of the lot of them.'

'I know it is – I just don't want anything to stress you out – especially now.'

Ellen slumps further into her chair. Whether that's with relief or disappointment is difficult to say.

22

'Book, check – brew, check – biscuits, check – right you've got the lot.' I tuck a cushion behind my wife on the recliner in our sun-drenched lounge. 'You keep your feet up.'

'Are you going to tell her about the twins?'

'I'll see what she wanted me for first. After all, she sent the text last night. I should have probably been over by now.'

'You've got a life of your own, haven't you?' Ellen looks sulky.

'Look, I won't be long.' I really won't be long at all if I don't get the reaction I'm hoping for from my mother when I tell her our latest news. But I don't say this to Ellen.

'I should be coming with you,' she says. 'After all, it's *me* who's carrying these babies.'

'No, honestly. You were there for Mum's initial reaction. It's not fair on you if we get a repeat performance.'

'Well I'm happy and you're happy,' she replies. 'In the scheme of things, that's all that matters.' Her hand flies to her belly. 'Twins!' She scrunches her face in excitement. At least *one* of us is getting used to the idea.

Bloody twins. Am I happy? I guess I would be if they were

truly my babies. Or if we'd done this properly through a fertility clinic, I'd feel more celebratory than I've been trying to fake. Ellen reckons they should feel even *more* mine because of the huge amount I've already paid to bring them into being, but I just can't feel that way. Every time I think about the hundred grand I've already parted with, my father's voice bounces around my brain, saying, *desperation drives the hardest bargains.* Another piece of wisdom he liked to offer.

I'm even more worried about breaking the news to my daughters than my mother, and have already decided to leave it until the weekend. It's Jasmine's first day back at school today after the summer break, and she's facing her exams this school year, so no doubt I'll receive some flack from my ex-wife for subjecting Jasmine to this added pressure at *such an important stage in her life.* Carmen and I always had each other's backs where the girls were concerned, but since I remarried, everything's changed. From amicably co-parenting, we're now at loggerheads.

To say we're now into September, there's little sign of Autumn as I trudge from our patio doors and around the edge of the vegetable patch towards Mum's cottage. It still feels like summer.

'Nice day for it.' Our gardener, clad in shorts and a t-shirt, leans on his spade as I reach the vegetable patch. 'And it looks like we're getting a bumper crop of veggies after the summer we've had.' He gestures across the garden.

'Good stuff.' I force a smile. 'I'll look forward to cooking up some soups. Thanks for all your hard work.'

'You OK, Oliver?' He stands up straight. 'You seem a bit down in the dumps.'

'I'm fine.' I force a smile. 'I'm just on my way to see my mother – I've got some news that I don't think she'll be too elated about, so I was just chewing it all over in my mind.'

'News, eh?' I've known Nick a long time but even so, I

certainly can't tell him anything before I've spoken to Mum. His quiet brown eyes seem to be inviting me to confide in him and I wish I could, but I can't tell the whole truth of my predicament to anyone.

'I'll tell you the news as soon as I'm able to.'

'How very intriguing.' He pulls his cap further over his face as if shielding his eyes from the early afternoon sun.

'Trust me – you'll know what it is soon enough.' The thought of a very heavily pregnant Ellen waddling around the garden almost amuses me.

'Actually, I haven't seen anything of Phyllis since I arrived here this morning.' Nick gestures towards her house. 'I'd have thought she'd have been out here on a day like today.'

Especially with me and Ellen out of the way. But I don't say this. We've been out of the house since early this morning. Firstly for the scan and a coffee, then we did some shopping and went for some lunch. I relented and allowed Ellen to buy some baby clothes. Not wishing to tempt fate, Carmen didn't buy *anything* until her second scan at twenty weeks, but I kept quiet about this. One skill any man who's on their second marriage has to master is when it is best to keep his mouth shut.

'She hasn't even brought me a brew.'

'That's not like her – anyway, I'll sort you one after I've been in to see her – we've got to keep our chief gardener happy.'

'Your *only* gardener.' He pulls his spade back from the ground.

'There'll be an extra bit of something in your pay this month,' I tell him. 'You do such an amazing job out here and I've seen how hard you've grafted over the summer.'

'Cheers boss.' His weathered face breaks into a smile. 'To be honest, I couldn't imagine working anywhere else.'

'I guess we're stuck with each other then.' I smile back at him. 'Right, I'd better go and see that mother of mine.' I glance back over at her cottage, noticing now that her front door's ajar. This shouldn't be unusual on a warm day like today, but like us, she *never* uses her front door. 'If you hear any shouting or swearing, try not to be alarmed. It won't be me, it'll be her.'

The gardener pulls a face. 'Mothers, eh? Mind you, I'd give my right arm just for an hour with mine again. I didn't realise how much I'd miss her until she was no longer around.'

'It's always the way, isn't it? Catch you soon.'

On that note, with thoughts of Dad now swirling around my mind, I continue onto the cottage. I wonder what he'd make of all this twin business and whether he'd be able to see through me as easily as Mum appears to have done. I reckon he'd be telling her to wind her neck in and just to let us get on with it.

The house is in silence which is also unusual. Mum normally has the radio blaring out, especially in the afternoon when she does her housework.

Even the birds seem to have stopped singing as I lift the latch on her gate and head for her open door. Her Mini was still on the drive when we arrived back, and the sandals she always wears have been kicked off here on the outside doormat so she must be around somewhere.

'Mum?' I push the door into the hallway, comforted by the familiar scent of her house. The wax she uses on her furniture combined with the perfume she's worn for as long as I can remember.

She doesn't reply. I make my way across the hallway to the lounge, gasping as I open the door. Her drawers have been emptied all over the floor. The TV lies smashed behind the cabinet it normally sits on and everything's in complete disarray. She's been burgled.

'Oh my God. Mum?' I dart from the lounge to the kitchen,

praying she's out for the day and hasn't tried to confront whoever's broken in head-on.

Why have they come *here*? Why haven't they burgled *our* house instead? After all, there's probably far more to steal from us, *and* we've been out of the way since first thing.

I let out a long breath. The kitchen's untouched but there's no sign of Mum apart from a cold cup of coffee and two uneaten slices of marmalade-topped toast on the side. This isn't looking good at all. As my panic levels continue to rise, I check her conservatory and her dining room where again, drawers have been tipped out. It looks like her silver cutlery's been targeted. Whoever's broken in has known what to go for. Things that are easy to carry and are likely to quickly fetch some funds. They must have been watching until Nick was out of the way, perhaps at the bottom end of our grounds.

My heart's banging against my rib cage. *Where is she? Where the hell is she?* Thank God I didn't bring Ellen over here. I'd better check upstairs, and then I'll call the police. At least whoever's got in here seems to have scarpered.

If I get my hands on the lowlifes who think it's OK to break into an elderly woman's house, I won't be responsible for how I'll deal with them.

'Mum?' I plant my foot on the bottom step. She can't be here – she'd have answered me the moment she heard my voice. As I continue to ascend the stairs, there's an even more eerie sense about the place than I felt from the silence in the garden. This house is usually warm and welcoming but there's a distinct chill about it today. Probably because it's been violated.

I take deep breaths and try to stay calm. Anything that's been taken or broken can be replaced. As long as Mum's OK, that's all that matters.

I don't usually come upstairs when I'm here so it's strange to be walking along her landing, looking at the pictures of my daughters at all stages of their childhood, along with photos of me and my sister, collaged over Mum's back wall. Once I've made sure she's alright, I'll have a proper look at them.

'Mum, it's me, Oliver – are you in there?' When she doesn't reply, steeling myself, I push the door into her bedroom.

23

'Oh no.' Mum's bedroom is in the same state as the lounge. A couple of pictures have been smashed from the wall. The contents of her handbag are strewn across her bed and her jewellery box is upturned on the dressing table.

I sink to the edge of the bed and slide my phone from my pocket. It's just *stuff*, I know it is, but there'll be items in that jewellery box that can never be replaced, and she'll also be heartbroken at the theft of her cutlery set which was passed down from her grandmother. It should have gone to mine and Hannah's kids one day. Worst of all, she'll no longer feel safe in her own home.

'Bastards.' My voice sounds louder in the silence of the room as I dial 101. There's no point ringing the emergency line as the thieves are no doubt long gone. Mum will have to stay at our house until whoever's done this to her is caught and she feels safe enough to return. I should check the other bedrooms but I'll get the police on their way here first. *For all the good they'll do.* But at least we'll get a crime number and might be able to claim back some of what's been taken on Mum's insurance.

'Emergency, which service please?'

'Police, my mum's been burgled.'

'Is the burglary in progress?'

'I'm not sure – I think they've gone but I haven't checked *everywhere*.'

I reach for Mum's overturned jewellery box but stop myself. My fingerprints might hinder their investigation.

'Is it a domestic dwelling?'

'It is.'

'And your mother's the householder?'

'Yes, but it's on the grounds of my house. I was just calling to see her and found it completely trashed.'

My eyes land on the smashed photo frame – Mum and Dad's wedding day, now shattered on the floor. The glass glints in the light, like jagged teeth. If I get my hands on whoever did this...

'Is she there with you?'

'No. To be honest, I – I don't know where she is.'

I rise from the edge of the bed to peer out of the window. And then I see it.

A foot – pale and motionless – just visible beyond the bed. 'Oh my God.'

The phone nearly slips from my hand. 'She's – she's here. She's lying on the floor. Just hang on – Mum!'

I drop the phone and propel myself around the foot of the bed. How the hell didn't I see her when I came in?

'Mum!' I fall to my knees. 'Mum, are you OK? Talk to me. Please.' My voice is shaking. The air feels thick, heavy, and unreal. It takes a second – no, a full eternity – to register what I'm seeing.

The pink carpet is soaked with blood. Not just spattered – soaked. The cast-iron lamp lies next to Mum's head, the one she also loved because it used to be her grandmother's.

Her hair is matted with blood. Her face is wrong – frozen

and drained of colour. Her eyes are wide open and staring at something far, far away.

'No, no, no—'

My fingers grope blindly for a pulse I already know I won't find. Her wrist is cool and her fingers slack.

The phone crackles from the bed, the operator's voice tinny and distant, 'Sir? Sir? Is everything alright?' I scramble back to it, almost dropping it again.

'It's... my mother.' I can barely speak. I can barely breathe. 'She's—they've—'

'Sir, try to stay calm. Tell me what's happened.'

'She's dead.' The words sound like they're coming from someone else. 'Please send someone. Please.'

'I'm escalating this now,' the operator says. 'Help is on the way. Hold the line, Sir.'

Tears blur everything. I never cry. But now, I can't stop. It's like something's broken inside me. Mum was solid and steady. The one person I thought I'd always have. Since Dad died, I've known – deep down – that her time would come eventually. But not like this – not bleeding to death on the carpet of her bedroom while some piece of filth rifles through her drawers for a bit of bloody jewellery.

The operator's voice breaks in again. 'We've traced your location and our officers will be with you in approximately twelve minutes.'

Twelve minutes. I want to scream. What am I supposed to do for twelve minutes?

'What do I do?' I whisper. 'What the hell am I supposed to do now?'

'I need you to wait outside the property until they arrive, Sir. It's important for the forensics team.'

'My DNA will be all over the place anyway.'

'It's just procedure. Is there anyone we can call to be with you?'

I think of my sister. Then immediately dismiss it. The operator can't be the one to tell her. Not yet. Not like this.

'A friend? A neighbour?'

'My wife,' I say. 'She's over at my house.' I immediately dismiss her as well. 'No, leave it,' I say. 'She's pregnant. I need to break it to her gently.'

'You're doing very well, Sir. Just stay on the phone with me. But wait outside please.'

'OK.' My voice is cracked and dry – a husk of a sound. Despite the operator's offer to remain on the phone, I end the call. The silence after we have disconnected is louder than anything.

I crouch again, gently brushing a lock of hair from Mum's forehead. She's smaller now, somehow. Deflated. As if someone let the air out of her life. 'Oh, Mum...'

I want to lie down beside her, close my eyes and wake up back in yesterday, when she was still alive. When there was still time to save her.

I don't know how I'm going to tell my girls. I don't know how I'm going to survive this moment, let alone all that will inevitably come next.

I get up – stumbling like I've just downed five brandies. And then I remember.

Mum's fridge. The bottle on the top of it. *Brandy for the shock*, she'd always say. Maybe that's what I need.

'Why the hell didn't you call me the moment you found her?' Ellen drops beside me onto the bench Mum always loved to sit on. 'Instead, I've been fast asleep on the sofa, oblivious to it all.'

'Why do you think?' It's made it all the more real now that Ellen's here with her tea and sympathy. What she doesn't know is that I've slopped another large measure of brandy into the steaming mug she brought to me. I need to be numb – I need to knock myself out — it's the only way I can cope. 'You've got the babies to think of, haven't you?' My voice is strangled. 'The babies Mum's never even going to get to meet.' A fresh wave of anguish crashes over me as our fresh reality hits even further home.

'How much longer are the police going to be in there?' She points at the lounge window.

I shrug. What does it even matter? Nothing can bring my mother back. 'As long as it takes.' I'm strangely coherent to say how much brandy I've poured down my neck in the last two or three hours. 'They told me just before you arrived that they'll be moving her soon.'

'And taking her *where*?' Ellen's eyes fill with tears as if the enormity of what's going on here is only just sinking in with her. 'Poor Phyllis – I can't believe it.'

'They've got to do a post-mortem,' I continue. 'How could those bastards have done this to her?' I can't swallow my drink for the melon-sized lump in my throat. 'How can they possibly go on, how will they be able to sleep tonight, knowing they've murdered a defenceless old lady?'

'Have the police *any* idea of who could have done it?' She gestures at the officer guarding the cordon.

'They're saying young 'uns or druggies at the moment,' I wipe my face onto my t-shirt. 'Because they've taken the *easy* stuff. But they must have been casing the place – after all, they've waited until we're not around. They must have waited until Nick's back was turned as well.' I gesture to where I was talking to the gardener before. As if I could have been cheerfully passing the time of day with him, when all the while, my mother was lying on the floor, dead.

'Where's Nick now?' She glances towards his shed.

'I've sent him home. He was in such a state, so sorry that he hadn't seen or heard anything – but I couldn't cope with him – I haven't even let my sister or the girls know yet.'

'Do you want me to contact them?'

'No.' I choke back fresh sobs. 'What's happened needs to come from me.'

'Could the burglars come back, do you think?' Ellen jumps up from the bench beside me, suddenly looking panic-stricken. 'What if they do? What if we're next on their hit list?'

'Our house is like Fort Knox. Mind you, this place is supposed to be as well.' I twist on the bench, looking at the sunny exterior of Mum's home. It's almost impossible to imagine that such evil has taken place within its walls today. 'Oh my God.'

'What is it?'

'For all I know, she could have even been lying there since last night – we haven't been seeing each other as much lately. And I promised Dad—'

'This isn't your fault, Oliver. How could you have known?'

'Mum always felt so safe in this house.' I drop my head into my hands and feel the weight of Ellen's hand on my back. Her perfume drifts up my nose. I'll never smell Mum's scent again, I'll never see the knowing way she'd look at me over the top of her spectacles or watch the familiarity of her back as she bustles around the kitchen.

'Oh God, what am I going to do, Ellen? I just want her back.'

'Of course you do.' Ellen pulls me closer and strokes the top of my head in a similar way to how Mum might have, once upon a time. I pull away, her attempt at comforting me only making me feel ten times worse.

'I'm sorry love, I just need to be on my own right now.' I stagger to my feet. 'I can't be here. I can't watch when they carry her out in a body bag.'

'Nobody would expect you to.'

'Just tell the police I'll be over at the house when they're ready to take my statement.'

'I'll come with you.' She starts getting to her feet. 'I can't bear to be here when they bring her out either.'

'No really. Please.' The tears are back again. 'Just leave me alone for a while. I'm sorry.'

24

SEPTEMBER 27

'OLIVER?' Ellen's voice echoes from the bottom of the stairs. 'Are you still up there?'

'I won't be a minute.' I don't move from where I've been kneeling for the last hour beside Mum's bed, rifling through a memory box I had no idea Mum created.

She peers around the door. 'The cars will be here in ten minutes.'

'I know.' What she means is that my mother's body will be arriving in ten minutes. I can't bear to see the coffin containing her, adorned with the M-U-M flowers we chose. Three weeks might have elapsed since that horrendous day when I found her body but I still feel like it hasn't really happened – like it's a nightmare from which I'm still awake. Who the hell could want to hurt my mother? She might have been outspoken at times, but fundamentally, she wouldn't have harmed a fly. The shock of it all has been unbearable. When Dad died, we knew it was coming but this — well, I'm not sure if I'll ever get over it.

'Are you ready?' Ellen steps right into the room, her hair pinned up and the slightest swell of a baby bump becoming visible beneath her clingy black dress. As she said, it won't be long before she needs maternity clothes.

'I'll never be ready.' I drag a hanky from my jacket. 'I don't know how I'm going to get through it.'

'I'll be right beside you.' I sense the weight of her hand on my shoulder. 'What are you looking at?' She kneels beside me and picks up a tiny leather boot. 'Aww, was this *yours*?'

'Yep. All of it.'

Ellen picks up what must have been my Christening outfit. 'I can't believe she's kept so many of your things.'

Resting it back down, her eyes roam from a *book of firsts* to a crocheted shawl and then to a school shirt covered in signatures. 'Wow,' she says. 'I'll have to do a box like this for our two, won't I?'

I don't want to think or talk about the twins today; the only person I can think or talk about is Mum. It's irrational, I know it is, but I keep thinking that if it wasn't for the pregnancy, the distance between Mum and I wouldn't have existed over the last few months. Plus, I might have been around to protect her the morning when it happened. The post-mortem confirmed that the burglars must have got in when we were at the scan appointment and that she died from two blows to the head. I wish I could talk about my guilt and regret with Ellen but I can't talk to *anyone*. There are times, often in the middle of the night when I feel like I could explode with my misery.

'Ouch, my knees.' Ellen hoists herself back to her feet.

I rise on my knees and without wanting or meaning to, my gaze rests on the spot at the other side of the bed, the vision of my mother slamming back into my mind, battered, broken and gone forever. It's an image that will probably never leave me. I haven't even been able to visit her at the funeral home, preferring to fight the final memory of what she looked like and instead remember the vibrant woman she was.

The police took the lamp away as evidence and I've told

them to dispose of it when they've finished. I never want to set eyes on it again. If it wasn't for the fact that we've got two babies due in five and a half months, I'd be selling up and moving. Every time, I return home and remember Mum's no longer pottering around in her cottage, the realisation winds me. But the enormity of how much there would be to organise is beyond anything I could cope with.

'Come on, we need to go back over to the house,' Ellen glances at her phone. 'Hannah's in the second car and says they're only a few minutes away.'

I rise to my feet and shake out my cramped legs. Ellen steps in front of me and reaches for my tie. 'You're all skewiff.'

'I don't think I can do this.' Following my wife down Mum's stairs, beside all our happy family photos, I feel devoid of all energy. I'm just relieved my sister's taken charge of the eulogy because there's no way I'd be able to stand up there and speak. I'd go to pieces. It was bad enough when the celebrant came around to see us and encouraged us to talk about her. Hannah seemed to welcome the chance to bring Mum's memory back to life whereas for me, as soon as he'd gone, I shut myself up in the office with a bottle of whiskey.

'It'll start to feel better once this is over,' Ellen says. 'It's true what they say about funerals bringing closure.'

'Is it?' I'd like to ask her how *she* knows. To my knowledge, she's *never* had anyone close to her pass away. She's been estranged from both her parents since her teens and refuses to talk about them. Whenever I've tried to get her to open up about *anything* to do with her past, she's always closed me down, saying she prefers not to wallow in what can never be changed.

25

MY SISTER'S voice sounds far away as she delivers her tearful eulogy at the front of the crematorium. She's doing brilliantly and Mum would be so proud of how she's getting through it. I stare at the large canvas resting on the easel beside the coffin. Mum when she was in her prime. With her blonde hair hanging down her back and her sparkling blue eyes, she radiates fun and vitality. In those days she used to travel everywhere on her bike and was always making something for the home – whether cushions, curtains or jam tarts for me and Hannah. I hope beyond all hope that wherever she's gone, she's somehow found peace after such a violent end to her life, and that she's been able to find Dad. As one of my tears lands on Ellen's arm, she squeezes my hand.

'You OK?' She whispers.

I want to say, *what do you think? I'm at my mother's funeral,* but that would be unfair. No one knows what to say at a time like this other than, *sorry for your loss,* or *if there's anything I can do...*

I run my hand behind my increasingly hot collar, wanting

to remove my jacket but not wanting to appear disrespectful. I glance across at Carmen who is sitting in the front row on the other side of the aisle from us. Tears pour down her face as she consoles our daughters who flank her at either side. She and Mum adored each other when they were mother and daughter-in-law, and I know Mum still went to see her for a coffee from time to time. The girls should have wanted to sit with me today but their feelings towards Ellen and me since they were told about the twins have been far from amicable. Perhaps I should have waited until *after* their grandmother's funeral before breaking the news like Carmen suggested. No matter what, I can't seem to do any right where they're concerned.

Hannah reaches the conclusion of her eulogy. I haven't heard a word but I already listened to her as she practiced it. We both repeatedly broke down in tears but somehow, she's kept it together up there this morning.

The stench of the flowers adorning Mum's coffin is making my head hurt. I don't know why she loved lilies so much – they stink. I twist in my seat to see if the police are still at the back of the room. I didn't want them here but I can't deny how supportive the two officers assigned to Mum's case have been since I found her body. They've both said they feel like they could have known Mum too after everything Hannah and I have told them.

Their presence at a funeral is a usual occurrence when the killer hasn't been caught. Sometimes, they told us, killers can be lurking among the congregation but more often, they'll wait *outside,* watching the final result of their actions with a kind of morbid pride.

As we followed the hearse into the crematorium, I combed the faces of people on the street before we turned in here, and then studied *everyone* who lined the lane leading from the entrance to the building. I was more focused on that than Mum at the time but there seemed to be no one untoward hanging around.

Hannah sits back down beside me. 'Well done, sis.' I lean away from Ellen and instead put my arm around my sister as she sobs into the lapel of my jacket. Finally, after her strength so far this morning in preparation for having to stand at the lectern and speak, she can now let it all out and properly grieve.

'I just can't believe she's gone, Oliver.'

We sit through a slideshow of photos while Mum's favourite song fills the packed room. *Somewhere Over the Rainbow.* I can hardly bear to look at the screen. It's a good job I helped to choose the photos and also that I vetted Hannah's eulogy beforehand, because not a word of this service is going in. I might as well not be here, I feel so removed from reality.

It's over. I watched the curtain draw around Mum's coffin and was the first one out of there to gasp in the late September air. Shrugging off the platitudes of well-wishers, I tunnel through their grabbing hands towards the Detective Inspector and the Sergeant in charge of Mum's case.

'Did you see anything – or anyone?'

DI Browne shakes her head. 'Not a thing, I'm afraid, but don't worry, the case will remain open for the foreseeable future and leads from the TV appeal are still trickling in.'

'It's been three weeks.' Something inside me sags. 'I can't lie, I'm starting to lose hope that you'll catch them.'

'As we've mentioned before, the thief or thieves were more sophisticated than we first suspected and must have been wearing gloves and head coverings. Other than some clothing fibres, we haven't found *anything* in your Mum's cottage to make any arrests.'

'I already know all this,' I snap. This is becoming more and more frustrating. What happened is horrendous enough but to know her killers are still on the loose is more than I can bear.

'I'm just scared they'll come back.' Ellen sidles up beside me. It's true. She's been as jumpy as a grasshopper since Mum died, which can't be any good for the twins. Like me, she speaks plurally about Mum's attackers. Mum might have been in her twilight years but it would have really taken something for just one person to trick their way into the house, then corner and overpower her before she could scream or ring 999 to raise the alarm.

'There's nothing to suggest they'll return,' replies DI Browne as Hannah also joins us. 'I just wish your cameras had been switched on when it happened.'

I sag some more.

'I'll *never* forgive myself.' Ellen stares at the ground.

Hannah's expression suggests that *she* doesn't forgive her either. I was initially furious that Ellen had unplugged something so vital for the sake of testing baby monitors, but I've had to let it drop. Ellen's punished herself enough without me pouring extra salt into her wounds. What's done is done and no amount of blame is going to change anything.

Kirsteen's watching on as she stands on the fringes of our attendees. Most people are gathered in small groups so she stands out a mile by herself. 'Are you OK?' She mouths the words at Ellen, patting her belly at the same time.

Ellen nods. 'Excuse me, Kirsteen's standing on her own.' She weaves her way past the other mourners to join her friend. I'm slightly irked my wife has left my side in the aftermath of Mum's funeral. However, it's not as if the police have anything new to tell me and I have got Hannah here for support.

The next ten minutes are a blur of handshakes and further *sorry for your loss* formalities.

As I finally manage to break myself away to rejoin my wife,

I'm greeted with the condolence of all condolences from Kirsteen.

'It's funny in families,' – she points at Ellen's stomach, – 'how births and deaths occur so close together. When one life ends, as they say, another begins.'

'How very profound.' I can't keep the sarcasm out of my voice.

26

DECEMBER 21

'I've got your ex-wife on the phone.' The receptionist's voice drifts through the intercom, slightly distorted, and echoey – like she's speaking from inside a snow globe. I picture her in the foyer, framed by the scale models of the buildings we've designed, visitors slouched on our angular grey sofas beside the monstrously large Christmas tree.

I lean back in my chair, the leather sighing beneath my weight.

'Thanks for calling me back, Carmen. Though I didn't expect it to take a week.'

My gaze flickers to the space where Carmen's photo used to sit –now replaced with one of Ellen. She's smiling, radiant and expectant. But something inside me twists as I realise how I preferred life when Carmen's photo took the pride of place on my desk. It's like my entire existence has been overwritten.

'I'm sorry, Oliver, but these things take time. And our girls —well, you know how stubborn they can both be.'

'Have you managed to get anywhere?'

I watch the open-plan office beyond my glass walls – people chatting, typing, laughing – all wearing their novelty jumpers and drinking festive coffees. They mostly look like they'll have places they want to go at the end of this, the final working day before we close the office for a fortnight. They'll have families they enjoy belonging to and Christmas traditions that won't cut them like broken glass.

Work is the only place I feel remotely normal. The sanctuary of my office is a buffer. From the house. From Ellen. From Mum's cottage, sitting so cold and empty. Today is the shortest day of the year and I can't remember a day when I've ever felt darker.

'I'm afraid neither of them will budge, Oliver.'

Carmen's voice has that soft melancholy that always used to ground me. It's warmer than my mother's voice and so much more familiar than Ellen's. Hearing it makes me ache.

'They won't even let me visit them for an hour on Christmas Day?'

Even as I ask it, I can hear how it might come across. Like I'm prepared to ditch my pregnant wife and leave her alone on Christmas Day. But Ellen's the main part of my daughters' problem and it's not like I could have taken her along.

'We're going to my mother's,' Carmen says.

I flinch. 'At least you've still got yours.' The words are out before I can stop myself. 'I'm sorry. That wasn't fair.'

'I'm only trying to help.' Her tone is calm and neutral which affects me more than if she'd shouted. 'But you haven't made it easy,' she continues. 'They've both said this – how you've put *that woman* head and shoulders above them.'

'But she's carrying my babies.'

'Is she really?'

I've time to dwell on the unfamiliar edge of sarcasm in Carmen's tone as a long beat of a pause hangs between us.

'Do you know, your mother saw straight through Ellen. And so can I.'

My stomach tightens. 'What's that supposed to mean?'

'It means you don't even *know* if the babies are yours, Oliver.'

'Of course, they're mine.'

'You had a vasectomy. I drove you there and picked you up, remember?'

'I had it reversed.'

'I know the score. Me and your mother still talked, you know. God rest her soul.'

Her words hang like a fog in the air as the density of my grief settles itself even more heavily over me. Soon I'll be returning home to my stunning wife, my beautiful house, and the twins are due in eight weeks. But without Mum—and without my daughters – everything feels meaningless.

And if I'm being honest, things with Ellen haven't been right since the deal with Anthony was sealed. The smiles might be still present, but something behind them has shifted. Or maybe they were never genuine in the first place.

'I don't want to talk about this with you, Carmen.'

'The woman's a golddigger. Everyone can see it apart from you. And I'm afraid, until you do, Jasmine and—'

'What have you said to them?'

'Don't lay this on me. They've made up their own minds. The other reason they haven't been back to see you is because they *can't* face your mother's house – not after what happened.'

'Neither can I.'

I bark the words louder than I mean to, and my PA twists in her seat just beyond my office. I turn towards the window to avoid her enquiring look. Outside, the sky is leaden and the streets sparkle with cold fairy lights.

'You're their father, Oliver.' Carmen sighs. 'They'll come around eventually – just keep trying and carry on messaging and calling. Maybe once the babies are born—'

'They'll want nothing more to do with me.'

'They were already hurting after we split. You were never there. Not at home. Not at their school events. Never—'

'Alright.' I grit my teeth. 'Talk about kicking a dog while it's down. Besides, I made up for it since. We were close, we were–'

'All they see is you bending over backwards for a woman they believe is shallow and opportunistic. While with them – and with *us*—' She trails off.

'I'm sorry, Carmen. I know I deserved the divorce, but I don't deserve this. I don't deserve my daughters ghosting me on *Christmas Day*, of all days.'

'You'll have to give it time. They're still broken over what happened to your mum. If someone had been caught, maybe they'd be healing by now.'

'Is it because they don't feel safe at my house? Because *that's* easy to fix.'

'It's not the house. It's *her*.' Carmen's voice dips to a whisper as if she doesn't want to be overheard. 'Look… just try to enjoy Christmas. And hopefully, the New Year will bring a shift.'

I end the call without saying goodbye. The New Year *will* bring a shift alright. Although my life is already unrecognisable.

And I'm not sure I've even reached the bottom of the dark pit of despair I've fallen into yet.

27

FEBRUARY 25

'Where've you been, love? You're supposed to be resting.' I look up at Ellen as she waddles into the lounge. I say waddles because that's how she moves. She went beyond *walking* a couple of months ago and looks like she's got triplets in there, never mind twins.

'I was climbing the walls with boredom so I had a drive over to Kirsteen's.' She holds a bag aloft, and I see tufts of pink and blue fur poking from the top. 'She had a present for the babies.'

'I'm surprised you managed to fit behind the steering wheel.' I force a laugh. 'Should you even be driving?'

She shrugs. 'I told you at the first scan I'd end up being the size of a house, didn't I?' She nods towards the mantlepiece where she had the first ever scan picture of the twins blown up in size and framed. It is positioned in between the husband and wife Valentine's cards we exchanged a couple of weeks ago. 'It's all getting real now, isn't it?'

I nod. I can hardly believe her induction date is tomorrow. The last few months have passed in a blur of grief, sorting out Mum's house and repeatedly trying to speak to my daughters, without success.

I've somehow endured a couple of the *firsts* I've heard mentioned so often concerning the grieving process. I spent my first Christmas without Mum, which was a subdued day, made harder because my daughters wouldn't answer their phones. I left messages which they eventually returned on Boxing Day. Even then, their voices were cold and clipped and I felt like they couldn't wait to get off the phone. I think Carmen must have forced them to call me.

Then there was the first of Mum's birthdays since she's died – she would have been seventy-eight. That was slightly easier than Christmas, in that the rest of the world carried on turning as normal.

But it's Mother's Day next month, which I'm dreading. Cards and gifts are already filling the shops, no matter how hard I try not to notice the tormenting pink flowers and sparkly hearts. Why can't the manufacturers consider the effect on those who no longer have a mum to celebrate? Or have *never* had a mum to celebrate?

However, it will be *Ellen's* first Mother's Day with the twins. Therefore, I'll have to make it special for *her* – even if I am only going through the motions. As the weeks pass by, I'm feeling increasingly detached from *everything*, even myself. Somehow, I need to get it together.

'This time tomorrow, they'll be here.' She points towards her case, packed and ready on the window seat in the bay window. 'I can hardly believe it.'

Ellen's more talkative this morning than she's been for months. I've challenged her several times about the lack of closeness that's come to be in our relationship, but her answer's always been the same – that she's giving me space while I work through all my turmoil. Once upon a time, I'd have been grateful for this, but since Mum died, I've changed. I want to

talk to Ellen, especially since my girls have distanced themselves from me, but like she's told me often enough, growing
two babies is already taking up most of her energy and
emotional reserves and, perhaps I need a more specialist ear
than she can afford me.

I'm grateful to Kirsteen for stepping up and supporting her
far beyond the normal call of a friend's duty while Ellen's been
pregnant. At least she's had someone to lean on while she feels
that we can't lean on each other.

'I'll put the kettle on.' I get to my feet, needing a breather
from the subject of the twins. It's the only thing we seem to talk
about when we converse. The relationship which briefly
existed between us in the short time from meeting to our
engagement then the wedding, and then from marriage until
the babies came into being, is a relationship which no longer
seems to exist.

We're having a boy and a girl – Ruben and Imogen. I can
only hope that when I hold them in my arms, a wave of
paternal love sweeps over me, as so far, I've felt nothing. Absolutely nothing.

'A cuppa would be lovely.' Ellen leans back into the cushions and plucks her phone from her handbag. 'Meanwhile, I'm
making the most of my last day of peace.'

I head across the carpet to the lounge door, still amazed
that Ellen's speaking to me so much this morning. Perhaps it's
because I'll be her support in that delivery room tomorrow. She
talked of having Kirsteen in there instead of me but that's a step
too far. If I'm going to have any chance of bonding with these
babies, I need to watch them being born. As I've repeatedly told
her, I wasn't there for their conception, so I *need* to be there for
the birth.

Boiling water slops over the rim of the mug, spilling all over the counter as the kitchen door slams into the wall.

Ellen storms in, her face thunderous, her hand clenched around her phone.

'I don't believe this.' She tosses it onto the breakfast bar like it's radioactive. 'How the hell's he got hold of my number?'

'*Who?*' I snatch it up, my heart thudding.

> Twins, eh? I guess congratulations are in order. As well as double bubble. Another hundred grand will cover it. Tell Oliver my Crypto details are still the same.

My blood turns to ice.

'How did he find out?' Ellen's voice is shaking. 'How *could* he have found out?' She's as white as a sheet, her breathing is too fast as she presses one hand protectively over her bump.

'Sit down.' I quickly pull out a stool. 'Please. Just – try to breathe. We don't want anything happening today.'

Today. The day before she's due to be induced. As if this wasn't already a minefield. She sinks onto the stool but doesn't stop shaking.

'Why's he messaging *me?*' She jabs a finger toward her phone. 'And why *now*? The timing can't be a coincidence.'

I don't answer. I'm too busy trying to process what the hell this means. What Anthony wants and how far he's willing to go.

I finish making her tea — an automatic gesture and, something to do with my hands — even though I feel utterly inadequate.

'I've gone the whole pregnancy without hearing a word,' she mutters. 'Not a whisper. Now, the *day before* I'm due to give birth, he crawls out of the shadows like—' She cuts herself off, shaking her head. 'Someone's told him. They *must* have.'

'Like who?'

'I don't know. Someone from the village? We're not exactly keeping the twins a secret, are we?'

'He might have seen something online,' I suggest. 'A photo or a comment. Perhaps you've shared more than you realise.'

'He's not even *on* Facebook! We *looked* – remember?'

I nod. I remember all too well. I spent hours trying to dig him up online — names, usernames, email addresses, any damn clue. And I found nothing.

'He could be operating under a business name,' I say. 'Maybe that's how he's found you. Maybe that's how he's been watching us.'

She stares at me, her eyes wide and moist. 'I feel *violated*,' she whispers. 'Like he's been lurking in the background this whole time. Waiting and watching me. And now, he's back. *Again*.'

I slide the mug across to her, and she wraps her hands around it like it's the only thing keeping her grounded.

'I have to admit...' I swallow hard. 'I didn't think we'd hear from him after paying him off.'

But of course, *deep down*, I always knew he'd be back. It's not possible to make deals like we have and to walk away unscathed.

'What are we going to do?'

I have no answer because the babies are coming tomorrow and suddenly, it's like we're not just bringing *them* into the world.

They're part of *him*. He's never going to go away.

28

'You're not going to worry about this, love.' I rest my hand on Ellen's shoulder. 'I'll deal with it.'

'Are you going to pay him?' The mug trembles between her fingers as she lifts it to her lips.

'I don't know yet, but you're not to give this another thought, do you hear me?'

'I just want to know how he got my number.'

'He'll have found it online somewhere,' I reply. 'From when you were working or selling something from when you still had your flat. Just block him and put him out of your head. You need to focus on tomorrow.'

'I'll try.' Her voice is small. 'But what—'

'Please Ellen – just leave it with me. You'll send your blood pressure through the roof again if you dwell on *him*.'

'I'm scared he'll *never* leave us alone.' Her face is puffier and pinker than normal. 'He's back for more now – and then it could be even more. But if we don't pay him, he—'

'You go and get comfy on the sofa.' I point in the direction of the lounge. 'I'll be along in a few minutes. You don't look at all comfy sitting there.' I don't add that the stool looks like it could collapse beneath Ellen's weight. She outgrew most of her maternity clothes over a month ago and constantly complains that her stretch marks have stretch marks.

'Are you sorting it *now*?'

I nod. 'Right now.'

Sighing, she takes her tea and waddles back towards the door. 'Thanks. I'll block him, like you said.'

I wait until the door's closed behind her then, unplugging my phone from the USB port, I scroll back through my messages for the person I'd hoped I'd never be forced to have anything to do with again. It pains me to reopen this channel of communication between us but I haven't got much choice.

> What the hell do you think you're doing, contacting my wife?

> > I heard about the twins.

> How?

> > The grapevine's a big place.

> We had an agreement. ONE hundred grand. Which you've already had.

> > That was for ONE baby.

> It was for ONE pregnancy. You signed the contract – I have it here in black and white.

> > You know as well as I do that contract isn't worth the paper it's written on. Our agreement isn't even legal. Neither is you putting your name on their birth certificates – which I could put a stop to, as you know.

> So you're threatening me?

> I'm reasoning with you. Another hundred grand for the second baby, same terms as before, and you'll never hear from me again.

> That's what you said last time.

The man's got me over a bloody barrel. But he's right. The agreement I drew up was a load of crap – it just made *me* feel better and more in control. Like I was *doing* something instead of just acting as a bystander.

I either pay him off or I risk all kinds of aggro. If he's somehow discovered that Ellen's induction date is tomorrow, he could even turn up at the hospital. He probably wouldn't get in but it would be damn awkward and wouldn't do Ellen any favours. Beyond that, he could demand all kinds of paternal rights, including being named on the twins' birth certificates. I need to put an end to this – I have to get him off our backs with the only thing he wants. Besides, it's the only thing I can give to him.

> I'm going to transfer the money to you now.

> I take it you don't want me to sign another contract this time?

I can imagine the bastard smirking as he types this message. What the hell was I thinking of – striking up a deal like this in the first place?

In my final message, I attempt to appeal to his better side. He seemed decent and genuine enough on the night he first turned up as he talked about his sister. I even joked that it was great to enjoy some male company for a change. I've always prided myself on being a reasonable judge of character and hope I haven't got it as badly wrong as I'm beginning to fear.

Like you said, there's no point in signing anything. But once you receive this money, that will be the end of it as far as I'm concerned and I hope it will be the end of it for you as well. You'll have been way more than compensated for your trouble.

For your trouble? But I've already hit send by the time I've considered what I'm saying. So I just need to transfer the funds. Hopefully, then, I can focus on what matters – looking after my wife, and tomorrow, bringing the twins safely into the world without any further drama.

Anthony's response reassures me that all should be straightforward from now on.

Yep. That's the end of it for me – you won't hear from me again.

Good luck.

PART II

29

MARCH 17

'If I could just take the first baby's name?'

'Ruben Oliver Holmes.' I always wanted a son. Someone to continue my name and my father's name. I smile at Ellen but she doesn't smile back. I'll have to take the health visitor to one side for a word when she arrives later to check on Ellen and the twins. My wife seems to be sinking further and further into herself by the day, and I'm getting worried. It's getting to the point where she might need something prescribed to lift her out of the fog of depression she's immersed under.

'And you're the father to be named on his birth certificate?' The woman looks at me over the top of her glasses. She'll be able to see that I don't look anywhere near young enough to have become a new father. In fact, after the time I've had over the last few months, I probably look ten years older. Jasmine was right, I *am* old enough to be a grandad.

'That's correct.' I shuffle from foot to foot. This is fraud and deception, I know it is, but it's what we signed up to that stormy night back in June, so I'm forced to see it through. I tug my hat off. Heat is belching from the heater in the corner but I'm sweating for other reasons beside the temperature.

I glance into the pram at Ruben, obliviously sleeping beside his sister, and a swell of love emerges from my chest. These babies need me to protect them, to give them everything they deserve – just as I've always tried to do with my girls. The twins didn't ask to be born and hopefully, they'll *never* discover the circumstances surrounding their conception. As far as they're concerned, I'll be their daddy and that will be that – just as long as Anthony will be true to his word and leaves us alone. I continue giving the registrar our information before she moves me onto Imogen.

'And your second baby has the same birth date as the first?' Her pen is poised above a second form.

'Yes, they're twins.'

'Congratulations.' She smiles. 'However, that doesn't always mean they have the same birth date – they could have been born either side of midnight.'

'True.' I nod. I'll have to Google what the odds of that are. Ellen would normally have poked fun at me for *being such a nerd* but these days, she's a long way from being able to raise a smile, let alone poking fun at me.

'Can I take the baby's gender and legal name?'

'Female. And it's Imogen Phyllis Holmes.' My voice wobbles as I say my mother's name and I glance at Ellen to make sure she hasn't changed her mind. She needed more than a little talking around to this idea, especially since Mum was so hostile towards her after we broke the news of her pregnancy, taking, as she put it, the shine off *everything* in those early weeks. About a month after Mum died, we argued about it, and Ellen gave me both barrels over how I'd allowed my mother to treat her. It was the last thing I needed at the time and she ended up going to stay with Kirsteen for a few days.

Thankfully, she's come to accept how much giving Imogen her grandmother's name for her middle name means to me and she remains silent as I continue giving the rest of the details.

The registrar gives Ellen one or two curious glances as we proceed through the formalities as if she's wondering what could be wrong, however, she doesn't comment. In her line of work, she must be accustomed to seeing new mothers like my wife. With unbrushed hair, perfunctory clothes and a face like a wet weekend in November. New mums in the throes of the baby blues.

Carmen suffered with it the first time around so I know all the signs – however, she was beyond it within a few days. It's been three weeks since the twins were born so if Ellen doesn't pick up soon, she might need some extra support. I should have probably left her at home today, after all, we're married so I could have registered the babies without her. But as always, she said she was frightened to be left alone. She's been this way since Mum's death but she was improving – until the day before she was induced when Anthony messaged her about wanting more money. If only he could have messaged me instead of her – she should never have known anything.

'It will take me ten minutes to produce your certificates,' the registrar announces as she gestures across the mosaic tiles. 'Would you like to have a seat?'

Ellen slumps to the bench in the waiting area and I wheel our double pram after her. It's surprisingly easy to move around, with its three fan-dangled wheels. It's certainly a step up from the prams Carmen and I used back in our days of early parenthood.

'Do you want to grab some lunch after she's done?' I nudge Ellen as I sit beside her, the sleeves of my heavy coat brushing against hers. 'We should make the most of them sleeping.' I yawn. Neither of us are getting much sleep at night with these nocturnal little creatures. They sleep hard all day but at night, they seem to take great delight in taking turns to wake us.

'The health visitor's supposed to be coming.' Ellen's voice is flat. 'Not that I want her to.'

'Not until later.'

'She'll probably say I'm doing a rubbish job anyway.' She picks at the stitching on her glove.

'Of course she won't. You're doing amazingly. Right,' – I attempt to load an enthusiasm into my voice that I'm not feeling. 'I'm not taking no for an answer – you've spent far too much time in that house.' The truth is I'm also going stir-crazy in there. Now the new baby visitors have more or less died off – mainly my work colleagues and some people I know in the village, I'm feeling increasingly isolated being stuck at home with two newborns and a wife who doesn't want to do anything other than sleep or stare into space.

'I'd rather just go home, Oliver.' Ellen checks into the pram as she's done around a dozen times since we arrived here. 'While we're out, it feels like Anthony could be watching us. The babies are safer from him at the house.'

I haven't got the energy to keep trying to persuade her to go for lunch somewhere that's not the house that's become our prison. Besides, even if I did, her heart's not in anything. So what's the point?

30

As I PURSUE Ellen from the registry office back to the car park, she's far more jumpy than usual, plus she's walking at around five hundred million miles an hour. It's one of our first outings since she was discharged from the hospital when Ruben and Imogen were three days old, and I hadn't realised until witnessing her in public, just how badly Ellen's anxiety has been eating away at her.

'We've paid him off, love.' I'm struggling to keep up with her pace. 'And we haven't heard a thing from him since.'

She strides in front of me, looking this way and that as she pushes the pram along as quickly as she can walk with people passing at either side of us. Most are happy to make way for the pram. Others tut at Ellen's supposed rudeness. I wonder if she's also acting this way because the birth was so long and hard. She was on the verge of a C-section when they finally managed a forceps delivery. By then, the room was crammed with a variety of midwives and doctors, all on alert in case she needed to be taken down to theatre.

'That means nothing.' She spins around. 'We didn't hear a thing from him for months while I was pregnant, did we?'

'It's my name on their birth certificates, isn't it?' I press the remote at the car as we reach it. 'So you just need to relax – if you're not careful, you're going to make yourself ill.'

'It's a bit late for that, besides, it isn't as if I can pour my heart out to anyone else about all this, can I?' She throws her hands in the air. 'I've never felt so alone in all my life. – you've forbidden me to even tell Kirsteen.'

'You can always talk to me.'

'No I can't,' she snaps. 'All you care about is your dead mother and your selfish daughters.'

'That's hurtful and unfair.' I unclip Ruben's car seat from the frame of the pram and slide him onto the back seat. 'I've been trying my best to be a support for you, but as for the girls – that's all out of my hands. They'll come around in time.'

'They haven't been anywhere near us for months, have they?' I search her face and all I see is venom spewing from it. 'They don't give a shit about anyone but themselves.'

I hate to see my wife tie herself in knots like this, but there seems to be little I can do to coax her out of her current mood. 'Get in the car, love.' I walk around to the other side and hold the door open. 'Let's get you home and I'll run you a bubble bath.'

'It's going to take more than a bubble bath,' she shrieks. 'Have you any idea what it's like?'

'Ellen. Please. People are staring.' I unclip Imogen's seat and slide her into the other side of the back seat. 'Just get in the car.'

'Every minute of every hour of every day,' she continues. 'It's as if he's going to suddenly turn up and snatch them.'

'You're blowing this all out of proportion.'

'Is she OK?' An elderly woman with kind eyes approaches us. 'Do you need any help?'

'See, I told you I'm useless,' Ellen sobs. 'Even *she* thinks so.'

'Of course I don't.' The woman reaches for her arm but Ellen tugs it away. 'It looks to me that you've got a touch of the baby blues.' Then she turns to me, and says, 'Are the two of you getting any support?'

'Look, I know you mean well but it's all in hand.' Tears stab at the back of my eyes which always happens when someone acts kindly towards me. Ever since Mum died, I've become a gibbering wreck. Nor can I get this bloody pram to collapse no matter how many buttons I push or levers I pull. I stand staring at it as if that's going to do any good.

'Here, let me help you. My daughter's got one just like it for her two. They're not twins like yours,' – she peers into the back seat, – 'but they're close enough in age for her to have her hands full.' I stand back, beaten, and allow her to intervene. Perhaps Mum's sent her my way. I've heard these stories before but have automatically dismissed them. With an upwards flick of the woman's foot against the central mechanism and a downwards press of the side lever, the pram frame lies collapsed at my feet.

'Thank you.' I hold out my hand to her as Ellen slams the passenger door. 'And I'm sorry for—'

'Don't you dare apologise.' The woman even has a look of Mum. It's the bobbed hair and her calm manner. 'Just insist she sees a professional. Take it from someone who's been there.'

'I will.' I stare down at the tarmac. 'She *is* getting worse.'

'I was convinced something was going to happen to my daughter when she was tiny,' the woman continues. 'I watched over her day and night, obsessed with her chest going up and down. They say *sleep when they sleep* but I couldn't. I was a bundle of nerves and from what I heard as I was locking my car up just then, your wife sounds to be suffering in much the same way.'

31

THEIR AGE two and age ten Christmas morning faces smile from the album. One daughter sits on the bike I built up on Christmas Eve, while the other is more interested in the boxes and wrapping paper. I had to battle with Carmen for these photos of my daughters as she wanted to keep all the photos of our girls in one place. But she yielded in the end and split her collection.

These were the days when I was the girls' hero, when I could do no wrong in their eyes. Now, they won't even pick up the phone to me. But while Ellen's upstairs taking a nap, I'll try them again.

This is the Vodafone messaging service... That's one of them not answering.

The other number rings twice then cuts off. *Hey, this is Jasmine, leave a message.* The sound of my daughter's voice would usually fill me with joy, but today, it makes my soul droop even more than the dreadful journey back from the Registry Office with Ellen. After she'd finished shouting at me for discussing her business with a stranger, she slumped into silence while the babies cried in the back, probably startled after being woken by their mother's angry voice.

Jasmine must have seen that it's me calling and has hit the reject button. That's what I feel like, an absolute reject. Perhaps the two of them are together and saying to each other, *look who it is – I'm not speaking to him.* I wonder if they're with Carmen – surely she'd be trying to reason with them and advise them not to cast me from their lives. Or maybe she agrees with their stance. It's not as though I can even pick up the phone and discuss it with her as I would have done in my pre-Ellen days. Before everything changed.

Why can't my daughters understand that just because Ruben and Imogen have come along, it doesn't make me love them any less? It makes me love them more if anything, as memories of giving *them* their bottles and watching over them when they were babies come flooding back. Not that I can ever reminisce to Ellen about my first-time-around experiences. She's already close enough to the edge.

Putting the album to the side, I rise from my armchair and cross the rug to where the twins are sleeping side by side in their pram. Imogen's mouth is moving as if she's suckling in her sleep and Ruben's smiling as if he's dreaming the happiest of dreams. It's too early to say who the babies look like – but I dearly hope it will be Ellen they resemble.

At least I've had no trouble bonding with the two of them like I feared, which is fortunate seeing as Ellen's struggling so much. It's also a good thing that I'm the director of my business and there's no limit to the time off I can take.

The doorbell echoes through the hallway, sounding louder than usual. I hold my breath for a moment, hoping the babies won't stir. They don't. The health visitor advised us not to keep the house quiet during the day as it will help the twins to differentiate between normal waking and sleeping hours and get them into a routine faster. But they're not due a feed for at least another hour and I, for one, am enjoying the peace.

I curse as the doorbell sounds again. I also hope it hasn't woken Ellen. She badly needs to sleep. It better not be more baby visitors turning up without checking with us first. I hoist myself from my chair, wishing I could see who it is before I answer. As an architect, I should have factored in being able to see the front porch from the lounge window when I designed the place.

Perhaps I'll look into installing one of the camera doorbells Ellen mentioned – for her peace of mind if nothing else. Especially after what happened to my poor mother last year. After all, the bastards were never caught.

The shape of a man is visible through the frosted glass. It must be a delivery driver – one who evidently can't read the note on the letterbox saying, *go to the side door.* I fumble in the drawer for the key and lunge towards the lock before whoever it is gets any ideas about ringing the doorbell for a third time.

I peer through the spy hole as I twist the key in the lock, unable to work out who the man with his back to me and his hands thrust into jeans pockets is. He doesn't appear to be holding a parcel, nor does he look like he's selling anything. As I pull the door open, he swings around. Suddenly I wish more than anything that I'd bothered to look into a doorbell camera instead of pushing it down my list of priorities.

'What the hell are *you* doing here?'

Anthony grins as he steps closer to the door. 'Well, that's not a very nice greeting to someone who's given you such a precious gift.' In his jeans and leather jacket, he looks to have bulked out even more since the last time I saw him and somehow seems more confident – more self-assured. It must be the money which has made such a difference.

'You're not welcome, Anthony. Our business with one another is over.'

'I've heard the babies have been born.' He points past me as if he expects to be invited over the threshold.

'So what if they have?' I hiss as I glance back into the hallway to make sure Ellen hasn't heard anything and got back out of bed. 'They have *nothing* to do with you – *nothing*.' This is all I need.

'Oh, come on, Oliver. Don't be like this with me.' He rolls his eyes. 'You made me so welcome the first time I turned up on your doorstep.'

'We had an agreement.' I'm relieved I haven't got any neighbours to witness the altercation I'm having with this awful man. I really can't believe he's back.

'Which, as we've already ascertained, isn't *really* an agreement. Not in the eyes of the law.'

'What do you want, Anthony?'

32

LIKE I NEED to ask Anthony what he wants. There will only be one reason he's sniffing around.

'You can't say I haven't given you a couple of weeks for things to settle down since the birth,' he begins.

'I said, *what do you want?*'

He leans against the side of the porch and looks at me with his slanted blue eyes. Eyes which I'm already certain Ruben and Imogen have inherited. 'Look, I'm going to level with you – the money you've paid so far has gone nowhere. I was in so much debt and difficulty that I should have asked for far more than that initial hundred grand.'

'You've had *two hundred grand*. And if I knew then what I know now, I—'

'Surely you can't put a price on the life of your son and daughter?' He screws up his mouth and cocks his head to the side as he waits for my response. Why couldn't I have seen who I was dealing with last year? And now he's back – just as I should have foreseen.

'How do you know we had a boy and a girl?'

He's getting his information from *somewhere*. I haven't

posted any pictures of the babies on social media so as not to inflame the situation any further with the girls, and I'm pretty sure Ellen hasn't either. She's been way too preoccupied and depressed since they were born.

'Let's just say we have a mutual friend—'

'Who?' Though it could be anyone. My business employs over fifty people and we know plenty of people in the village.

'That doesn't matter.' His leather jacket, no doubt paid for with my money, creaks as he waves his arm. 'But what does matter is that we keep our little arrangement as neatly tied up as it has been up to present – I'm sure you wouldn't want the truth to get out – to risk damaging your impeccable reputation.'

I was right – he's here to extort more money. 'Do your worst, Anthony. You're not getting another penny.'

'I've got rights.' He folds his arms. 'Just in case you need reminding – paternal rights.'

'You've *never* had any paternal rights.'

'All I've got to do is see a solicitor and demand a blood test to prove I'm their father. There isn't a judge in the land who won't grant me regular access – or even partial custody.' I survey him from the spike of his hair to his cheap trainers. *Partial custody.* The prospect doesn't bear contemplating. No wonder Ellen's been so paranoid about this scenario and all I've done is dismiss her angst.

'Oliver?' Her muffled voice drifts from upstairs. 'Who are you talking to?'

'No one. I'll just be a minute.' Shit – she's awake. I step out onto the doormat. 'You've got *no* right turning up at our home,' I hiss. 'This was never part of the deal.'

'Maybe I'd like to meet the two of them now I'm here.'

'No chance.'

'I only want to see if they take after me.' He tries to look beyond my shoulder as if they're going to suddenly appear behind me in the hallway. 'After all, blood's thicker than water. Let's just hope you don't have to find this out the hard way.'

I pull the door behind me. 'I'd like you off my property.'

'Another three hundred grand and I'll be out of your hair.'

'What?' I stare at him, desperation flooding my veins. He's never going to leave us alone. So long as I keep paying him, he's always going to keep coming back. This will never end.

'So what do you say, Oliver? Do we have a deal?' He stretches out his hand just like he did that night across my kitchen counter.

'Fuck off, is what I say.' Fury courses through me. If I had something in my hand, I'd probably clout him with it.

'Now that isn't the language of a middle-class businessman.' He lets his hand drop back to his side.

'It's the language of someone who's absolutely at the end of his tether. If you don't leave us alone—' Mad ideas are marching through my mind. If I ask around, maybe I can find out exactly where Anthony lives and spends the majority of his time. There's a lot I could do with far less than three hundred grand – it probably wouldn't cost that much to get rid of him *permanently* – to ensure he *can't* return. Oh my God, as if I'm even thinking along these lines. That's what this man's done to me – to *us.*

'You'll *what?*' His nonchalant expression is sending me into a tailspin. He believes he holds all the cards here and maybe, he does.

I need to get a grip and get rid of him. Any minute now, Ellen will head down the stairs and if she sees *him* standing here, she'll go to pieces, that's if she hasn't already heard his voice and chosen to cower upstairs until I get rid of him. Anthony being at our front door means all her fears have rolled into one.

'My wife's under enough stress without you doing this to her.' I step closer to him, almost forgetting how much he towers over me. I've never initiated violence in my life and if I were to start now, he'd, no doubt, wipe the floor with me. I might run a little and play golf but judging by the muscular legs beneath those jeans and the thick neck poking from his leather collar, I'd barely stand a chance.

'I'm their father.' The tranquillity in Anthony's voice angers me even more. It's as if he *believes* this.

'I'm named on their birth certificates,' I snap. 'It's *me* that takes care of them, and *me* who gets up with them in the night.' I jab my finger at him. 'We *paid* you for this. And we've already paid you well over the odds.'

'Falsifying birth certificates can be imprisonable.' Anthony uncrosses his arms as if readying himself to fight me off if it becomes necessary. Evidently, he's not intimidated by me in the slightest. 'Added to you already paying me to impregnate your wife, you could be in trouble.'

'Rubbish,' I reply. 'The police wouldn't even be interested. They've got far more important things to deal with.'

'Look it up,' he says. 'And you'll find I'm right.'

I already know he is. I know from my research that *everything* we've done to bring these babies into being *could* be thrown out by the police and the courts, but equally, it could also be treated as a criminal matter. And even if it wasn't, there's still the damage to my reputation and my already fragile relationship with my daughters to consider.

'You'd be in as much trouble as me and Ellen,' I retort. 'Plus, I could throw blackmail into the mix.'

'You'd have to prove it first.'

He's right but I'm not going to admit it.

'I'll tell them how you took advantage of me,' he continues. 'That you coerced me with your fancy promises of big money. I could even tell them how you locked me in the house until I agreed to give you what you wanted. Well, to give Ellen what *she* wanted, more to the point.'

My hands ball into fists. 'I want you to leave – *now.*'

'I understand that you must be grumpy with all the sleepless nights and the shitty—.'

'I mean it, Anthony. There's no more money. Not a penny.'

'So I'll give you the rest of the day to think about it. After that—'

'I said, I want you off my property.'

'Next time, Oliver, I won't be quite so polite.' He steps back. 'In fact, I won't even ring the doorbell. Don't say you haven't been warned. You've got until the end of today.'

33

'WE MUST LOCK the doors and windows – night and day.' My voice bounces around the walls as I pace up and down the hallway, hardly daring to read the reaction on my wife's face to what I've just told her.

'I heard most of it.' Ellen drops her head into her hands as she sits on the bottom step. 'When I realised who it was, I crept down here to listen.'

'We're going to have to report him to the police.' I pull back the curtain at the hallway window to ensure he's gone. I didn't notice a vehicle on the drive when I was at the door but he's probably prevented me from seeing it by parking at the bottom of our lane. 'For continuing to blackmail us. We can't just keep paying.'

'But we don't know where he lives, the name of his business, or *anything*.' She raises her head. Her hair is more on end than I've ever seen it. 'Have you carried on paying him in Crypto?'

'Yep – which, as I told you, is untraceable. But maybe the police could do something with the phone number I've got on WhatsApp.'

'You'll probably come to a dead end there too – I bet he's using a Pay-As-You-Go SIM.'

'He seems to know how to fly under the radar.' I stare at the door, still unable to believe or understand the situation we've found ourselves trapped in. 'Plus he was right in saying that *we'd* be in trouble too.'

'I heard what he said about the birth certificates.' Ellen wraps her arms around her crumpled clothes as if hugging herself. The weight's dropping from her since giving birth and she looks far more gaunt in the face than Carmen ever did. 'And he's right – we both knew it was fraud.'

'I'm more bothered about his threat to gain rights over the twins. If he got a court order for a DNA—'

Ellen's face drops before I've even finished my sentence and I instantly know I've said too much.

'He could try to fight me for access?' She stares at the tiles beneath her bare feet. 'What if he goes for custody?'

'You're their legal mother.' I hitch my jeans up and sit beside her on the step. 'Nothing can change that.' Right on cue, one of them stirs from the lounge.

'Yeah, but I'm not a very good mother.' She freezes as I rest my hand on her arm. There's been very little physical affection between us since her positive pregnancy test last year. What there has been between us has been perfunctory, a peck on the lips here, the briefest of hugs there. It's partly my fault we've become strangers. As I always do in the face of turmoil, before the twins' arrival, I buried myself in my work as a distraction.

'We're both finding our way through all this.' I point at the lounge door. 'Babies don't come with an instruction book. And with everything else, we've had going on, and losing Mum, it's little wonder we're struggling.'

Our marriage has had more adversity swirling within and around it over the last year than many couples endure in a life-time. Firstly, came the stress of the 'arrangement' with

Anthony, then weathering the hostility of Carmen and my girls amidst news of Ellen's pregnancy. Then, on the same day we were allowing the shock news of twins to sink in, we had the trauma of Mum's senseless murder. So it will be nothing short of a miracle if we manage to get ourselves back on track after coping with all this. If we get beyond it all, we can get through anything.

'I'm just so tired,' – she goes on, – 'I can't remember the last time I laughed, or even smiled. I look at people on the TV or in the street and I think, *what on earth could there be to smile about?*' Her voice is wobbling and I can tell she's trying to fight her tears.

'Come here, love.' I try to pull her towards me but she freezes even harder as if she can no longer stand to be in my vicinity. 'Just let it out. You've got a touch of postnatal depression, like that woman said.'

'It was none of her business.' Ellen jumps to her feet, no doubt, using what I've just said as an excuse to create some distance. 'It isn't *anybody's* business. I'm sick of people turning up here, judging me, then—'

'Nobody's *judging*. It's difficult enough with *one* newborn baby, let alone two.' Imogen's cries – at least, I'm almost certain it's Imogen, are getting louder. I'll have to go into her in a moment but getting through to my wife feels like the priority. 'It's little wonder you're finding things tough - plus you've been trying to feed them yourself.'

'*Trying* is the operative word – they're going to have to go on formula milk. Look, I can't face the health visitor when she gets here. I can't stand the way she'll look at me when I tell her I'm on the verge of giving up.' Tears are spilling from Ellen's eyes as she rests against the sideboard. 'I don't want *anyone* here today.'

'The visitors have all died down.' I get up from the step and lean against the bannister. 'Everyone's seen the twins.' *Everyone apart from my daughters*, I don't add. If one or both of them were to turn up here now, it would probably send Ellen off the deep end. 'Look, I'll deal with the health visitor when she arrives. You go back upstairs when you've fed the twins and I'll tell her you're sleeping.'

Fat tears roll down Ellen's cheeks. 'I didn't – want all this, you know. I – didn't know – what I was doing – it's all gone – so wrong and I—' She gasps the words out between her sobs. 'He's going to take them away – I just know it.'

'He isn't.' It's becoming a struggle to keep my voice calm as I recall what he said about getting into the house without ringing the bell in the future. I must make sure the patio doors into the kitchen are always locked, *and* the doors out of the conservatory beyond the dining room. 'He wouldn't have a clue where to start with two newborn babies. Who would?' I force a laugh even though there's little to laugh about really.

'How do you know? His sister's had a baby, hasn't she?' Ellen pushes her hair back, hair that's clinging to the sides of her face like seaweed. I'm not even sure when she last washed it.

'Look, love, you've got to calm down.' I won't repeat what the health visitor said about stress and depression being the factors that will be affecting Ellen's milk supply. 'Shall we go through and see to the twins – together?'

'He said he'd be back – I heard him.' Her voice is a wail.

Amidst his mother's hysteria and his sister's crying, Ruben's also started to mewl.

'We need to feed the babies.' I glance towards the door.

'We need to pay Anthony what he's demanding.' Ellen's voice is small. 'It's the only way I'm going to feel safe. It's the only way I can keep the two of *them* safe.'

'He. Won't. Do. Anything.' I speak to her as I'd speak to a child, slowly and firmly, as I thrust my hands deeper into my pockets. How the hell am I going to feed these babies if Ellen doesn't pull herself together? There's no expressed milk left in the fridge so I'll have to drive down to the village and get them started on some formula. Ellen might be saying that's what she wants but I reckon it will make her feel even worse. 'Look you overheard our conversation. He went away as easily as he arrived.'

'Please, Oliver. We can't risk him demanding blood tests.' She presses her hands together as if she's begging. 'Or threatening to force his way in here to get to the twins. We need to pay him off again – it's not as if we haven't got the money.'

'That's not the point at all – if we were to pay, he'll only come back.' I let out a long breath. 'And then back again. No matter how much money we pay him, he'll keep coming back.'

'Not if we can get away.' Her voice rises. 'Well away from here, I mean. We could move to–'

'But this house—' I begin. 'You can't ask me to leave. I built it from scratch.'

'It's just bricks and mortar.' She flails her arms from left to right. 'We could rent somewhere until you've built another – somewhere miles away where Anthony won't think of looking.'

He'll *always* find us if he's so inclined. I want to voice this but I don't. I'll let her turn this runaway fantasy around in her mind until she sees it for what it is. They say we're only ever at six degrees of separation from anyone else in the world, so no matter where we go, I've little doubt he'll be able to find us.

'If we pay him now, that should buy us a few months to rent somewhere until this house is sold.' The idea of moving has buoyed Ellen and she appears brighter at the prospect. She's even stopped crying. 'This place is full of ghosts – and I, for one, don't want to live among them.'

She's probably referring to Mum. But I'm the opposite of Ellen – I'm comforted by the *ghosts* she's referring to. Mum having lived over at the cottage gives me something to grasp onto. Sometimes, I can almost feel her presence, and it's the same with the girls – they've spent so much time in this house, it's as if their essence has etched itself into its walls. This familiarity grounds me at a time when it feels like *anything* could happen. I used to be so in control of my life and now it feels like I'm anything *but.*

'You told me last year you'd do whatever it took to make me happy.' Ellen dabs her eyes on the sleeve of her shapeless cardigan.

'And I will. I always will. It's just—'

'Then pay Anthony off and put this place on the market.' She stretches the sleeves over her wrists. 'If you don't, I'm taking the babies and we'll stay with Kirsteen. At least we'll be safer at her house.'

34

APRIL 18

NORMALLY, I love this time of year. Spring – the time of new beginnings. I twist the blind in the ensuite to let the day in.

With two-month-old twin babies and a For Sale sign nailed into the wall at the end of the drive, this year is certainly offering plenty of new beginnings. But the control I used to have over my own life has slipped away and, I can't even recall the faces of my daughters without logging into Facebook and looking them up. I miss them so much, it's become a physical ache. But the last person I can discuss how miserable it's making me is with my wife. I don't know what I'm going to do about it but I've got to do *something*.

I reach the bottom of the stairs and sweep the post from the mat. I can't look at the front door now without thinking about Anthony.

He's gone back to ground, thank God. He's now had a straight half a million in total from us, which I'm still trying to work out how I'm going to justify to my accountant. But if and when the blackmailing slimeball comes back for more, we'll be long gone. I've not only put my house up for sale but also my business. Ellen and I have agreed not to post a single thing on social media and we've both locked our accounts down so they're as impenetrable as a high-security prison.

'I need to nip to the office,' I tell my wife. She's slumped in front of morning TV. It feels good to have shaved, showered and to be wearing a shirt and a proper pair of trousers. I've just caught sight of myself in the hallway mirror and barely recognised who I was seeing. I can't wait to be among the camaraderie of my colleagues and to feel normal for a change, albeit briefly.

'Why?' My wife doesn't even look at me. She never does.

'I'm meeting a prospective buyer.' Ellen's wearing *my* joggers and a shapeless baby-sick-stained hoodie, even though it's fairly warm today. Therefore, I'm not going to suggest she and the twins accompany me to the office with a view to going somewhere else afterwards. People would think I wasn't taking care of her.

All I can do is keep on coaxing. She still refuses to take tablets and even though it's been over a month since Anthony reared his ugly head, Ellen remains obsessed with the possibility that he'll come back *before* we move into the rented house we've found on the Yorkshire coast.

'Is everywhere locked?' She doesn't take her eyes away from the TV and makes no effort to move. She's dead behind the eyes and it's painful to witness.

'I think so but I'll double-check before I leave.'

'Do I need to do anything with the twins?'

'I've only just fed and changed them both.' I've covered all bases which clears my conscience at having to leave them all for two or three hours.

I've barely been back into the office since they were born – I haven't been able to create the space. My world has shrunk beyond all recognition and there are times when I understand why Ellen doesn't bother getting showered or properly dressed all day. Even I wonder what the point is on occasion. The two of us barely speak to one another – not unless it's about the twins' needs or something else that's a necessity. There's little chatting or reminiscing.

'How about we book you a doctor's appointment when I get back from the office?'

'What for?'

'You know *what for*. You can't go on like this. None of us can.'

'I'm perfectly fine. As soon as I get away from this house and I no longer feel like Anthony's sitting duck, everything will get back to normal.'

'We could at least sit in the garden when I get home.' I gesture towards the back of the house. 'It's lovely out there today. Besides, the twins could do with some fresh air.'

'I'll see.' She sniffs.

I return to my Range Rover, not looking forward to having to go back home. Resting my head on the steering wheel, I contemplate my options.

Of which there really aren't many from which to choose.

I've felt almost like *me* again this morning. My team were over the moon to see me, clapping me on the back and telling me they'll never get a boss they respect as much. My PA asked me to reconsider what I'm doing, and my second-in-command looked almost tearful. It was the moment when I shook hands with our buyer, sealing the first stage of the deal. There was a sense in the air of the end of a long and happy era. They all think I'm on the verge of an exciting new one and I'd give *anything* for that to be the case. But little do they all know...

If anyone knew what I'm returning home to and the existence which is now my reality, they'd think I was nuts. I stare across at the clean, white building, which stands proud against the clear blue sky. *Homes from Holmes Architects.* I'll have to call my next business something else. Something which doesn't include my name. I'm still not convinced Anthony won't be able to find us once we've moved so I need to make things as difficult as possible for him.

My bank account's going to be extremely healthy once the sale of the business hits it, not to mention the sale of the house, so I'll be able to rebuild and set up whatever and wherever I want. Mum always said to me, that money doesn't fix things and it certainly doesn't buy happiness. Yet I still believe it can. Without the money I've amassed, I wouldn't have the power to get us out of here and to build a new home and life somewhere new.

My phone vibrates from my glovebox. I've only been in the office for a couple of hours and in that time, I've had eighteen missed calls.

All from Ellen. But also one from my eldest daughter.

35

I'M CALLING BELLA FIRST. It's the first time she's rung me for months.

'Hey, it's Dad.'

'Yeah – your name came up on my phone.' Her voice is sulky and she sounds more like her sixteen-year-old sister than the now twenty-four-year-old she's grown into.

'To what do I owe this pleasure?'

'Do I need a reason to call?'

'Of course not. It's just—'

'It's just that you never bother with us anymore. Not now you've got your *new* family.'

'Oh come on, Bella, that isn't fair.' I wave at my receptionist as she strides from the main entrance. 'I've lost count of how many times I've tried calling and texting. You *never* answer and you never reply.'

'What's there to say? We haven't seen you since last year.'

'I'm always here for you, sweetheart. Both of you. Life's just become a bit mad, that's all. But I mean what I say – you could pick up the phone or come to the house *anytime*.'

'*She* doesn't want us there though, does she?'

'That's not true – you're always welcome. It's still your second home.' Now isn't the time to tell her that a move is on the cards. Bloody hell, she'd have a meltdown if she knew I was seriously considering taking off. But I can't lie, the sound of Bella's voice is already causing me to have a rethink. I don't like the idea of running away – I never have.

'Plus, I can't bear the place without Grandma around.' Bella's voice dips. 'I miss her so much.'

'Me too.' I catch sight of myself in the mirror as I talk. My eyes are lined and heavy with lack of sleep, not to mention misery and worry.

'Can we meet up over the weekend?' Her tone brightens slightly. Just *us* though. Me, you and Jasmine?'

'Of course we can – I'd love to.' But a wisp of worry blows into my thoughts. How will Ellen react?

'I'll call you tomorrow.'

'Do you promise?' I inject a mock-sternness into my voice.

'I need to get to bed,' she says. 'I'm on nights at the moment. But after I've slept, I can meet anytime over the weekend.'

'I'm so proud of you, Bella, and I don't tell you often enough.'

'Yeah, whatever.' Suddenly she sounds more like herself.

'And I can't wait to see you both.'

After the turmoil of late, finally having my eldest daughter reach out to me is exactly what I needed. I allow myself a few moments of basking in the warmth of knowing I'm going to see them over the next couple of days, before hitting the callback button next to Ellen's name.

She answers almost immediately. 'Why the hell haven't you been answering?'

'What's the matter? Has something happened with the twins?'

'I've tried calling you over and over.'

'I'm sorry, my phone was on silent while I was in my meeting. What is it?' She still hasn't confirmed if the twins are alright.

'He's been here,' she shrieks. 'Inside the house.'

'Who has?'

'Who do you think?' She sounds hysterical. 'You said you were checking all the doors and windows.'

'I did.' I scratch my head. 'He can't have got inside – there's no way.'

'I was sleeping on the sofa and I woke to find him standing over the twins' sleeping basket.'

'Oh my God.' I press the button to start the engine and hit the loudspeaker button on the dashboard. 'Have you called the police?'

'I didn't know what to do.' Her voice is full of tears and it's clear she's worked herself up into a right state while I haven't been answering. 'I wanted to talk to you before I did *anything*.'

'I'm really sorry.' I check over my shoulder and reverse out of the car park. 'I'm on my way back.'

'He wants more money from us, Oliver,' she cries. It's the first time she's used my name for ages, or referred to the two of us as *us*. Sometimes she looks at me as if she's forgotten who I am or what she's doing with me. 'He says he's going for joint custody if we don't pay up, and he reckons he's got proof of me being an unstable mother.'

'He's talking absolute crap.' I pull up at the traffic lights, silently cursing. I just need to get home. The *one* time I decide to leave them alone in the house, *this* happens. It wouldn't surprise me if he's been hanging around, waiting for me to leave. 'Surely you don't need *me* to convince you of that.'

'But, he's right – I *have* been unstable. I don't know how he's found anything out, but he *must* have *something* on me.'

'He's clutching at straws, Ellen.' I set off again, looking at vans as I drive on. Maybe I'll pass the weasel as I'm heading home and run him off the road. 'He's got *nothing* on you – how could he have?'

'The bottom line is we weren't quick enough to move out after the last payment to him, were we?'

'These things take time.' This tone again, the one I used to reserve for Bella and Jasmine when trying to reason with them. All this might be going on but nothing's going to get in the way of my seeing them this weekend.

'We suspected he'd be back for more, didn't we? We should have been out of that house long before now but *you* wouldn't listen.' Her voice is filled with accusation.

'How much does he want this time?' I glance in my rearview mirror, half expecting him to be behind me. The man's a nightmare but Ellen's right. I always knew he'd be back for more, however, I didn't dream it would be so quickly. 'Not that I'm intending to give in and pay.'

'Another five hundred.'

'Pounds?' Maybe I could do that – especially if it will buy us more time.

'Thousand.' Ellen's voice is filled with panic. 'And we're going to have to pay him – when I tell you everything else he's said, you'll see that we've got no choice.'

'No chance.' I let a long breath out as a police car screeches past me, making me jump. 'Listen, I'm getting off this phone and I'll be back in twenty minutes. Get yourself in the shower, it'll help you to calm down, and we'll talk shortly.'

As if I'm telling my wife when to shower. But this is what things have come to.

36

EVERYTHING'S LOCKED when I arrive back at the house. Every door, every window. I painstakingly checked it all before I left, so the only way he could have got in is if Ellen let him in – or if he somehow stole a key when he was here that night last year. Why the hell didn't I pre-empt this and change the locks? What an idiot.

'Have you locked or unlocked anything since I left?' I tug at the hallway window, just making sure.

'I haven't touched a *thing*,' she rubs at her hair with a towel, thankfully having taken my advice. I can't recall the last time she showered but I think it's been several days. 'I've only just moved myself from the sofa.'

'I'm going to have to get all the locks changed.' I tug out my phone. 'I'm not taking any chances.' I glance at the clock that used to sit in my mother's hallway and makes me sad every time it chimes. 'Hopefully, I can get someone out today.'

'Just hang fire a minute – you're missing the point.' Wrapping her arms around herself, Ellen sits at the foot of the stairs. 'You need to listen.'

'The only thing we *need* right now is to ensure he doesn't get into this house.' I pull the sideboard drawer open where the keys are kept but am none-the-wiser as I sweep my eyes over what's in there. I don't know which key is for what or how many we should have of each. The girls have spares and Mum had spares. 'If everything was locked and you're saying you didn't let him in, the only other explanation is that he took a key when he was here last year.'

'Whether he has or not doesn't alter what he's been threatening me with.' She hooks her towel around the back of her neck.

'There's *nothing* he can do to prove you're an unfit mother – you've got to get that out of your head.'

'He wants joint custody.' She looks straight at me as if trying to gauge my reaction.

I let out a strangled laugh. 'Don't be daft. He hasn't got a leg to stand on.'

'You can't say that.' She rubs at the side of her head, no doubt fending off another migraine. They seemed to ease off when she was pregnant but are now back with a vengeance. 'And you definitely won't be able to say that when I tell you what he said next.'

'What?' I close my eyes as I lean onto the sideboard. It's only just gone lunchtime and already, I want to crawl back into bed. I haven't got the energy to deal with this level of drama anymore. I yearn for the days Ellen used to refer to as me living in my 'man cave.' She claimed to have rolled the boulder away from the entrance to it and has often said she'll never let me have it back. I used to be happy with this but these days I'm not so sure. The days of baggy boxers and pizza deliveries in front of Netflix are increasingly enticing.

'He's taken cheek swabs from the babies.' She screws her eyes together as though she's frightened of seeing how I'm going to react.

'What? *How?*'

'I was dead to the world on the sofa. It was only when Imogen made a noise that I woke up as he was swabbing her cheek.'

'And you didn't try to stop him?' I stand up straight.

'He'd already done it.' She rises from the step. 'There was nothing I could do. He's got us bang to rights, Oliver. The only thing we can do is pay him off.'

'No chance.' I stride into the lounge. I'm not having this conversation.

'But it won't make so much as a dent in your finances.' She follows me in. 'But it will get him well away from us for a few weeks, or even months – it'll give us the chance to move before he can come back.' The rise of her voice suggests she truly believes what she's saying.

'He's already had half a million pounds.' I throw myself into the armchair, glancing across our turning circle and down the nearest part of our lane in case he's hanging around. Wherever he is, he'll be laughing his head off at the power and control he's managed to yield over us during the last ten months. 'So if you think he's going to blackmail us into *another* half a million, you must be insane.'

'Please Oliver. I can't risk him going all the way. He's got their DNA – he meant what he said – he's going to go after custody.'

I stare back. There's something in my wife's expression I don't like. And even more than that, suddenly there's something in her face that I don't trust. 'I think you're holding something back from me, Ellen.'

She sits in the chair facing me.

'Come on then, out with it.'

37

'OK, look I haven't told you the full story, love.' Ellen folds her arms in her lap as she glances from me to the twins' Moses baskets. Her voice is calmer and more considered as if she's trying to steady herself. I can't remember the last time she called me *love*.

'Then I think it's time you did, don't you?' I sit up straighter.

I haven't a clue what she's going to come out with but it seems my daughters and my mother could have been right about my second wife, and how I've been oblivious to a side of her they all claimed to see. So whatever Ellen's about to divulge, I suspect I'm not going to like it.

'Anthony turning up here last June wasn't just out of the blue.' She shuffles in the chair.

At first, I think I'm hearing things. 'What the hell are you talking about?'

'I'd already met him before.' Suddenly she can't meet my eye. It's little wonder.

'Before when? Before he turned up *here*?' I think back to the night of the storm. There's no way in a million years I'd have suspected they were already acquainted. But *how* acquainted? That's the question.

'It was a couple of months before.' Her eyes are fixed on the floor as if the rug her feet are resting on is the most interesting thing ever. 'Just after your reversal op.'

'And?' Tension throbs through my jaw. I can't believe what I'm hearing here. *Has she cooked this whole 'baby' arrangement up with him beforehand? Surely not.*

'It was when I was meeting Kirsteen, but she was late and well, the two of us got talking.' Ellen's face is flaming red and she's stuttering.

'You and *him*. Where?'

'We were in a pub.'

'Why are you telling me *now*? After all these months.' I rise from my chair and stride to the window, tugging my shirt out of my waistband. 'All these bloody months.'

'We haven't been having an affair if that's what you're thinking.' Her voice becomes more affirmative but I can't look at her any more than she seems able to look at me. 'Like I said, we just got talking.'

'About what?' I unclench the fists that are bunched at my sides. I need to hear her out. A slight relief is alleviating my anger at her reassurance that they haven't been having an affair, but that's all it is – a *slight* relief. And that's if she's telling the truth.

'A few things really – it started as small talk over a drink while I was waiting for Kirsteen. What stood out was him telling me he was into manifestation. This was why, he said, he was going to a property auction but had called into the pub first for some Dutch courage.'

'Eh? What are you on about?'

'He was telling me how he couldn't afford to bid on anything but that he wanted to get among the people who could.'

'What?' I'm not going to apologise for how incredulous I sound as I spin around from the window to look at her. 'What's a property auction got to do with anything?'

'His words were that *he didn't have a pot to piss in*,' – she draws air quotes around her words, – 'but that he wanted to *better himself.*' She looks straight at me now. 'He'd been listening to podcasts and watching YouTube videos on manifesting what you want, then putting yourself in the way of it.'

'So you were having such a deep discussion with a complete stranger – is that what you're trying to tell me?' Her damp hair curls around the sides of her face as it always does when it's drying. I've always loved looking at her when she's natural – when she's not hidden beneath layers of make-up and straightened hair.

'I was being polite by listening to him – I didn't have anything better to do while Kirsteen was running late.' She fiddles with the buttons of her cardigan and the soft leather of the sofa creaks beneath her as she moves. 'He was going on about how he was desperate to get into the property game but just needed a lucky break.'

'What I want to know,' – I fold my arms, – 'is how it went from him talking mumbo-jumbo about *manifestation* to him turning up on our doorstep that night?'

She takes a deep breath. 'Because I made a stupid joke about how I should be spending time in a maternity ward or at an antenatal clinic if manifestation works so well.' She lowers her voice as one of the twins stirs.

'Oh, I see.' Strangely enough, since we began this conversation, Ellen seems so much more 'together' than she has since the babies were born. I really don't know what to think.

'You can probably imagine how the rest of the conversation went.' She fiddles with the edge of a cushion. 'He suggested we could help each other. He could make me pregnant and in return, I could help him get the money together for his first property, so he *would* be able to bid in the not-too-distant future. He said it was fate that had got us talking.' She raises her eyes to look at me.

'That figures.' His face fills my mind as I recall his comment about *fate* in the dining room that evening. 'You've both played a blinder here, haven't you?' I bite my lip, too shocked to be angry but no doubt, anger will follow. 'I had *no idea* you'd ever met before – you should both be on stage with your acting abilities.' I cast my mind back to how she reacted when he initially turned up and then to when the text came through the day before her due date. 'In fact, you deserve a bloody Oscar for your performance.'

'I'm sorry, Oliver. But—'

'I take it you were sleeping with him *before* I had the pleasure of meeting him?'

'No.' It's Ellen's turn to sound incredulous. 'Of course not – it was purely a business arrangement – which is where *you* came in.'

'How do you mean?'

'Well, I couldn't lay my hands on the kind of money he was asking for, could I?' Shame creeps into her expression. 'Not on the measly amount I saved up from working in the poxy bar before I met you. Look, I hated deceiving you but he was offering everything I wanted on a plate. How was I to know he'd keep coming back for more?'

'You're telling me his extra demands have had *nothing* to do with you?'

'Of course they haven't.' She hangs her head. 'I only went along with the initial arrangement. I had no idea he'd get so greedy?'

What a fool I've been. I invited the man into my home, drank beer with him, and offered him a meal – I even felt grateful to my wife, at least initially, for being so hospitable. And all the while—

'Why do you think I spent most of the time in the kitchen while you were speaking to him?' She doesn't give me a chance to answer as she continues. 'I was bloody terrified I'd give something away, that's why.'

'I knew you were desperate but—' It's on the tip of my tongue to repeat what Mum's view of her was but what would be the point? We are where we are and somehow I need to dig us out of it.

'As you've said yourself, we only had a *five per cent* chance,' – she holds up five fingers as if I'm an imbecile, – 'of the second reversal being a success. I'm thirty-eight, Oliver. It's not as if time was on my side. So when Anthony suggested he'd be willing to help us, of course, I grabbed at it.'

'Oh, of course.' My voice drips with sarcasm. 'Like *anyone* would.'

'I wasn't sure the whole thing would work or whether you'd even go along with it,' – she shrugs, – 'But I guess the amount of drink you'd put away helped.'

'When did you arrange it?'

'When we checked the forecast a couple of days before and learned about the storm that might be coming, we decided it was then or never.'

'*We* decided.' My tone is more sarcastic still. I'm fuming, bloody fuming, yet my anger isn't going to alleviate any of this. The extra money he's demanding and the fact that he's now got swabs of the twins' DNA.

'I just knew you wouldn't turn someone who was stranded on the doorstep away. You're like your father in that respect.'

'You never even knew my father.' Yet I can't deny this comparison has softened me somewhat. To the man I've always aspired to be.

'I just can't believe I've been duped like this. I've spent years running a multi-million-pound company and prided myself on being more astute.' I should probably give myself a shake. As

Mum used to tell me, when it comes to matters of the heart, I've always been a pushover.

Ellen's shoulders slump. 'I just can't believe how horribly wrong it's all gone.'

'So why tell me all this *now*? Especially since we've gone all this time without me knowing.'

'Anthony said he was planning to tell you himself – unless I ensured the money for him. So I decided the truth was better coming from *me* than him.'

'How did he *really* get in here today, Ellen?' I tilt my head to the side as I await her answer.

38

I ALREADY KNOW Ellen's answer before I've finished asking the question.

'I let him in.' She hangs her head again.

'But why?'

'He's been hounding me like I just told you. I needed to try and reason with him.' She wrings her hands in her lap as her wide blue eyes implore my understanding. 'I had to stop him from telling you. But unless I talked you into paying him more, he warned me you were going to know I'd been in it from the start.'

'And you're sure he's managed to swab both babies' DNA?' I gesture at them. The possibilities of where we might go from here chase one another around and around my mind. My head's killing me – I need some painkillers. I can't even think straight.

'I lied when I said they were asleep.' She closes her eyes. 'The truth is that they were both screaming.'

I want to scream too, I want to scream at her that she wouldn't know the truth if it bit her on the arse.

'That still doesn't explain how he managed to shove a swab

inside their cheeks or whatever he's done to take their DNA. Unless you left him alone with them?' My voice hardens. I want to hit something – I'd never hit my wife but rage is coursing through me faster than a flood-swollen river.

'Only for a moment while I warmed their milk in the kitchen.' Her voice is low.

'How could you have been so *stupid*?' I spit the words *stupid* out like it's something nasty in my mouth.

'He wasn't going to just *take* them, was he?' She throws her hands in the air. 'And they were screaming.'

'How could you have known he wouldn't take them? How can you say that?' My neck cracks as I tilt my head back to the ceiling. I don't know whether I'm trying to summon divine intervention or whether I just can't bear to look at my wife.

'We're going to have to pay him, Oliver.' She rises from the chair. 'We need to pay him and then take off from here,' – she points along the drive, – 'just like we've been planning. Nothing needs to change.'

'This is absurd. And what if I don't want to *take off* with you anymore?' It's my turn to throw my hands in the air. 'What if I can no longer trust you after what you've admitted to?'

Mum was spot on when I broke the news of the pregnancy. *And* before that when she all but admitted her distrust of Ellen. I just couldn't see it myself. All I saw was this beautiful younger woman who'd brought so much colour into my life. I'd become infatuated with her to a point where I couldn't countenance a return to a pre-Ellen existence. I'd have done anything for her, as I've stupidly proven.

'I made a huge mistake,' – she steps closer to me and I step away, deeper into the sunny bay window. 'I know I did. He said he'd be satisfied with the initial hundred grand – it was all he would need to get him started so he could buy his first property, and that we'd never see each other again after I became pregnant. Please, Oliver, you've got to forgive me.'

'How can I?' I rest my burning forehead against the chill of the window pane. How did my life come to this?

'Because Anthony lied to me too – and he's made numerous threats to tell you the truth.' I can tell from the proximity of Ellen's voice that she's standing right behind me. 'He's been blackmailing me as well.'

I lift my head from the window and angle my neck to look at her again. She's so thin compared to how she was when we met. Carmen struggled to lose weight after the births of our two girls, but other than the stretch marks the twins have left behind, no one would ever suspect Ellen had carried them.

'You don't know how horrendous it's all been.' She reaches for my shoulder and I allow her hand to rest there for a moment before shrugging it away. 'I've been coping with two newborn babies, lying to you and trying to get *him* to leave me alone. It's been a nightmare.'

I turn to face her fully. It *does* sound like she's been really going through it, whether she started all this or not. 'We're going to have to report him to the police – there's no other way.'

'You're joking, aren't you?' She steps back, her face filled with anguish. 'But *we've* broken the law too. By entering this agreement in the first place, as well as putting *your* name on the birth certificates.'

'We'll just have to take our chances, won't we?'

'No, Oliver – we need to think this through. Aside from what could happen legally, I thought you didn't want this getting out?'

'Well, I've supposedly sold my business so I don't give a rat's arse what anyone thinks in a professional sense.' I say *supposedly* as right now, our future isn't quite as certain as it used to be. I *do* care about my daughters finding out what I've been involved with though. Just as we're arranging to see each other again, it could all come crashing back down.

'I don't really believe that.'

A thought occurs to me. 'For all you know, he could have been targeting *you* all along.'

'That's crossed my mind as well.' She pushes her hair back from her face. 'My longing for a baby wasn't exactly a secret.'

'So you must agree then – that he's left us no choice other than to report him?'

'No, Oliver, please! I can't face all that. We'll have social workers sniffing around us – wanting to prove that we're unfit parents. I came from a childhood of social workers – I can't put myself through that.' This is probably the most information she's ever divulged about her childhood, but that's a conversation we can return to in the future. If we have a future.

'We'll soon convince them there's nothing for them to sniff around at.' Much as I detest the prospect of us being assessed in this way, it feels like the least of our worries.

'But Anthony will seek rights over *our* children.' Her eyes glisten with tears as she leans against the wall. There was a time when the slightest inclination of her being upset would melt me down faster than butter in a hot pan. But not today. I'm too stressed to be able to offer her any comfort. 'And they *are* ours,' she continues, 'I can't risk Anthony gaining joint custody of them.'

'He'll be too busy in prison after he's been done for extortion.'

'But you heard what he said about—'

'You've got an answer for everything, haven't you?' I glare at her. 'Whose side are you on?'

'He'll just spin a story about *us* exploiting *him*. I heard what he said at the door.' Her voice is becoming more and more high-pitched. '*We* could end up in prison – and what will happen to our babies *then*?'

'You're catastrophising, just like you always do.'

'No, I am not.' She juts her chin out in a similar way to how Jasmine does when I refuse one of her requests.

'You're also forgetting that I can afford the best lawyer money can buy – unlike Anthony.' I turn back to the window, still half expecting him to turn up here again now that I'm back at home. After all, as Ellen so rightly pointed out, it's me who controls the money. She's asked for my accounts to be turned into joint ones but I didn't even do that with Carmen. 'So just trust me on this and I'll sort it out.'

As Mum used to say, *good will always triumph over bad.* And one positive thing to be coming out of this mess is how it appears to have dragged Ellen out of her perpetual state of apathy and fired her with some determination and drive.

'I just want you to pay him off and for us to leave this house. I really can't cope with anything else. You've already seen how much I've been struggling.' She strides over to the mantelpiece, tugs a tissue from the box and dabs at her eyes. 'Please Oliver – if you still love me, you'll do this for me. You'll do it for *them.*' She points at the babies' baskets.

'Don't you see?' I pace forward and face her in front of the fireplace. 'We can't pay the man another penny. Blackmailers always come back for more.'

'But he won't know where we are to come back.' She blows her nose.

'We could move to Timbucktoo and he'd find us.' I gesture to the sunny window. 'Slimeballs like him always do.' I can't tell her I'm having serious second thoughts about moving, especially now Bella's been in touch. I'll bring that up later.

'So after all I've said, after all I've told you, you're still *refusing* to pay him, is that what you're saying?'

'I'm still refusing to pay him.' I nod. 'And no matter what you say, Ellen – I'm reporting him to the police.'

'And you're going to tell the police *everything*, are you?' Her eyes widen and she speaks in the tone of voice she always reserves for when she's trying to get around me. If I'm honest, it's a struggle not to yield to the power she usually holds over me. 'Including what I've admitted to *today*?'

'I've *got* to tell them everything.' I throw myself onto the sofa. 'It's the only way we can stop him. How many other couples could he bend over a barrel like he has with us, either now *or* in the future?'

'I don't care about other couples. I only care about us. Please, Oliver, think about this. We could have a fresh start – we could go further than the Yorkshire coast, we could move *anywhere*.' She spreads her arms out as if demonstrating just how far we could go. 'We could even move abroad, just me, you and our babies. But if you burst this can of worms open, that's it – who knows what will happen.'

'I'm sorry, Ellen.' I drop my head into my hands. I've no idea why I'm apologising to her but there it is. 'I've made my mind up.'

'In that case,' – she heads towards the baby's baskets. – 'You've left me with no choice for what I'll have to do next.'

39

'If you don't pay him, I'm leaving here on my own.' Ellen lifts Imogen from her basket and holds her against her shoulder. 'And I'm taking the twins with me. It's the only way I can keep us all safe.'

'And where the hell would you go?' I rise from the sofa. I don't know whether to sit, stand, pace around or thump a wall. I really don't know what to do with myself.

'I'll stay with Kirsteen. Or I'll find a hostel. But I can't wait around to see what he's going to do next.' She rocks from side to side with the baby in her arms. 'You either sort this my way or we're out of here.'

'So *you're* effectively blackmailing *me*? Pay up, or you're leaving?' I hook my thumbs into the waistband of my trousers. 'You're no better than *he* is, but having said that, you cooked all this up with him in the first place, didn't you?'

'Only the first part of things,' she cries. 'Not what's happened since.'

'I need to make some calls.'

'Have you not heard a word I've just said?' She rests Imogen back down in her basket. 'I meant what I said, Oliver.'

'Just leave me alone for an hour.' I march toward the door without looking at her. 'I'm going to my office – I need some space to think.'

'You can't just dump me on my own like this,' she cries. 'You know I haven't been coping – I don't know what to do.'

'Neither do I, look Ellen, please – just leave me alone.' I yank at the door handle.

'Well don't blame me if I'm not here by the time you've *thought*,' she yells. 'At least I can see how important we are.'

I slam the office door. I've had just about enough. After confessing to what she's set up, she thinks she can threaten to leave if I don't bow to her wishes.

My eyes fall on a photo she framed of the twins to cheer me up for my last birthday and something inside me gives way. When Ellen was carrying Imogen and Ruben, I feared I'd never bond with them, but as soon as they came into the world, I fell for them, hook, line and sinker. They're my son and daughter and all I want is to love and protect them. With a vulture like Anthony circling their world, they need all the protection I can offer.

I flick through my contacts until I reach Joe – he's more of a conveyancing solicitor but he's extremely well-connected, so should be able to put me in touch with someone who can give me some advice.

As I outline the situation to him, I realise even more how stupid I've been, but if Joe thinks this too, he's kind enough not to say so. Instead, he lets out a long whistle and then takes a deep breath. 'OK, well, as you know, this sort of thing isn't my bag, so I'm going to ask around to find the best person to take you on.'

'Discreetly, of course.' My eyes rest on the glass trophy on top of my filing cabinet. *Company of the Year.* Yes, I might be selling Homes from Holmes but I still want my employees and associates to remember my time in the driving seat with respect and positivity. I don't want their enduring memory to be of someone who let his heart rule his head, of someone who, when drunk, entered into such an ill-thought-out agreement before becoming a victim of blackmail. Then there's the prospect of action being taken against me for paying a sperm donor in the first place, not to mention falsifying the twins' birth certificates.

'Without question, this will be handled discreetly. Look, Oliver, it's a mess – I can't deny that. But I'll get onto it today and hopefully have someone calling you to discuss it all before the close of play.'

'Do you think I should ring the police in the meantime?'

'I'd hang fire until you've had some proper advice.' He lets a long breath out as though considering how to handle my question. 'We need to get you through this with as little damage to your record and standing as possible.'

'What would you do?' I ask. 'Would you pay him? Bearing in mind that I need to protect the twins.'

The line falls silent for a moment. He's probably wondering how to phrase what he's thinking – that he'd never have been as stupid as I've been. *Stupid* is an understatement. Not only did I never suspect Anthony and Ellen of being in league at the beginning of all this, but I've allowed the man to extort large amounts of money from me *three times* since. And my continued stupidity has led to virtual estrangement from my girls and forced me to put my home *and* business on the market.

'You may lose the twins anyway by the sounds of it.' Joe's voice takes on an edge of sadness. 'They're not yours – not genetically speaking. This means you don't hold any of the cards here – only the wallet strings. In my view, you need to look out for *yourself*.'

'But I love them as if they were my own, Joe.'

'I can tell.' His voice becomes more sympathetic. 'Look, let me get off this phone and make some proper enquiries. I'll find you the best I can, Oliver. It's just with it being a donor arrangement, especially one where your neck's on the line, we need someone with a certain level of expertise.'

I'm heartened by his use of the word *we*. For the first time in nearly a year, I feel less alone. I wish I'd rung Joe in the first place but perhaps it's taken Ellen's admission of her involvement in all this to force my hand. Before that, I thought me and her were in it together.

One thing he's right about is that I really *could* lose them – *all* of them.

~

Ellen jumps as I enter the lounge and Imogen startles in her arms as her feed is disturbed.

'So what's happening? What are you going to do?'

I glance into the basket at Ruben who has a milk dribble on his chin. They're so much more settled since we moved them to formula milk – it's just a shame the same can't be said for us. I feel so displaced, I can't imagine ever feeling *settled* again.

'My conveyancing lawyer is on it,' I reply. 'He's got a few contacts and he's going to find me the best advice.'

'You've told him *everything*?' She holds Imogen up against her shoulder and rubs her back.

'I had to.'

She nuzzles her nose into Imogen's downy hair. 'God only knows what he must be thinking of me. What I'm thinking about myself is bad enough.'

'I told it as it is.' I sit beside her on the sofa. 'It's perhaps difficult for us men to understand a woman's yearning to be a mother but most of us have *some* idea. Like I explained to him, you'd have done almost *anything* to make it happen.' What I don't add is, *as you've demonstrated.*

'How did he react?' She rubs more vigorously at Imogen's back.

'He was pretty understanding.'

This is a complete lie, but then lies seem to have become the currency of mine and Ellen's marriage. When I pushed Joe for his opinion, what he *really* said was that women like Ellen give the rest of them a bad name and, that if he were in my shoes, he'd get out while he was still able to. He seemed more focused on exploring damage limitation options for *me* as opposed to sorting the situation as a whole.

'I suppose he's advised you *not* to pay Anthony.' Her words slip out in a resigned sigh as Imogen finally does the burp Ellen's evidently been waiting for. 'And I suppose he's also advised you just to risk the fallout all this is creating – after all, lawyers just want to line their own pockets, don't they?' She holds Imogen out to me. 'They both need changing.'

'He's a friend as it happens, so he isn't charging me a dime.' I linger for a moment with Imogen against my shoulder, enjoying her warmth. I can't help but wonder how much longer I'll be able to do this. Everything has taken on a new fragility. 'But I'm waiting for him to put me in touch with someone more specialised.'

'And how long's that going to take? We need to be acting *today*. Those DNA results could be back by tomorrow and Anthony's got the money to fast-track all this through the courts if he wants to.'

'Has he hell.' I lay Imogen into her basket as Joe's words, *you may lose the twins* float back into my mind. 'Anthony's only come running back for more because he's spent everything he's had so far. Anyway,' I glance at the clock on top of the Welsh dresser. 'I thought you were going to Kirsteen's.'

'You sound like you want us to go.' The hurt look is back –

the look that suggests everything's all my fault. The fact that she's still here suggests her previous threats were empty to provoke a reaction.

'I understand if you feel safer at her house until all this dies down. I'll drive the three of you there myself.' Perhaps I'm calling her bluff, I don't know. The truth is that I don't want them to go but, equally, after what Ellen's admitted to, I need to unravel whether I want her to stay. She brought this man into our lives and now that he's turned it upside down, she's looking to me to sort it all out. Plus if these babies are going to be wrenched from my life, I need to start detaching myself.

'I'll feel *safer*,' – she glares at me, – 'if you just pay him what he's asking for. It's like you don't *want* to get him off our backs so we can disappear. Instead, you're messing about with *legal advice* and wasting precious time.'

She's beginning to sound like a broken record.

'I can't pay him, Ellen. Nor am I *disappearing*.'

'I thought we had a plan.'

'Let's just see what the solicitor says when he or she calls.'

40

THE GARDENER CLOCKED off an hour ago and the shadows in the garden are lengthening as afternoon stares evening in the face. This time a year ago, Mum was alive, I was in, albeit *limited*, contact with my daughters, and Ellen and I were thinking about a second vasectomy reversal. To my knowledge, she hadn't yet encountered Anthony, and the prospect of selling my home and my business would have been laughable.

I let myself into the summer house, and drop into my comfy chair which overlooks what we've always called our little lake. It's a large pond really, but so still and peaceful, that if it can plant just a fraction of that stillness and peace into me, it's the best place for me while I continue to wait.

Ellen didn't listen to my suggestion of us wheeling the twins out here for some fresh air. As the afternoon has worn on, she's become increasingly agitated and jumpy. She doesn't know whether to go or stay and says she can't bear being so powerless over whatever might happen next. The best thing I could do in the circumstances was to put some distance between us.

I've tried calling Joe twice since we initially spoke but he's *still* waiting on a ringback from a favour he's called in.

I drop my head into my hands as I breathe in the musty air, mingled with the wood treatment Nick painted on the outside of the summerhouse. The scent reminds me of childhood, of my dad's deckchair in his shed, his *oasis of calm* as he called it, a place filled with projects and things he was taking apart and putting back together. I inherited the *putting things together* gene from him and knew from a young age I was going to be an architect. I miss his involvement in my business and his pride in what I achieved. But who knows what he would make of what a mangled mess I've made of things now.

I grab my phone as it vibrates in my pocket. 'Joe – at last – we've been going out of our minds.'

'I'm sorry it's taken longer than we might have been hoping but, I've identified the guy you need to speak to.'

'Go on.' I stand from the deckchair.

'His name's George Ellison, from Ellison, Steeton and Powers. He's the best you're going to get, really he is and, he's agreed to fit you in first thing tomorrow.'

'*Tomorrow?*' My stomach sags. 'But I could do with speaking to him *today*. Ellen's threatening to leave and to be honest, with the threats Anthony's been making—'

'George had a family commitment this evening,' Joe explains, quite possibly resisting the urge to tell me I should just let Ellen go. 'It's something to do with one of his daughters. So, I'm sorry but tomorrow is the earliest he can call.'

'OK.' I sigh as I watch the dust particles dancing in the early evening sunshine. 'Do you still think I should hang fire on reporting all this to the police?'

'I'd still say wait until you've spoken to George. I've given him a brief overview of your predicament so he'll be chewing it over before he speaks to you in the morning.'

'Did he say *anything* to you about his initial thoughts?'

'Only what I've already thought – that on the face of it, if

Anthony can prove he's the twin's biological father, he *will* have rights, no matter what prior arrangement has been agreed.'

'He's not fit to be anywhere near those babies.' Anger bubbles within me at the prospect of him playing dad after how he's used them as pawns in his game.

'I know it's easy for me to say but try and relax tonight, get some sleep and you can hit the ground running tomorrow. George *will* get you the best possible outcome.'

'OK – thanks, Joe. I appreciate all your help. Hopefully, I'll soon be able to take you for a pint or three to celebrate all this being in the rearview mirror.'

'I'll hold you to that.' I can hear the smile in Joe's voice. 'Good luck. Keep me posted.'

After he hangs up, the summerhouse seems more silent than before. As if my surroundings are holding their breath with me - waiting to see what tomorrow will bring – the call from George Ellison and potentially, Anthony's DNA results.

Just as I'm considering returning to the house, a robin lands on the windowsill outside, seeming to be looking straight at me. I sit back into the deckchair and stare back at it, wishing I had its freedom and simplicity. All it probably has to worry about is finding some food to take back to its nesting mate and it will find plenty of that in this garden, thanks to Nick's painstaking care of birds as well as the flowers and plants.

Something Carmen once mentioned slides into my mind. Her father died several years into our marriage and she told me about what she thought was the same robin, visiting her every morning since her dad's passing. It would perch on the patio while she ate breakfast with the girls and she insisted it was her father hanging around to comfort her. *Robins appear when loved ones are near*, she would say. I didn't pay too much attention at the time and filed her story under *mumbo jumbo* to join other theories she had associated with butterflies and random feathers.

However, as I continue to hold eye contact with this beautiful bird that seems to have taken a special interest in me, all I can hope is that Carmen was right, that this robin is somehow the spirit of my mother, and that everything's going to turn out OK.

41

APRIL 19

THE CREDITS ARE ROLLING on the film I started watching to distract myself and to pass the time. My chin is coated with a layer of drool and my leg is dead as I try to sit up on the sofa. Rubbing my eyes, I check the bottle on the coffee table. I haven't drunk as much whiskey as I'd planned to before dropping off. However, the large one I got down me as the film began thankfully bestowed an hour or two of oblivion.

Ellen took the twins upstairs what feels like hours ago, saying she was exhausted. I told her I'd follow her up after I'd had a nightcap. And now I might just have another. I reach for the bottle and slop a large measure into the tumbler, breathing in its sweet and oaky aroma. If I'm to have any chance of falling asleep when I climb into bed beside my wife, I need to knock myself out again.

Before she went up, Ellen seemed slightly more at peace and even kissed the top of my head as she passed me. Her threats of going to Kirsteen's house seem to have been empty. Hopefully, she's been reassured that something's being done, rather than us just sitting around, waiting for Anthony to call the shots.

In the faint light of the flickering TV, I can just about read the clock. It's already after two am so there are only a few hours to wait until I can speak to the solicitor and we can come up with some kind of action plan. Joe sounded confident that nothing I've done will invite *criminal* proceedings but caveated that with a reminder that he's not an expert in this area of the law. Still, I'm trying to hang onto his positivity.

All I know is that when I looked into the newborn eyes of Imogen and Ruben two months ago, I promised I'd always look after and protect them. It's a promise I'll honour for as long as I'm able. As long as it's not snatched out of my hands.

I'd better go up shortly. If the twins wake for a feed, I'll take charge so Ellen can continue sleeping. Some parents moan about the nightfeeds but actually, I enjoy them, and given the state of play, I need to hang onto every moment. When they're soft and warm in my arms, Imogen likes to grasp my little finger as she greedily gulps from her bottle, while Ruben just likes to stare at my face. I can picture them now, wrapped in their swaddling robes, lying side by side in the cot next to our bed. We've said we'll put them into their own room and probably individual cots when they get to six months or so, but for now, their place at night is with us. For as long as there is still an *us*. For now, there is. But who knows what will happen tomorrow...

I screw the lid back onto the whiskey and point the remote at the TV, plunging the room into complete darkness. I'm going to tip the whiskey I've poured down the sink and instead pour myself a pint of water. The twins don't need me breathing whiskey fumes over them and I don't need a fuzzy head in the morning. Not when I've got so much to face.

My bare feet slap against the hallway tiles as I check the front door for what must be the tenth time in the last twelve hours before making my way back to the kitchen. I love the house when it's still and sleeping – this house I created. I love the place full stop. Ellen keeps saying it's just bricks and mortar which can be recreated *anywhere*. I agree to a point, that home is the *who*, not the *what*, and that's how things used to be here. I just wish, with every fibre of my being, that my mother was still alive and that the girls still came to stay at the weekends.

I fill a glass with water, downing it in one before refilling it. Its chill slides to my stomach as I head to the patio door. Shit. I can't have locked it after I returned from the summer house. I lecture Ellen for being lackadaisical when it comes to keeping the place under lock and key but here I am, leaving the rear of the house vulnerable. I open the door and poke my head outside, shivering as I breathe in the middle-of-the-night air.

The days might be warming up but the nights are still chilly and suddenly, the room upstairs containing my wife and children seems far more inviting than being on my own down here.

It's an effort not to let my attention settle on Mum's pitch-black cottage. Ellen's told me several times that I should pack the place up but I can't bear to. After what happened, we got it all cleaned up and now it's as it was when she was alive – which is the way I want it to stay. However, if I'm forced into this move to the Yorkshire coast, I'll be left with no choice other than to box up Mum's belongings.

I close the door, twisting the key in the lock before grabbing a couple of extra bottles of milk from the fridge just in case Ellen didn't take enough up for the babies earlier. Then I check the side door out of the utility room followed by the conservatory door out of the dining room. Everything's safe and secure. With a sense of relief, I trudge up the stairs, my feet sinking into the thick carpet pile as I ascend. Yes, I was careless with the patio door but there's no harm done.

I shower in the main bathroom to minimise the risk of waking everyone by using the ensuite, then I towel down before wrapping myself in my bathrobe. Warm from the towel rail, it feels like a warm hug which is a very welcome sensation. Other than the twins, it feels like a long time since I've known the proximity of another human being. It might have been at Mum's funeral. Everyone was hugging me that day whether I wanted them to or not.

The bedroom is steeped in darkness, shadows draped over every surface. I pause at the door, letting my eyes adjust.

I can just make out Ellen's form beneath the covers — a still, hunched silhouette, facing towards the wall. The air smells of formula and baby powder, clean and faintly sweet. Once, this room held the musk of aftershave, Ellen's perfume, and the heady scent of skin and sex. Back when I used to reach for her without thinking.

I set the bottles down gently on the dressing table. My eyes drift to the cot at the foot of our bed, and as always, a fragile smile touches my lips. No matter how hard yesterday was, one glimpse of their tiny, sleeping bodies never fails to anchor me. To remind me what all of this is about.

I step closer, the floorboard creaking beneath my foot. I peer over the cot's edge, already picturing the slow stretch of a tiny arm, the crumpled peace of their faces, the soft rustle of sleep. I reach down, expecting warmth, fleece, and the velvet smoothness of a cheek. Instead, my hand brushes cool cotton.

The surface is flat and empty. My fingers sweep wider across the mattress. There's nothing. No weight, no shape, no warmth.

A cold pulse of dread shoots through my body. I blink, as I continue to stare into the dark.

I reach again, frantic now, my hands splaying across the

sheet, under the muslin at the foot of the cot, then beneath the blanket. As if they could be hidden there. As if this could somehow be a mistake. But the cot is bare and abandoned. My breath catches in my throat.

They're gone.

42

Perhaps Ellen left the twins in their pram or their baskets in the lounge without me realising. Surely I wasn't paying *that* little attention? The room was dark but I *must* have known if they were still in the room. I was certain she'd taken them up to bed.

Tightening the cord on my robe, I race across the landing and back down the stairs. I gasp as I notice the front door that I checked only twenty minutes ago.

It's ajar.

Darting to it, I'm just in time to catch the tail lights of a vehicle as it disappears around the corner of the lane.

I stagger back, my heart hammering. The air seems thinner and everything inside me lurches with a single, unbearable thought, *someone's taken them.*

What the hell's happening? I snatch my keys from the hallway windowsill and slam my feet into trainers before hurtling out of the door towards my Range Rover. I've got to get after them.

It *must* be Anthony. Who else could it be? He must have snuck into the house when the patio door was unlocked and taken the twins while I was in the shower. Ellen clearly hasn't heard a thing so far but, perhaps she'll now hear the roar of my Range Rover's engine as I leave. I spin it around, leaving a cloud of dust as it churns up the gravel.

If Ellen does wake, the first thing she'll do is to check inside the cot. I could break what's happened more gently to her but there's no time to go back up there and explain. If I'm going to have any chance of catching up with Anthony, I have to chase after him *now*.

I hurtle along our lane as fast as the bends will allow, praying I'll catch up with those tail lights before they get too far away. I didn't catch the registration so I haven't got anything to report to the police. Nor have I got my phone with me. But I can't go back. All I can do is catch up with him and rescue my twins.

Ellen was right, she was bloody right, but I wouldn't listen. If I'd paid Anthony what he was demanding this would never have happened. Imogen and Ruben would still be snug, side-by-side in their cot instead of being snatched by someone who won't take proper care of them. He's probably got no milk or nappies, and God only knows how he'll be transporting them but I can't imagine they'll be safely strapped in. I promised I'd protect the two of them and look what I've allowed to happen.

'Mum, if you can hear me,' I mutter into the darkness of my car. 'Please, please, please let them be safe. Please help me to catch up with them.' How I'll make him stop when I get behind him remains to be seen. The priority is the safety of the twins but even if I can get the registration number, that will be something. Or I can follow without him realising until he stops somewhere...

I can't believe I didn't grab my phone so can't call for any help. 'Come on, come on, come on.' There's a screech as I wrench the car from the end of my private lane and out onto the country road leading away. But a T-junction is coming up shortly, and I'm going to be forced to guess which of the two routes Anthony could have taken.

'No, no, no.' I slap my palm against the steering wheel, Joe's words bouncing around my brain, *if he's proven to be the natural father, he's got rights.* Maybe he's had the DNA results back already if he's paid a premium for them to be fast-tracked. Perhaps that's why he felt he could sneak into our home and snatch them.

And it was *me* who left the patio door open while I slept on the sofa – it's all my fault. Ellen's never going to forgive me – and whether she does or not, I'm never going to forgive myself.

I twist my head from right to left at the junction. Will Anthony be driving deeper into the Dales towards Settle, or do I take the road towards Skipton? Since he's more likely to live in an urban than a rural area, Skipton, which then branches off towards Leeds or Bradford, has to be the safest bet. Really, I'm just taking stabs in the dark.

Now I'm off the twisty B-roads, I can get some speed up. Some poxy kitchen fitter's van will be no match for my Range Rover once I get my foot down. If he's turned this way, I'll soon catch up with the bastard. *Please, God, let him have turned this way.*

My breath catches as I spot stationary tail lights in a layby. I swerve into it after them, tugging on the handbrake and darting from the car. But what might have looked like a van as I approached it from behind in the darkness is just a pick-up truck delivering milk.

I thump at the window, and the man behind the wheel jumps. I tug on his door.

'Have you seen a van?' I shout.

If the milkman is taken aback at a wild-eyed man in a dressing gown throwing open the door of his milk float, he says nothing. 'There was something parked further up there.' He points forward. 'It could have been a van now you come to mention it. Why what's the matter?' I'm almost reassured by his thick Yorkshire accent – he sounds just like my Dad.

'I've no time to explain, I'm sorry. I need to get after it before it sets off again. Thank you.'

I slam the door as he's shouting *drive carefully* and race back to my car. With a bit of luck, Anthony will still be parked up. One or both of the twins must have been crying and he's pulled over to tend to whichever of them is making a noise. As well they would after being dragged from their warm cot in the dead of night by a stranger. Why couldn't they have cried earlier? Why couldn't they have alerted me to his presence when I was still in the shower?

I'm almost into Skipton before I admit defeat. Whoever that milkman saw must have set off again before I reached them. I can't guarantee that Anthony even turned in this direction. He could be practically at Settle now in the time I've wasted. There's nothing else for it. I'll have to go back to the house, wake Ellen and call the police. We can't wait for George Ellison to call in the morning. The babies' lives are at risk.

Whether or not Anthony's had the DNA results, nothing gives him the right to creep into my house and snatch the twins from their cot.

I can't bear to imagine Ellen's fear and confusion when I wake her to break the news – and it's all my bloody fault. I should have locked the patio door. I should have gone to bed when they all went. I should have had a shower in the ensuite. I should have had my phone on me when I rushed from the house.

Should-have, should-have, should-have. I've done nothing of what I should have done for the last year and now, it seems, two vulnerable and innocent babies are going to pay the price.

43

THE FRONT DOOR is still ajar. The gravel crunches beneath the weight of my wheels and I steel myself for the news I'm about to break.

It's well after three so perhaps, tuned in as she is to the routine of the twins, my wife will already be awake. I should have probably woken her as soon as I realised Imogen and Ruben had been taken but I wasn't thinking straight. All I could focus on was getting after those tail lights. And I couldn't even manage to catch up with him. I feel even more of a failure now than I did earlier. As if that's even possible.

I slam the front door shut and pound across the hallway. I hit the stairs at full speed, taking them two at a time.

'Ellen! Ellen, wake up!' My voice is ragged with panic, I'm yelling her name before I even reach the top. My heart is smashing against my ribcage like it's trying to escape. 'He's taken the babies!'

I burst into our bedroom, heading straight for the bed – my hand flying out, expecting to find her still sleeping. But the duvet sinks under my palm. The pillows give way, soft and hollow beneath the surface. There's no warmth. No shape. Just silence.

She's not here. I stare at the dented bedding, every nerve in my body screaming. My brain claws for explanations. Maybe she got up to look for them. Maybe she just couldn't sleep.

But the pillows... they've been *arranged*. Like a decoy. Like something Hannah would do as a teenager when she snuck out and stuffed her bed to fake a sleeping shape.

No, no, no.

I snap the light on. The bottles I brought up earlier sit untouched beside the cot. My eyes sting. My throat burns. I stumble toward the ensuite. The mirrored cabinet is wide open.

Her toothbrush has gone. So has her daily medication — the little blister pack of thyroid tablets. It's always there. Always. Racing back into the bedroom, I rip open the wardrobe doors. Empty hangers swing where her clothes used to hang, rattling against each other like bones.

I drop to my knees. Slide my hand under the bed. The suitcase we took on our honeymoon is still here. But the smaller one — the one she uses for weekends away, easy to carry, easy to pack fast, is gone. I lurch upright, my heart thudding so loudly I can barely hear myself think.

Maybe I've got it wrong. She could have started packing for the move. Or perhaps she went to Kirsteen's as she threatened. Maybe that was a taxi I saw outside, not a van. Maybe she just didn't want to wake me from where she thought I was sleeping on the sofa.

But the sick, sloshing dread in my stomach says otherwise.

I lurch across the landing and shove open the nursery drawers. The top two are empty. All the sleepsuits, the tiny vests, and the little socks I folded just the other day are gone. The bulk box of nappies we bought last week? It's been torn open and two packs are missing.

She's taken everything she needs. This wasn't panic – it was a plan. She said she'd do this – she *threatened* me. But is she really with Anthony? Did he help them leave?

I crash back into the bedroom, lungs burning, and grab my phone from the bedside table with shaking hands. I have to find her. I have to get the babies back to the safety of their cot.

Hi, it's Ellen. Leave a message after the tone.

Bloody hell. I hurl the phone onto our bed. As fast as it hits the duvet, I launch myself after it. I need to call the police. But as my finger hovers above the nine button, my thinking changes yet again. If I *were* to ring the police, what the hell could I even tell them? What would they even do, if anything? Ellen's left here of her own volition. More to the point, those babies aren't even biologically mine. Oh God, what the hell? Why did she feel the need to do this? I offered to drive her to Kirsteen's myself, there was no need for her to drag the twins from their cot and take off from here in the dead of night.

I pace onto the landing and then back into the bedroom. *Get a grip, get a grip.* I don't know what to do for the best. I raise the phone to my ear for a second time.

Hi, it's Ellen. Leave a message after the tone.

I take a deep breath to calm myself. There's no chance she'll call me back if I start ranting into her voicemail, 'Ellen, please, love. Call me. Just let me know you're all safe. I'm going out of my mind here.'

I throw off my dressing gown and tug fresh clothes from the cupboard. All I can do is wait for her to contact me. She'll have to call me sooner or later. However, I don't know how I'll survive the night in this state. I'll probably drive myself insane.

I head back down the stairs, turning the lights on as I go, hoping to also cancel out the darkness inside me. I'd give anything for Mum still to be over in her cottage – for her to be there for me, like she always was. Resisting the urge to pour more whiskey in case I need to drive again, I flick the switch to boil the kettle, shaking my head at the absurdity of what I'm doing. My wife and two-month-old twins have taken off into the night and I'm just standing here doing something as mundane as making a cup of tea. I tug my phone from the pocket of my joggers. 'Ring me,' I shout at the screen. 'Please, just ring me.'

Within moments – as if summoned by sheer will – the screen lights up. *Unknown number.* My thumb hovers above the accept call button, my heartbeat skittering.

'It's Ellen.' Her voice is brittle like it's being dragged through wire.

'Where the hell are you? What's going on?'

'He wants another million.' She pauses then adds, 'From *us.*'

That word — *us* — nearly knocks the air out of my lungs. There *is* still an *us.* It's like a sliver of light in a black room.

'He says he needs to get out of the country,' she continues. 'And once he's gone, we'll never see him again.'

'He's said that before,' I snap. My voice shakes with fury and fear. 'He promised he'd disappear last time. And yet here we are.'

In the background, a baby starts to cry. It's Imogen. I know that cry, I *know* it. *He* doesn't – he doesn't have the first clue about our babies. She always sounds like she's pleading when she's hungry — not wailing, not demanding. Just... *needing.* I press the phone tighter to my ear, like I can get closer.

I imagine her face. The downy fuzz of hair that always sticks to her temples when she's warm. The way her tiny fingers curl instinctively whenever they're wrapped around mine. The faint birthmark on her cheek shaped almost like a comma.

'Oliver,' Ellen shrieks. 'I don't care what he's said before. You didn't see his face when he ordered me out of bed and made me pack some things – he's desperate.' Her voice is cracking now. Bordering on hysteria.

I close my eyes. Grip the edge of the worktop. My knuckles turn white. 'Are you safe?' I ask. 'Are you all OK?'

'If you transfer the money right now, he'll tell you exactly where he's going to leave us. You can come straight away. You'll get us back safely.'

'Ellen... where are you *now*? Just tell me. I'll come straight away, this second.'

Another cry joins the first.

Ruben. His cry is lower-pitched and throaty. He always cries like he's angry at the world — fists balled, red-faced, eyes scrunched shut. My brave little boy. I can't breathe.

'I *can't* just wire him another million based on promises,' I choke. 'I need to know you're alright. Where the hell are you?'

44

'I can't tell you where we are.' Ellen's voice cracks. 'If I do, he says he'll—' her words die away. 'Look, please, just transfer the money.' The twins' cries are picking up pace. 'And you *can't* involve the police.' Her tone becomes firm again.

'You must be joking. I've *got* to call them. He can't get away with this.'

'You mustn't! Please, Oliver. We've got to do exactly as he's telling us.'

'Why the hell did you leave the house with him? Was it when I was in the shower? Why didn't you scream, for God's sake?' I'm firing questions she probably can't reply to – not if he's standing over her.

'He had a knife.' She sounds terrified. 'He's *still* got a knife.'

I stare at the gap in the knife block. He's taken the biggest and best one. The one I never usually use because it's so lethal looking.

'He needs to do as you're telling him if he wants you all to stay safe.' Anthony's voice is muffled behind the babies' cries. I was right – he *is* standing over her. Over all of them. The maniac abducted my family at knifepoint while I, the person supposed to protect them, was obliviously soaping myself in the shower.

'Just do it!' she cries. 'Please, Oliver!'

'Put him on the phone.' I grit my teeth.

After a few seconds, Anthony's smarmy voice fills my ear. 'Nice family outing, this. Shame you're not holding all the cards *now*, eh, Oliver?'

'If you think—'

'Message me through WhatsApp when the transfer's sorted.'

There's a burst of static, a muffled scuffle, then nothing apart from silence. The bastard's cut me off. And I'm left standing in the kitchen, the phone clutched in my shaking hand, the last echoes of the twins' cries still ringing in my ears.

There's no number to call back so I try calling Anthony through WhatsApp. It just rings out. *What to do? What to do?* I pace up and down the kitchen, as I chase myself in and out of the only three options I've got.

I could ring the police, I *should* ring the police, but the maniac still has the knife he forced them out of the house with. The minute he knows the police are onto him – no I can't do that. But if I transfer the money, how do I know he won't carry out his threats to hurt them anyway?

However, I can't leave any of this to chance and have little choice other than to send him what he wants. Then, to hope and pray he'll drop them off somewhere like Ellen said he would. After that, we can inform the police and hopefully he won't get very far. At least they'll be able to pick him up on the ANPR cameras.

With trembling hands, I log into my crypto account and make the transfer to the wallet address where I've already paid half a million pounds. He's now had one-and-a-half million of my money. I take a screenshot of the confirmation screen, and then type the message.

> It's done. So where are you going to leave them?

> I need proof.

I attach the screenshot and hit send.

> I'll message you an hour from now when the money's cleared with where to pick them up, once I've got myself away from them. Any funny business – any police, and you'll never see them again.

> Just leave them somewhere safe, do you hear me?

I wait a few moments for his reply. A reply that doesn't arrive. He can't possibly expect to get away with what he's doing to us. Mum's voice echoes in my brain. *Call the police, son. Just call the police.*

If I did, there'd, no doubt, be a massive alert through the media. The police would be crawling all over the nearest airports and ferry docks, doing everything they could to find them all and stop him. But if Anthony realised they were closing in on him, he'd be capable of doing *anything*. So there's nothing I can do until I've picked the three of them up safely and only then will I call the police. He's not going to get anywhere fast in an hour.

It's after four. All I can do is wait. I head into the hallway to check the twin's all-in-one coats have gone and heave a sigh of relief when I spot the gap on the pegs inside the cloakroom. Ellen's long Superdry coat has also disappeared. At least if he dumps them outside, they'll be warm enough until I get there. I'd set off now but there's no way of knowing which direction I should head towards. I'm around an equal distance between the Manchester and Leeds Bradford airports. It's the same with the ferries, I'd have to choose between Hull and Liverpool. If I set off in the wrong direction, I can't bear to think of Ellen, Imogen and Ruben being forced to wait any longer than necessary.

I have never felt so powerless or as stressed. I need some air. I unlock the patio doors, the same doors I so stupidly left unlocked yesterday. I slide my feet into the crocs that my girls say are an embarrassment and, by the light of the nearly-full moon, I navigate my way over the decking and around the patio that Ellen and I have enjoyed so many glasses of wine on in our fifteen-month relationship. Then I head towards the summerhouse where I was sitting merely hours ago.

A fool and his money are easily parted. It's Dad's voice again, back from the days when he told me to thump the lad who was robbing my dinner money. I *did* thump him but things never improved. Instead, his mates jumped on the bandwagon and before long, I was fighting half a dozen of them. It was only when Dad threatened to remove me from the school that the staff finally took action. Here I am, being robbed from again, yet on a much larger scale.

The pond's a mirror in the ground reflecting the clear sky. If I were to peer into it, I'd see a face etched with grief and worry. I've already lost Mum, and now the safety of my wife and two youngest children is severely threatened. How I'm going to wait for an hour without going out of my mind, I really don't know.

45

I JUMP as my phone beeps and sit bolt upright in the deckchair. I must have dropped off to sleep. Adrenaline courses through my chilled-through body as I pat the sides of the chair, feeling for my phone. I shift my foot, sending it skidding across the wooden floor of the summerhouse. It must have fallen from my hand when my fingers relaxed as I dozed.

> Surprise View. Otley Chevin.

That's it. That's all he's telling me. With numb fingers, I type the location into Google Maps. It's a forty-five-minute drive.

I stumble into the early morning air where night is giving way to dawn. I break into a run towards the lit-up windows at the rear of the house.

In the hallway, I quickly swap the crocs for trainers, tug on a jacket and snatch up the keys for the Range Rover.

The familiarity of its throaty engine as it fires up is an almost comforting sound. I glance into the back, expecting to see the two baby seats which will hopefully soon be filled. But they're not there.

As I tear off down my lane for the second time, I imagine my wife, waiting alone in the emerging dawn at the top of Otley Chevin, shivering in her coat with the twins in their car seats at either side of her. I've got to get to them – fast.

The bastard must be planning to jump on a plane straight out of Leeds Bradford Airport as it's only a five-minute drive from Otley Chevin. I just hope he can be stopped before he leaves, but until Ellen and the babies are safely in this car, I'm doing nothing. I'm not prepared to risk their lives.

The roads are empty apart from the occasional tractor and a couple of delivery vans. It's a relief to get onto the more open roads where I can stretch the legs of my Range Rover. There's not likely to be any police around with speed guns at this hour so I can get my foot down and reach my family.

Dad used to take me to Surprise View as a boy. He was a keen photographer and, I can recall a sunset photo where I was standing on a rock, holding our labrador. He took loads more photos as the scenery is stunning up there but that's the one which sticks in my mind. At the age I was, the main attractions of The Chevin were the rope swing in the woods and the ice cream van at the edge of the car park. It's a place of beauty and enjoyment, not a place to leave a lone new mother and two vulnerable babies who've been abducted at knifepoint.

Sunrise is imminent as I turn the final corner towards the car park where I pray I'll find my family waiting. As I slow the Range Rover to ease over the gravel and potholes, I scan the vicinity for any sign of them. But all that's visible is the shape of the rocks against the awakening sky.

Ellen and the twins must be hiding amongst them, petrified at the prospect of Anthony returning. I'd have thought she'd have emerged by now, having heard my engine or seen the headlights.

I swing into a bay at the side, lock the car and rush to the front of the car park where the ice cream van usually spends the day.

'Ellen.' I scan the benches that look out over Otley. 'I'm here.' My voice echoes back at me above the dawn chorus. After a few moments I call out again. 'It's Oliver, love.' I shout louder this time. 'It's safe to come out.'

I scan from left to right over the rocks as I edge closer to the dry stone wall. Has he lied about where he was planning to leave them? I tug my phone from my pocket in case he's sent another message.

But there's nothing.

Perhaps I need to head deeper in, to search among the rocks or go down to the forest. But *this* part of the Chevin is Surprise View. This is where he said they'd be waiting. I pace up and down, my breath and the crunching of my trainers against gravel loud in the silence of the morning. Before long there'll be other people here, dog walkers, joggers and early-morning photographers. A place like this doesn't remain silent and empty for very long when it's daylight.

A distant humming cuts into the quiet. I pause in front of the wall to listen. It's growing louder. After a few more moments, there's no doubt that it's the engine of a van or a small truck. And it's heading this way.

I hold my breath as headlights light up the road beyond the car park. Then it appears. A white combi van. If it's him, it's not signwritten which I'd expect with Anthony being a kitchen fitter. However, it's probably new, having been bought with his ill-gotten gains. But what's going on? He was supposed to have dropped them off here ages ago and be long gone by now. I guess this means the police will be able to stop him before he gets to the airport – if it's him. I must make sure I get a good look at the number plate.

The van swerves off the main road and veers into the car

park, gravel pinging out in all directions as the headlights cut through the sunrise.

I freeze. It doesn't pull into a space. It doesn't park. Instead, it rolls to a slow stop about two hundred feet away, the engine still idling.

A cold spike of dread pierces my spine. I squint into the glare, trying to make out who's inside, how many people — but the headlights are high-beamed and brutal, masking everything behind them.

I wait for the engine to cut. For the lights to dip. For something — *anything* — to shift. But nothing happens. Except for the revving.

It's low at first. Then louder. A deliberate snarl of the engine, rhythmic and relentless, like an animal pacing behind bars.

What's he doing? Is he trying to intimidate me? Is he playing mind games? It's too late for those. I lift my hand to my brow, shielding my eyes from the full force of the glare. The beam makes my head throb, and my vision swims.

Still, I walk forward. Deliberately. Steadily. He's done enough damage hiding within his shadows. The gravel shifts beneath my feet as I close the distance. My heart is pounding — loud in my ears — but I don't slow. I won't give him the satisfaction of seeing my fear.

Then, all at once, the engine howls. The wheels spin, kicking up a storm of dust and loose stones pepper the air like shrapnel. It lurches forward with a sudden, jerking fury.

My breath catches. He's not bluffing. He's coming at me. There's no time to think. There's nowhere to hide. There's just the blinding light, the roar of the engine, and the scream of spinning tyres.

He's going to hit me. Instinct takes over and I hurl myself sideways. The sound swells — a deafening crescendo of rage.

Then white-hot agony tears through me as metal meets my

flesh. My body lifts — weightless for a second — before slamming down. A thousand needles of pain explode across my side, my head, and my chest.

The sky above twists. Flashes of black and grey, headlights spinning like a carousel. And then – darkness.

46

BELLA

'There's no time like the present to put that CPR training into practice. Come on Bella – *now!*'

Even after my sergeant's command, I can't move, nor can I find the words to tell him why. All I can do is stare at what's in front of me. At the collapsed dry stone wall and the bent metal railing behind it. But mainly, I'm staring at the bloodied and broken man lying there.

There's a hiss from beneath the bonnet of the van. Smoke's rising from a pool of liquid. It smells like petrol, and it's continuing to drip onto the ground. The ground where he's sprawled out in front of me. I rub my eyes. I can't believe what I'm seeing. Maybe I'm hallucinating. Perhaps I'm overtired.

'Bella, come on. I've got you here. We need to move, we've still got a few minutes before the ambulance arrives. For goodness sake, you need to frame yourself.'

It's a phrase Dad used to use to get me up in the mornings with when I was late for school. *Come on, Bella, frame yourself, you're going to make us all late.*

'PC Holmes!'

'I can't—' Finally. I find my voice. I gesture at the lifeless form. 'It's–it's my dad.'

'What? What are you talking about?'

I gesture to the ground, tears blurring my vision.

'It's your *dad*? You're bloody joking, aren't you?' Jon rushes forward and clutches my arm. 'Come on Bella – please, get a grip – we *have* to get him clear of the van.'

'Is he—' I close my eyes as Jon bends forward to search Dad's wrist for a pulse. What the hell is Dad doing, here in Otley at six in the morning, lying in front of a crashed van? We only spoke yesterday – we've arranged to meet up over the next couple of days. I rub my eyes again in case this isn't real – in case I'm just trapped in a bad dream.

'He's still alive. But I need you to help me move him to safety.' Jon's voice is more urgent than I've ever heard.

'But his neck.' I can't take my eyes off him. 'We could make things worse if we move him.'

'Things can't get any worse than this van going up while he's inches from it. Come on Bella, get it together – we need to help him. *Now.*'

The boom of my sergeant's voice propels me forward, and with tears rolling down my face, I grab Dad's trainers as Jon hooks his arms under Dad's shoulders.

'One step to your left,' Jon shouts. 'And another. Keep going.'

Together, we move him well back from immediate danger onto the soft grass beside one of the benches and I drop beside him, huffing and blowing, checking again for his pulse.

'Dad.' There's a trickle of blood from his ear down his neck. 'Oh my God, Dad. It's Bella. Can you hear me?' He's as still as the rocks which preside over us, his ashen face bathed in the peachy-pink sunrise. How can such a beautiful dawn illuminate something so dark and dreadful? 'Dad, come on. Please,

please open your eyes.' I'm sobbing so hard I can barely breathe.

'I need you over here.'

Glancing around to where Jon's tugging at one of the doors to the van, I can now see the swirl of blue lights in the sky beyond the car park. 'Help's coming, Dad. Just hang in there for me.' I take his hand. 'Thank God we spoke before this happened.' My chest is so tight, it feels like it's trapped in a vice. 'I can't lose you now. Please Dad, please just wake up.' I wrench my jacket off and lay it over his top half. I don't know what else to do – I feel utterly helpless.

'Bella! Now!'

'I can't leave him on his own.' I can't take my eyes away from my father. This whirlwind of a man, who's constantly on the go with his work and his gym workouts, is *never* this still. 'He's my dad.' My words are filled with anguish. '*He's my dad.* I can't lose him.' I reach for his hand.

'We've got another two people we need to rescue. I don't trust this van not to go up.' The stench of petrol *has* become more pungent.

'I'll be back in a minute, Dad. I promise I will.' I stare at him for a moment longer. I don't want to leave him – not for a second. What will I do if he dies while I'm helping someone else? 'Help's coming.' I rise to my feet and lurch over the uneven ground towards my colleague. If the van were to explode right now, it would also take Jon and I couldn't live with that on my conscience – not when he's been imploring me to help him. The ambulance will pull into this car park at any moment. They'll save my dad, I know they will. He's as tough as old boots - he'll be alright.

He's got to be.

I arrive at the opposite side of the van to where Jon's bent over one of the casualties. There's so much blood, it's impossible to see where one person ends and the other begins. A cursory glance tells me one of them wasn't wearing a seatbelt. However, the airbags have deployed which could be their saving grace. I tug at the door handle. 'It won't open.' I race around to Jon's side, looking back over at my dad, willing him to suddenly wake and sit up on the ground.

'Oh my God.' I clasp my hand over my mouth as I take in the bloodied face in the shadows of the van and the slight flutter of a dark fringe. 'It's *her.*'

'*What*? You know *her* as well?'

'It's–it's my dad's wife. It's my stepmother. Her name's Ellen Holmes.' Despite the circumstances, her surname still sticks in my throat. I can't stand that she's got our surname. I tried when he first introduced her to us to warm to her but I just couldn't. I could see straight through the woman even if Dad was unable to. We all could.

'We've got a pulse so I'm going to lift her beneath her shoulders, just like I did with your Dad,' he says, then if you could inch her feet little by little out of the van as I guide you.'

I've got to *try* to help her – but I'm only doing this for Dad. I'm also doing it because I wouldn't be able to live with myself if I didn't. But I'm not doing it for *her.*

Just as he starts getting hold of her below her arms, two ambulances appear at the entrance to the car park with a fire engine waiting behind them. It's one of the most hopeful sights I've ever seen.

'Thank God.' Jon looks down at Ellen. 'We'll let the fire crew take care of this. We don't want to aggravate these injuries any further.'

I rush back over to Dad, re-checking his pulse. 'They're here – the paramedics are going to sort you out now. You're going to be alright.'

Maybe he'll suddenly open his eyes and reassure me. But he remains deathly still.

'Please don't die. Please, please don't die.' I'm sobbing like a four-year-old as I continue to hold his hand.

'What the hell's happened to you both?' More questions march through my mind, starting with, *whose van is it*? And *who the hell is the other man*?

Doors bang, voices bark instructions and the car park fills up with paramedics and fire crew. I remain kneeling as close to Dad as I can while paramedics begin tending to him. Now that they're here, I'm not leaving his side.

'Time of death. Six twenty-eight am,' a voice pronounces from beside the van.

'Dead? Who's dead?' My voice is a screech. 'Is it *her*?'

Jon emerges from the crowd at the other side of the van and heads towards me. 'The man.' He wipes his hand across his forehead, leaving a streak of blood. 'The force of the impact sent one of his tools flying from the back to the front of the van. It's smashed into the back of his head.'

Bile bubbles at the back of my throat. 'Who is he anyway?' I can't look over there again. No wonder there was so much blood.

'We don't know yet.' The weight of Jon's hand on my shoulder is a small comfort. I still feel like I'm going to wake up in a cold pool of sweat with one of my housemates standing over me.

'I need to go with my Dad.' I jerk my head in the direction of the ambulance. 'I can't do anything else.'

'Of course you do. More officers are arriving, they'll take over here.'

'Is Ellen going to make it?' I glance over to where paramedics are gathered around her. 'How come she was inside the van and yet Dad was on the ground in front of it? What the hell happened?'

The other question is – if *both* Dad and Ellen are *here*, who's looking after their two babies? A wave of concern washes over me. They're two months old and I haven't even set eyes on them. They might be Ellen's, but they're also Dad's, which means they're still my brother and sister. If anything's happened to them, I'll never forgive myself.

'They've got two kids as well – babies – where are they?'

'Over here, *now.*'

Responding to the urgent shouting of one of the fire crew, Jon lets go of my shoulder and hurtles back to the van. I rise from the ground.

'How the hell didn't you see this?' The fire officer's tugging at the darkened windows of the van's rear cabin, his voice heavy with desperation. 'We've got two baby seats in the back.'

And suddenly I know what the phrase, *blood running cold* means.

47

OLIVER

'He's waking up. Nurse?' There's a scuffling to my right.

I force my eyes open, just a slit. 'Dad?' A blurry Bella's leaning over me from one side, Jasmine from the other. I close my eyes again.

'If you could both stand back for a moment,' a brisk voice commands as footsteps quicken towards me.

'He's going to be alright. See I told you,' Bella hisses, presumably at her sister.

'It's good to have you back with us, Oliver. How are you doing?'

'Erm, groggy.' My voice is feeble. It doesn't even sound like me.

'You might feel like that for a while – at least until the anaesthetic fully wears off.' I wince as a torch is shone into one eye and then into the other. All I see is headlights. They're coming straight at me. I stiffen in anticipation, bracing myself for the slam followed by the agony.

'It's OK, Dad.' Bella's voice is back at my side and I feel the warmth of her hand on my arm. 'You're safe in hospital now.'

I turn my head the other way, towards the nurse and try to force my eyes open a little further.

'What's – the – damage?'

'You've suffered a concussion.' She turns from a monitor she's checking and looks at me. 'And we've had to operate on your hip and femur.'

'Really?' I don't recall being brought in here, let alone being taken for an operation.

'Both needed pinning in two places.'

'Oh.' I reach down, my fingers brushing against my gown and reaching a bulk of bandages beneath it.

'How's your pain? On a one to ten?'

'Probably a four.'

'The morphine's doing its job then. We'll see how you go but we'll look to lowering it over the next few hours. From what I've heard you've been very lucky.'

She's right. Anthony drove his van straight at me and yet, I'm still here. Not only that, both my daughters have been at my side, waiting for me to wake up and, no doubt, tearing themselves apart at the state of me. I stretch my fingers out to Jasmine and she takes my hand in hers.

'Ellen? The twins?'

Her voice wobbles. 'They're all safe, Dad.'

My eyes burn with tears behind their lids. 'Thank God.'

'You need to rest, Oliver.' The nurse hooks a chart onto the end of my bed. 'Can I suggest that your daughters go home and return in the morning?'

'Can't we stay?' Jasmine sounds tearful. 'I don't want to leave him.'

'Your dad's not going to be up to much tonight in the way of conversation.' Her voice moves further away. She must be heading back to the door. 'But by the morning, as long as his pain's under control, we should be able to move him onto a normal ward.'

I want to affirm what the nurse has said and urge them to go home and rest, but sleep is overtaking me.

'The nurse is right – we *should* go,' Bella says. 'I've been awake for over twenty-four hours *and* worked a night shift. If I stay here much longer, I'll have to crawl in that bed beside him.'

'We'll take good care of your dad,' the nurse says. 'And if anything changes, we'll let you know straight away.'

'Why what could change?' Jasmine's voice is filled with panic. 'You just said—'

'Go home, girls.' The nurse's voice is sterner now. 'He'll need you far more in the morning. Go and get some rest.'

48

APRIL 20

'HEY.' I glance up to where my daughters are framed in the doorway of the ward, their identical blue eyes filled with love and concern. 'The two of you are a sight for sore eyes.'

'I'm glad you're on a proper ward.' Jasmine flicks her hair behind her shoulder as she lifts two chairs from the stack by the door and assembles them at my bedside. 'That High Dependency Unit was scary.'

'It was just because they needed to keep a closer eye on me.' I squeeze her hand as it reaches for mine. 'But aside from a headache, some cuts and bruises and a couple of broken bones, it looks like I'm made of tough stuff. No, don't put the big light on.' I point as Bella reaches for the switch. 'This overbed light's kinder on my head at the moment.

'Are you in a lot of pain, Dad?'

'It's all a bit tender but this stuff's pretty good.' I point at the IV which is administering the morphine. 'They've lowered my dose but I'm still getting enough to keep things at bay. 'I'll be out of action for a few weeks but then I'll be just fine.'

'It stinks in here.' Bella wrinkles her nose as she sits beside her sister. 'I hate the smell of hospitals.'

'Me too.' Jasmine nods towards my feet. 'Cool socks, Dad.' We all look at my surgical stockings and I wiggle my toes. They both laugh but Bella's smile fades as quickly as it arrived.

'Has anyone been in to see you yet? From the police, I mean?'

I shake my head which swoons with the movement. However, I've been told I've sustained nothing more sinister than a concussion, probably from when my head hit the ground.

'I've been told very little, to be honest. I gather I wasn't up to it last night after my op so I've been hoping you girls will enlighten me?' I look from one of them to the other. 'I recall arriving at the Chevin and I don't think I'll ever forget those headlights, but after that, I don't really remember anything.'

Jasmine's face clouds over. 'I couldn't believe it when Bella called to let me know what had happened.'

'I said I'd let the station know when you're up to talking.' Bella glances at the clock above the door. 'When do you think you'll be ready?'

'As soon as they want.' I grab at the edges of my mattress to slide myself up into a seated position. 'I might as well get it over with.'

'That hospital gown suits you too.' Jasmine laughs and Bella glares at her. 'You should ask if you can take it home.'

'I vaguely remember you saying last night that Ellen and the twins are safe.' I look towards the door as if they might miraculously appear. 'So where are they? What the hell happened?'

My daughters look at each other.

'Just tell me.'

'Ellen's been taken to a different hospital.' Bella's hands are trembling in her lap.

'Why? What's wrong with her?' Panic washes over me.

Jasmine hides behind the curtain of her hair as she often

does when she's uncomfortable. The silence between us is palpable, only broken by footsteps which pass by out in the corridor.

'Things might have been rocky between everybody but she's still my wife. Was she in the van?'

Bella takes in a long breath. 'Maybe we should wait until my sergeant gets here.'

'What won't you tell me? Where are the twins?'

'It's OK – *they* weren't in the van.' Bella's expression is the most serious I think I've ever seen. 'They were being looked after, thank God.'

'By *who*?' I close my eyes. 'It was the middle of the night when they left the house.'

'By the mother of the bloke in the van,' Jasmine replies.

'*Anthony's* mother?' I haven't a clue what to make of this. What the hell was he playing at, leaving them there? Maybe his plan was to extort even more money from me before he'd hand them over. But if that was the case, why drive the van at me? None of it makes any sense.

'When the man's mother found out about the crash, she no longer wanted the twins there and demanded that *we* take them.'

'*You*? How did she know how to contact you?' I close my eyes. Perhaps she must have known Ellen well enough to have learned her surname.

'She looked us all up on Facebook.' Jasmine points at her phone on my overbed table. 'But she said it had taken a while to find us.'

'Who are you talking about?'

'Me, Mum, and Bella.' Jasmine jerks her head in her sister's direction. 'We all got messages, and calls from her. Quite a few of them. 'Here – look. She thrusts her phone at me and with a shaking hand, I take it.

> They were only supposed to be with me for an hour.

> There's nothing I can do. I'm at the hospital with my Dad – we all are.

> There's no milk – there's no nappies. I can't cope with them for much longer – I've got enough to cope with as it is.

> Please – I need someone to take them off my hands.

> Right then – I'll have to get social workers involved. They'll have to take them.

An hour or so has elapsed before Jasmine's sent a reply.

> OK. My mum and sister are going to come. Can I have your address?

'Jasmine stayed here with you and I went to pick them up with Mum.' Bella's face clouds over. 'The woman was shaking like a leaf. There's clearly been some substance misuse going on there.'

A surge of pride courses through me for the daughter who's grown up enough to make these observations and is making a huge difference in the world. From this day forward, neither of them will ever be in any doubt of how proud I am of them.

'Wait, *who's* got them now?' I sit bolt upright and both girls jump to their feet, possibly concerned that I'm going to suddenly try leaping out of bed. Chance would be a fine thing. 'Are they *still* with your mum?'

Jasmine nods.

'Where's my phone?' I glance towards the cabinet at my side. 'Did it survive what happened? I need to call her.'

'We found it on the floor. It's a bit scratched but it's still working.' She points at the cabinet.

'Your Mum— she can't—'

'Don't worry – she's fine, the babies are fine, *everything's* fine.'

'But their stuff. They need—'

'Mum drove to yours yesterday — she called in here for my keys. Anyway, she got milk, clothes and nappies for them so you've got nothing to worry about.'

I relax back into my pillows for a moment but then stiffen again. 'Wait, are you *sure* she's alright looking after them?' The thought of my ex-wife, the person who pressured me into having a vasectomy, coping with two-month-old twins at the age of fifty-two is both bewildering and amusing in equal measure.

'*Someone* had to take care of them. Anyway, Dad, let it go,' Bella says. 'It's this Anthony Powell we need to know about.' I'm unsure whether she's in daughter or police mode. 'Was Ellen having an affair with him? Is that why they were in the van together when it crashed?'

'It's a long story.' I lean further back into my pillows, already worn out and I've only been awake for an hour. Perhaps the morphine's wearing off faster than I thought. Maybe I should ask for enough to send me into a welcome oblivion.

'We're going to need to hear this story.'

'Where is he now?' Fresh panic surges through me as I suddenly realise how at risk I could be from the man who's already tried to kill me. 'Is this ward locked, Bella? I need to know that Anthony isn't going to come charging in here to finish what he started.'

'How do you mean?' Worry etches itself across Bella's face. 'And yes, it's locked, we had to buzz on the intercom to get in.'

'Well the bastard, sorry, excuse my French,' – I pat Jasmine's hand, – 'Clearly wanted to wipe me out when he drove his van at me, didn't he? So—'

'I don't know how to tell you this, Dad.' Bella and Jasmine exchange glances again and Jasmine pulls a face.

'What – is he dead? You can tell me straight, you know – I'm not exactly going to be upset.'

Who knows how they'd react if they knew I'd sent one-and-a-half million pounds to the lowlife. Money that could have set them both up for life if only I could have redirected it their way.

Bella nods. 'A hammer from the back of the van smashed into his head at the point of impact. My sergeant said it would have taken him out instantly.'

I rub at my own head, feeling spaced out.

'But that's not all,' Bella continues. 'And I don't quite know how to tell you this.'

'Just tell him.' Jasmine stares at the floor. 'He needs to know.'

'Yes, whatever it is, just tell me. I might be lying in a hospital bed but I'll be back out of it before you know it.'

'Anthony Powell wasn't the person driving that van.' The way Bella reaches for my hand tells me I don't want to hear what she's about to tell me.

'So who was it?' I stare back at her. 'To my knowledge, there's nobody else who'd have it in them to drive at me like that. *Nobody.*' The last word escapes me as a whisper. I shiver, even though it's as warm as the Sahara Desert in here.

'It was Ellen, Dad.' Jasmine squeezes my other hand.

'When we found the crashed van,' Bella continues. 'It was your *wife*, – she spits the word out like a glob of gristle, – 'who was sitting in the driver's seat.'

49

FOUR MONTHS LATER - AUGUST 22

'THIS HAS COME FOR YOU.' I glance up from feeding the twins. The expression on Bella's face says it all as she saunters into the kitchen, dressed in shorts and a t-shirt, while waving a letter. She's moved into Mum's cottage with her boyfriend, and I couldn't be happier to see her every day, and also to see the place lit up again at night.

Mum would be delighted that her cherished home has gone to her beloved granddaughter, rather than me renting it out to a stranger. And like Mum used to in my pre-Ellen days, they both tend to join me on the patio in the evenings for a glass of something when their shift patterns allow. Like Bella, her boyfriend, Sam, is in the police.

Her blonde ponytail swings from side to side like her childhood skipping rope as she crosses the kitchen. She thrusts the envelope in front of my face. 'It's *her* again. You haven't been writing back, have you? I can't understand why she keeps sending these.'

'Of course I haven't.' I rest Imogen's bowl of mush on the counter. 'I wouldn't even know what to say.'

'She shouldn't be allowed to contact you. I can't understand why they're letting her. Do you want me to have a word?'

'I'm quite capable of fighting my own battles.' I laugh. 'Anyway, I know you mean well, but actually, I consented.' I avoid my daughter's gaze. 'Just for now. I need to understand what—'

'Please tell me you're not going to forgive her, Dad.' Bella's voice is laced with worry. 'That you're not going to allow her back into your life. Into *their* lives.' She gestures to Imogen and Ruben, in their matching summer all-in-one suits, one blue and one pink, both impatiently waiting in their highchairs for further influxes of their lunch. The kitchen's filled with the sweet aroma of mashed swede and carrot.

'Of course not.'

'Ellen might be their mother but she doesn't deserve them in her life.' Bella smiles back at Imogen's toothy grin. It would take a hard heart not to melt at the sight of it.

'Can we swap while I have a quick read?' I gesture to the letter. 'And don't worry, Ellen writing to me doesn't change a thing.'

Bella holds out her hand and I pass the spoon. 'Give Imogen a couple, and then switch to Ruben. If you give one of them more than two spoonfuls at a time, the other starts to perform. They're demons, the pair of them, but at least they've begun to sleep through the night.'

I chuckle as I take the letter stamped with the crest of the medium secure hospital Ellen was sent to. With their blonde hair and blue eyes, the twins couldn't look any *less* like demons. Or their father. A vision of when Anthony first came to my door floods my mind. When I assumed he was a decent guy just needing some shelter from the storm and a helping hand to get his van back on the road.

'Really,' – Bella begins spooning the gravy-infused mush into Imogen's mouth, – 'You should do what Mum suggested and just bin Ellen's letters. Unopened. I mean, hasn't she caused you enough damage?' She throws her free hand into the air and shakes her head.

'I need to stay on top of whatever's going on.' I sink onto a stool at the breakfast bar, wincing in discomfort. My hip's healing better than my leg and I have a physio coming to the house most days, but I've still got a fair way to go before I can even dream about getting near the gym again or going for a run. 'At least until after the hearing.'

'But why?'

'For their sakes.' I nod towards the babies, smiling at Ruben's wide-open mouth. There's no need to make aeroplane or choo-choo train noises to get these two to eat. They didn't become so dimpled and chubby without devouring everything that's put in front of them.

I came clean to the police about the money I transferred to Anthony's crypto wallet, and the fraudulent birth certificates. Miraculously, I haven't been prosecuted, but an order was made for the births to be re-registered with Anthony Powell named as their father. But thankfully, the court granted me temporary residency of the twins. Meanwhile, an array of social workers and other professionals have been parading through our lives, just as Ellen often feared.

'I don't know how you can bear to read words she's written.' Bella wipes Imogen's mouth. It's heartening to see how my girls behave around the twins. They may not all be genetically related but a bond's certainly growing. 'You'll be able to hear her voice as you read.' She pulls a face.

'Listen to me, love. I've researched Postpartum Psychosis.' I slice a knife through the top of the letter. 'And it can be a horrendous illness.'

'That's if she hasn't invented being ill to be treated more leniently.' Bella sniffs. She doesn't possess an ounce of forgiveness or compassion towards her stepmother. As far as *both* my daughters are concerned, the woman wanted their dad to die and drove a van at him. It's completely black and white.

'I knew she was prone to anxiety and depression,' I explain, needing to help Bella understand. 'And from what I can recall, it must have taken hold of her even while she was still pregnant.'

'You wouldn't have known a thing of her having *anxiety and depression* when *we* first met her.' I can tell by Bella's face that she still has no sympathy for her stepmother. 'Grandma used to call her *Miss High and Mighty*. Well, look how the mighty have fallen.'

'Come on, love.' I slide the letter from the envelope. 'The training you've had in mental health should make you a little more forgiving, surely?'

'The woman tried to kill you, Dad.' Bella's voice rises to the top of its range and Imogen studies her with curious eyes. 'Look, I'm sorry but I'll never forgive her. Plus, I think she's playing on her hormones to disguise how evil she is.' She scrapes the last of the food from Ruben's bowl and holds the spoon towards his mouth. 'How did the two of them get so gorgeous with the parents they've got?'

'Give them a drink for me, would you, love?' I point at their sippy cups next to the sink. 'Just let me have a quick scan through this then I'll be right back with you.'

50

This will be the last time I write to you as I'm done with explaining myself, and I'll be in court soon anyway. The meds are working, the shrinks have wrung the whole story out of me, and now you're going to hear it too.

I REST the letter on the breakfast bar and stare absently at the cloudless sky beyond the breezy patio doors. I already know about Ellen being the one who drove Anthony's van at me. She tried to kill me that morning.

What can she possibly have to tell me which is *the whole story*?

The truth is, I never loved you. I saw what you were – rich, clueless, and desperate for someone – anyone, which is why I took my chance.

You kept digging into my past, so here it is. My father was in prison, my mother was sick in the head, so I ended up in care. My first husband beat the crap out of me and I escaped from him with nothing. Life's taught me to survive by any means.

'Shall I give them a yoghurt, Dad? They both still seem hungry.'

'Hmm, yes – if you wouldn't mind, love.'

I raise the letter so it's in front of my face. The girls keep laughing that I'm too vain to get my eyes tested and to finally admit that I should be wearing glasses.

I lied when I said I'd only just met Anthony. We were together all along. He was in the bar that night, watching you throw yourself at me. We saw the opportunity and went for it.

Marrying you was part of the plan. Having your baby became part of the plan. But the money wasn't coming fast enough, so we changed direction. We were going to take as much as we could and then walk.

You probably don't need me to remind you how much of a problem your mother was. I tried to tolerate her, the same way I pretended to want a relationship with your daughters, but I hated the lot of them. Then Phyllis followed me the night before the first scan, saw me with Anthony, and started digging. We couldn't risk her telling you what she'd seen. She was a threat, and threats have to be dealt with. Which is what Anthony did when we were out for the morning at the hospital.

'What's the matter, Dad?' Bella drops the spoon into the bowl. 'You look like you've seen a ghost.'

'Take the babies into the other room for me, love.'

'Why, what does it say.' Bella grabs at the letter but I swipe it away. No way can she read this. If Ellen means what I think she does here, I'm going to have to break this news to Bella and Jasmine gently.

The news that their so-called stepmother and her secret boyfriend were involved in their grandmother's murder. And that the bastard who attacked her in her own bedroom will never even be brought to justice for it – because he's dead. Death's far too good for him. Instead, he should be locked in the misery of a life sentence with his fellow inmates knowing he's inside for murdering a defenceless old lady in her home. And for what? So they could carry on working on *me*? Fleecing *me*?

'Please love. Just give me a few minutes and then I'll come to talk to you. Can you give Jasmine and your Mum a call too and get them to come over as soon as they can? I think we need to all talk together.'

Right now, I need the stability of my ex-wife. I can't handle this on my own. She's been my absolute rock over the last few months.

> You were still sending money, but Anthony had already burned through most of it. If your mother had spoken to you, everything would have been over. We weren't walking away with nothing. So we had no choice other than to make sure she could never tell you anything.

I stride over to the fridge. I need a beer. I can't believe what I'm reading.

The fridge mainly consists of bottles of formula and pureed food but I still have one or two beers nestling amongst it all. I grab one and hold it against my throbbing temple for a moment, relishing in the chill to cool me down.

I liked the life you gave me, and I wasn't ready to give it up. The night we left, I knew the million wouldn't be enough – plus you only agreed to send it because you thought you were coming to collect me and the babies. That's when we decided we'd have to get you out of the way as well.

The plan was supposed to be simple. Run you over where there were no cameras, pretend it was an accident, and then cry like a wounded widow in front of the police. If you weren't dead the first time, I was going to run back over you until I'd finished the job. I just didn't expect the van to hit that steel post and knock me out.

Ellen's utterly evil. How the hell didn't I see this? The two of them murdered my mother. And they planned to murder me too.

Somehow, fate intervened. Ellen knocked herself out at the first point of impact. If she hadn't, she would have reversed the van and run over me again. She wouldn't have stopped until she was certain I was dead.

I was hearing voices. They told me what I already knew, that you were in the way. You didn't belong in that house. I did, and whether you like it or not, I still do.

Anyway, I've been told to plead guilty. That way, I won't be inside for as long. I'll be back for my babies – that much you can count on.

Oh, and one final thing – Anthony never sent those DNA swabs off. So maybe they're yours... or maybe they're not – who knows?
    Ellen

She'll be back for the babies? Over my dead body. As it so very nearly was.

I swig from my bottle. I can't go through to the other room and face Bella. Not yet. She'll take one look at me and I'll feel compelled to spill the contents of this letter. What will she think when she finds out what a fool her father's been? I've never considered this before but, there's the remotest chance they could be mine – after all, I had sex with Ellen the night before Anthony did. However, I'm not going to take any DNA swabs – I'd rather leave things as they are. If the tests came back negative, as they no doubt would, it would just be another blow. And I've more than my fair share of those from Ellen already.

A flicker of movement beyond the patio doors catches my eye as I fold the letter into quarters.

It's a robin. I hold its gaze until the tears burning my eyes blur my vision.

Could it be the same robin that watched me from outside the summer house in April? Could there be truth in what Carmen once told me about robins?

It hops closer to the window as if trying to convince me. Through my tears, I smile.

EPILOGUE
3 MONTHS LATER - NOVEMBER 4

'IT'S ME, Oliver. It's over. We're outside the court.' I can only just make Carmen's voice out amid the noise of the traffic in her background.

'Did both the girls stay with you for the verdict?' I balance the phone between my shoulder and my ear as I push the twins on the baby swings.

'Of course they did – but it all went just as we were told it would.'

'A psychiatric treatment order?' I glance around the playground as normal life carries on. A group of kids trying to knock conkers from a tree, another dad sending his two kids dizzy on the roundabout. The ice cream van that parks up at the edge of the playground all year round, whatever the weather.

'Yes. She's gone back to the same hospital. Which is a cushy number if you ask me.'

Like the girls, Carmen doesn't have a forgiving bone in her body when it comes to Ellen. In the end, I just had to let them all read the letter. I couldn't put what she'd written into my own words and I've now blocked her from being able to contact me again.

'Will she be transferred to a prison when they deem her to be well enough?'

'Prison would be too good for her. She should have died with *him*.' I can hear Bella in the background.

I'm hoping Carmen and the girls might begin to feel like justice has been done to some degree when Ellen's finally discharged from the secure hospital and placed in a proper prison cell.

I've been hanging onto the fact that she was badly afflicted with Postpartum Psychosis, and my vitriol has been more directed at Anthony. But there are moments when my hatred towards Ellen creeps in and I'm having counselling to deal with it all. To start to let it go instead of turning it all inwards.

'Ellen seemed perfectly compos mentis when I was eyeballing her across the courtroom.' I can picture Carmen's normally calm and smiley face, etched with the grief my second wife has caused for us all.

'She's had seven months of therapy and treatment since she drove that van into me.'

Ruben shrieks with enjoyment as I push him higher. I've just been given the all-clear to go through the courts to legally adopt the two of them but have been told this won't necessarily negate any rights Ellen might have when she's released one day – whenever that day might arrive.

'How did she react when they passed her sentence?'

'She was as meek and as mild as a dormouse,' Carmen replies. 'Yes, OK,' – her voice muffles for a moment, – 'sorry Oliver, I was just replying to Jasmine. They're going over to the bakery. We're all starving.'

'I haven't been able to eat a thing all day.' I shiver. I've lost so much weight this year with the stress of what's happened and the toll of caring for two babies, especially now I'm in my mid–

fifties. Many men my age are staring grandfatherhood in the face, not single parenthood to nine-month-old twins. I've been incredibly lucky that I've had the support of my girls – and Carmen. I couldn't have got through all this without them.

'It's all over now.' Her voice grounds me. 'We can all get on with getting back to some kind of normal.'

'Whatever that is.' I stare at the top of Imogen's woolly hat as she swings into the air. 'I just hope to have you still in my life as much as you have been, now that the hearing's over with.'

'Oh, this again.' She laughs.

'What's so funny?'

'It's just that I've already had both girls going on at me today before we went into court.' She laughs again. 'Pointing out how well we get on to say we're divorced. Even their friends are going on about it.'

'It should never have happened.' I push Imogen. Really I should take them from the swing to allow for another parent who's waiting in the wings with her toddler, but the conversation with Carmen feels more important. 'I'll just be a few minutes.' I mouth the words at her and point to my phone.

'What shouldn't have happened?'

'Me and you splitting up.'

'You were married to your work, Oliver. We never saw you.'

'I know.' I let out a long sigh. 'At the time I thought earning the money to give you all the best of the best was the most important thing. I believed I was doing my bit.'

'It was a lonely life,' she replies. 'It was *you* we wanted at home, not your money.'

'I know that now.' Mum's face floods my brain as her words come back. *Money can't fix everything, Oliver. Nor can it buy your happiness.* Then she added, *some things just aren't meant to be.*

But some things are.

'All that matters to me is my family, Carmen. Me, you, our wonderful girls and now the twins.' I push Imogen and then

Ruben, ignoring the waiting mother's hard stare. 'It's just a shame it took all this for me to realise what a mistake I made in neglecting you.'

'How about the three of us meet you all back at the house? We can open a bottle of something, order a takeaway, and well, you never know where tonight might take us.'

'You're on.' And for the first time in ages, a weight lifts from my shoulders.

Before you Go

Thank you for reading *Ties That Bind* – I hope you enjoyed it and would be hugely grateful if you would consider leaving a review on Amazon, which will help other readers to find it too!

If you want to read more of my work, check out *Their Last Day of Summer on Amazon*, my next psychological thriller, where you'll meet Tina, Jo, Becky and Siobhan, who are celebrating their fiftieth birthdays in Aruba with their other halves.

It's a week packed with exciting activities, one in particular, but it's after this activity that they realise one of the group is missing.

With the chance of finding their group member alive being minuscule, panic rises as fingers begin to be pointed.

At each other.

And for a FREE novella, please Join my 'keep in touch' list where I can also keep you posted of special offers and new releases. You can join by visiting my website www.mariafrank land.co.uk.

BOOK CLUB DISCUSSION QUESTIONS

1. Ellen and Oliver's marriage is built on secrets and hidden motives. At what point do you think their relationship was beyond saving? Was there ever a moment where things could have turned out differently?

2. Ellen's desperation to have a child plays a major role in her decisions. Do you think she would have gone to such extreme lengths if Oliver had been able to have children with her? Or was something deeper at play?

3. Anthony appears to be a catalyst for destruction, but do you think Ellen was already on a dangerous path before he came into her life? How much do you think his influence shaped her actions?

4. Ellen's letter reveals shocking confessions, including her involvement in Oliver's mother's murder. Do you think Ellen truly regrets her actions, or is she simply trying to justify them? Can her postpartum psychosis fully explain her crimes?

5. How does wealth and class play into the novel? Oliver was "born with a silver spoon," whereas Ellen had to fight for everything. Do you think their financial imbalance played a role in their toxic relationship?

6. Oliver's ex-wife is a surprising source of stability for him. How do you think their co-parenting relationship affects the story? What does this say about the contrast between his first and second marriages?

7. The letter offers a rare glimpse into Ellen's mindset. Did your perception of her change after reading it? Did you feel any sympathy for her by the end?

8. Ellen describes hearing voices that influenced her actions. How much do you think mental illness contributed to her crimes, and how much of it was her own free will? Should she be punished in the same way as someone without mental illness?

9. The title *Ties That Bind* suggests strong emotional or psychological connections. What do you think it refers to most —Ellen's attachment to motherhood, her toxic relationship with Anthony, or something else?

10. The novel's ending leaves some uncertainty about Ellen's future. If you were Oliver, would you ever allow her back into the twins' lives? Why or why not?

PROLOGUE – THEIR LAST DAY OF SUMMER

I can't close my eyes without seeing the light-dappled waves. Nor can I breathe without feeling the weight of what we brought back to the shore.

Or more to the point, *who* we didn't.

I look at the photos from our first day – our sun-flushed skin, matching cocktails, and smiles frozen in time.

I want to scream at the others. I yearn to go back and be able to warn them – *by the end of the week, one of us will be dead and another of us will be a murderer.*

I keep wondering what might have happened if I'd spoken up sooner. If I hadn't played along. If I hadn't let it all spiral out of control.

But it's too late for *what-ifs* now.

Find out more on Amazon

INTERVIEW WITH THE AUTHOR

Q: Where do your ideas come from?

A: I'm no stranger to turbulent times, and these provide lots of raw material. People, places, situations, experiences – they're all great novel fodder!

Q: Why do you write psychological thrillers?

A: I'm intrigued why people can be most at risk from someone who should love them. Novels are a safe place to explore the worst of toxic relationships.

Q: Does that mean you're a dark person?

A: We thriller writers pour our darkness into stories, so we're the nicest people you could meet – it's those romance writers you should watch...

Q: What do readers say?

A: That I write gripping stories with unexpected twists, about people you could know and situations that could happen to anyone. So beware...

Q: What's the best thing about being a writer?

A: You lovely readers. I read all my reviews, and answer all emails and social media comments. Hearing from readers absolutely makes my day, whether it's via email or through social media.

Q: Who are you and where are you from?

A: A born 'n' bred Yorkshire lass, now officially in my early fifties. I have two grown up sons and a Sproodle called Molly. (Springer/Poodle!) The last decade has been the best: I've done an MA in Creative Writing, made writing my full time job, and found the happy-ever-after that doesn't exist in my writing - after marrying for the second time just before the pandemic.

Q: Do you have a newsletter I could join?

A: I certainly do. Go to www.mariafrankland.co.uk or click here through your eBook to join my awesome community of readers. When you do, I'll send you a free novella – 'The Brother in Law.'

ACKNOWLEDGMENTS

Thank you, as always, to my amazing husband, Michael. He's my first reader, and is vital with my editing process for each of my novels. His belief in me means more than I can say.

A special acknowledgement goes to my wonderful advance reader team, who took the time and trouble to read an advance copy of Ties That Bind and offer feedback. They are a vital part of my author business and I don't know what I would do without them. This is my twenty-third full-length novel and it becomes harder and harder to think of first names for my characters. Therefore, I'm really grateful to members of the group who offered their own names up for me to use! They are:

Anthony (Put forward by Pheadra Farah)
    Phyllis (Phyllis Kaplan Fried)
    Ellen (Ellen Squire)
    Oliver (Put forward by Claire Harrison Walker)
    Ruben (Put forward by Joanna Elliott)
    Kirsteen (Put forward by Ann McGonnell)
    Bella and Jasmine (Put forward by Michelle Davis)
    Carmen (Put forward by Mary Schwickrath Busema)

I will always be grateful to Leeds Trinity University and my MA in Creative Writing Tutors there, Martyn, Amina and Oz. My Masters degree in 2015 was the springboard into being able to write as a profession.

And thanks especially, to you, the reader. Thank you for taking the time to read this story. I really hope you enjoyed it.